DREAMS

SOMETH

THEIR ABILITY TO SHATTER.

Michaela

Going from a record label back to my home town was something I never imagined. When I realized my dream was nothing but a nightmare, I couldn't run fast enough. I wasn't expecting everyone to see me as a some big star... and I definitely wasn't expecting my older brother's best friend to be living down the hall.

West Abbott starred in every single one of my teenage daydreams. And now he's quickly becoming the subject of every adult fantasy too. He's my brother's best friend, but that does nothing to stop the fire that sparks when he touches me.

But will he still want me when he finds out the dream world I've told him about is nothing but make believe?

West

The Mikey I remember is still the two-year-old with platinum blonde dandelion fluff for hair. But that's not who I find in the kitchen at three in the morning. Mikey is now Michaela, and I can't ignore that she's all woman now. And that I want all of her.

She's a famous singer. I'm a broke history teacher. She's my best friend's baby sister. And for every excuse I come up with to stay away from her, my attraction to her grows until I can't resist her any more.

But I can't help feeling like she's hiding something from me. And one lesson I learned after my last relationship crashed and burned? Never again fall in love with someone keeping secrets.

EMBRACING THE BEAT

HEART BEATS BOOK 4

BREANNA LYNN

Names, characters, businesses, places, events, locales, and incidents are either the products of the author's imagination or used in a fictitious manner. Any resemblance to actual persons, living or dead, businesses, companies, locales, or actual events is purely coincidental.

Designations used by companies to distinguish their products are often claimed as trademarks. All brand names and product names used in this book and on its cover are trade names, service marks, trademarks and registered trademarks or their respective owners. The publishers and the book are not associated with any product or vendor mentioned in this book. None of the companies referenced within the book have endorsed the book. *I Think We're Alone Now*© Claire Hastings, used with permission.

ISBN: 978-1-955359-08-5 (ebook)

ISBN: 978-1-955359-09-2 (paperback)

Cover Design by: Y'all That Graphic
Photographer: CJC Photography
Cover Models: Eric Taylor Guilmette & Skyler Simpson

Edited by: Jessica Snyder Edits and VB Proofreads

Printed in United States of America

https://breannalynnauthor.com

For my Family...
For supporting my dream,
For being there,
For your love.

FROM THE AUTHOR

Recommended for ages 18 and over.
Trigger warning/content warning for attempted sexual assault.

CHAPTER 1

MICHAELA

A sliminess coats my skin as I finish the last song in my set. The crowd may see a singer who hasn't quite hit the next level—let's be honest, I'm nowhere near where I thought I would be by now—but the dingy bar, the drunk patrons, and the cigarette smoke that chokes me, all scream *nobody*.

"Thank you," I rasp into the crackling microphone, waving a little and trying to keep the smile on my face as I grip my guitar.

The strings digging into my fingers help ward off the tears threatening to make an appearance. They'll still come, but later. Once I'm alone in the motel on the outskirts of Atlantic City—our stop for the night.

A year and a half ago, I was in Chicago, high on the excitement of signing with Reverb Records after they'd promised sold-out shows and stadium tours. But for the last three months, it's been dingy bars and clubs with makeshift stages. It's been two-star motels—if I'm lucky.

Shane was my label rep then—a happily married man with two kids who treated me like a little sister. But Shane had been replaced almost a year ago with Brad.

And the two men couldn't be more different.

No applause follows me off stage, and my shoulders slump as I stand next to the table where Brad lounges with several empty shot glasses and a basket of soggy French fries.

"Hungry?" he asks around a mouthful of food.

"No." I am, but I'll wait until we're back at the hotel. Hopefully they have a vending machine, or if I'm lucky, I can grab something edible at a gas station close by.

He shrugs one shoulder. "Suit yourself." Standing, he drains the rest of a bottle of beer and motions at me to put my guitar in its case. "C'mon, princess, we don't have all day."

I open my mouth, ready to hurl his attitude right back, but just as quickly snap it shut. He wants a reaction from me. But the less I give him, the sooner he'll go back to ignoring me.

Instead, I gently place the guitar in its case. The Gibson was a graduation present from my parents. They wanted me to chase my dreams. Do nightmares count? Asking for a friend.

I snap the latches shut, and Brad pushes me toward the exit. The guitar case slams against a column, making me flinch at the thud. Hopefully it's not broken. He steps around me and storms out into the darkness.

At least he isn't leaving me this time. I hurry to catch up with him. He's only done it once, but it left a strong enough impression to reinforce that I never want it to happen again.

The summer night in New Jersey is hot and sticky, and adds to the dirty feeling of my skin. Thank God it's the last night of the tour Brad booked. Back to LA in the morning to start the next album. A whole different kind of torture, but a change of pace from the lecherous stares Brad's been giving me more frequently over these last few weeks.

For most of the tour, he's made comments to me about how he likes my ass and how I need to show a little more skin for more recognition. He even went so far as to take over my wardrobe choices. Tonight's skirt barely brushes the bottom of my ass, and the shirt could double as a bikini top.

One more day. I can do this.

I set my guitar in the back of his rental car and carefully fold myself into the passenger seat to avoid flashing him. He smirks and punches the accelerator. I close the door quickly and drag the seatbelt across my body at the same time.

The silence is awkward, but I'll take the discomfort over the awful death metal he listens to, so I don't say anything as we drive the ten minutes back to the motel.

"You want to grab a drink to celebrate the end of your tour?" he asks as he parks the car.

"No, thanks. I'm tired, and our flight is pretty early, so I think I'll just go to bed."

Hasn't he had enough?

My parents and my brothers would kill me for getting into a car with someone who drank as much as he had tonight. But they're not here. None of them understands what my life has been like.

If I told them, they'd encourage me to come home. There would be offers to take care of me, to help. But I can't be a failure at this too. Calls to my family are short, infrequent, and filled with lies about what an amazing time I'm having. About how all my dreams are coming true.

I step out of the car, then open the back door to grab my guitar case.

"I'll walk you to your room. This neighborhood's not so great."

Who is this guy who gives a damn and what did he do with the Brad I've gotten to know over the last year? Maybe he's as relieved to be done with this tour as I am? No one would willingly sign up for this. Right?

"Okay."

The only sounds come from the motel lounge and restaurant. The air is polluted with dirt and neglect, and it seems like only half of the lights work, casting shadows in the flickering of the bulbs. At least the smoky smell of cigarettes is gone, and the headache throbbing behind my eyes is clearing too.

"Thanks, Brad. I'm sure there are other things you want to do. I can take it from here," I say, turning from my door to face him.

"I have other things I want to do," he says with a creepy smile. "But I don't need to go anywhere to do them."

He presses close, surrounding me with his thick arms and body odor.

I'm trapped between the solid door at my back and the two-hundred-pound guy whose hands shift behind me to grab my ass. His fingers dig painfully into my flesh.

I yank my guitar case up between us to push him away, but he blocks it with his hip.

"Stop."

"'Stop,'" he mimics, chuckling. "Aren't you cute?"

"I m-mean it."

He slides his hand down my backside, his fingers reaching under the skirt.

"B-Brad. Stop."

"You know you want this too, princess. Why else would you dress like you do?"

I squirm between him and the door, trying to dislodge his fingers from yanking at my panties. Turning my head, I search for someone to help me, but there's no one.

I'm alone.

"I don't. You t-told me I had to dress like this. Stop." Freeing a hand, I shove at his chest.

He pushes more of his weight against me and slides one leg between mine. "You could have said no," he says.

I could have. But I didn't. Too caught up in wanting to be successful at this, I went along with most of his demands. But not this. My body is still mine, and I won't sleep with him.

"I'm saying no now."

He tugs at my underwear again, and the distinct ripping

sound is echoed by him groaning in my ear. Then he licks it. Ice freezes in my veins as my heart thunders against my chest.

No!

I'm going to be sick. Air saws in and out of my lungs, but my vision still blurs with light-headedness.

I need to get away.

I push against Brad, but he only grunts.

"That eager for me, princess?"

Bile coats the back of my throat. If I don't do something, I'm going to end up raped against my motel room door.

Deep breath, Mikey.

I recognize that voice.

West.

Breathe and think.

Brad moves one of his hands to the cup of my top, yanking it aside to pinch my nipple. The bolt of pain steals my breath.

Michaela, you need to breathe. Save yourself.

I push out the unwelcome sensations tunneling my senses and take a deep breath. My guitar case hangs heavy in my hand, and I nearly laugh at the absurdity of being attacked while still managing to hold on to the case.

Bingo!

"Maybe we should take this inside," I offer. "Privacy."

"Now you're talking. Where's your key?"

"My pocket. But I can't reach it."

He shifts away a little, and I tug the key from my pocket. He doesn't give me enough room to turn around, so I fumble until the key slides into the slot and the beep tells me the door is unlocked. Gripping the door handle, I yank at the same time I position the neck of my guitar case between Brad's legs.

With one step back, I bring it up as hard as I can. Brad falls backward, clutching himself and groaning.

"You fucking bitch." The hatred on his face is the last thing I see before I slam the door, latching the chain as quickly as I can with shaky fingers.

The door vibrates as Brad pounds on it. I sink down against it, drawing my knees up to my chest. One breast is still hanging out of my shirt. I tug the material of my top back into place and wrap my arms around my knees and focus on slow, deep breaths.

"Think you're hot shit, do you? We'll see about that." His voice fades, but I don't move, terrified he's coming back. Or worse. He's still there. Waiting.

I sit in front of the door until my legs start to tingle, then stand stiffly and peek out the moldy curtains. The car is still there. No sign of Brad.

But what about tomorrow?

I can't. I can't do this anymore. I can't keep pretending this will be my path to success. Stepping into the bathroom, I lock myself inside before twisting the water as hot as it will go. While the room fills with steam, I stare at myself in the mirror.

The girl I was eighteen months ago—happy, excited, and optimistic about the future spun for her with lies and pretty words—is gone. My reflection shows someone who's been worn down by each obstacle the last year has thrown.

"Maybe I should just admit I failed," I whisper.

Each piece of clothing I strip off gets kicked into a pile behind the toilet before I step under the hot spray. The complimentary bar of soap is little, but it does the job. The air conditioning in the room freezes me as I step out of the bathroom wrapped in a towel, the frigid air clearing the fog of the last hour. Hell, of the last three months of this tour.

I pull my pajamas on quickly and glance at my phone.

BRAD

See you tomorrow.

Tears blur my vision, and I drop the phone, pacing the small room and nearly tripping over my guitar case lying forgotten by the door. With a sigh, I lean over and pick it up, placing it on top of the dresser and unlocking the latches.

It looks the same as it did when I started this journey. But *I'm* different. No longer the naïve girl who thinks she'll be an overnight superstar. I'm not sure who I am now. Except tired. I rub my fingers along the strings and up the soft lining of the case. They snag on the hidden pocket Mom was so excited to show me. She told me to keep something safe there if I needed to.

There's a hard ridge under the pocket, and I study it curiously for a moment before I dig my fingers into the small space.

It's a credit card with a sticky note on it.

For Emergencies Only in Mom's handwriting.

I'm eighty-one miles from home and scared to find out what comes next with Brad. Does this count as an emergency?

Better to ask for forgiveness than permission.

Working through the best way to do this, I pull up Uber on my phone, plug in the credit card information, and order the least expensive ride I can. Finding the Atlantic City bus station on my own after midnight seems scary as hell. And this is cheaper than a cab. My ride is accepted, and I sigh in relief when I see the driver who has accepted my ride is a woman about my age.

I trade my pajamas for jeans and a hoodie and toss the remainder of my meager belongings into my duffel bag. House-keeping can throw away the clothes piled behind the toilet tomorrow. Once the guitar is secure in its case again, I watch the little car on the app get closer and closer. Finally, I check the peephole to make sure that Brad is nowhere in sight, then slowly open the door and scan both directions. No Brad.

I sprint to the car and don't take a full breath until I'm in the back seat.

"Michaela?" the driver asks.

"Yes. Thank you so much," I say as she pulls onto the main road.

She shrugs. "No problem. I usually drive at night, and you're my first request today. Now my only one."

"I still appreciate it."

"You're welcome. Umm…do you mind me asking why you were at that motel? You don't seem like the normal type to stay there."

I glance down at the jeans and hoodie I tossed on before leaving the room.

"I don't?"

"No. Most of the time, those rooms come with hourly rates, if you catch my meaning."

"Oh. Uh, someone else booked the room." *Brad.* "I didn't know."

She nods. "Makes sense."

She's quiet for a while, and my eyelids droop as I lean my head against the window.

"You mind if I play some music?" she asks, and I sit back up, blinking.

"Sure. Sorry, I'm not great company tonight."

She laughs. "Most nights I chauffeur a bunch of drunks around. You're just fine."

She hits the button for the radio, and music fills the small car. I'm not sure whether to laugh or cry.

It's "Possibilities"—the duet I recorded with Jax when I was on top of the world.

The irony of this particular song after tonight is more than I want to deal with now. Attempting to ignore it, I lean my head back against the window, relieved when sleep silences the memories.

CHAPTER 2

WEST

I bolt upright in bed in the pitch dark. A quick glance at my alarm clock tells me it's almost three in the morning.

"Ugh. Abbott, go back to bed. First day of school tomorrow." I adjust my pillow a little too harshly, then flop back down.

I thought as a teacher, the first day jitters would dissipate. Blame the hormones of youth. Whatever. Turns out, I'm still anxious about school starting tomorrow. Granted, it's my first day at a new school, but even after seven years of teaching at the same school, I had still been a little nervous the night before every first day.

I'm almost asleep when a thud downstairs has me sitting up again. It's not Dan or Kelly—they left for a three-week cruise on Saturday. What the hell is going on?

I toss on a pair of pajama pants and grab my phone before creeping downstairs, automatically avoiding the one tread that has squeaked since Sawyer and I would sneak out as teenagers.

The light in the kitchen is on, the sound of the coffee maker loud in the otherwise quiet of the middle of the night. I squint at my phone again to see if I have any missed texts. Maybe Sawyer planned to stop by his parents' house. Nothing. But he wouldn't think twice about not sending a text either.

My palms are sweaty as I ease across the living room toward the kitchen doorway. I blink against the bright overhead lights. Turning in the direction of the coffee maker on the opposite counter, I brace myself for either a burglar or my best friend—I'm not sure what to expect.

Certainly not the cascade of honey-colored hair falling halfway down a light pink hoodie.

"Mikey?" I croak, my voice raspy with sleep.

She gasps and spins away from the counter.

"West?" The confusion on her face would be adorable if it wasn't the middle of the goddamned night.

"What the hell are you doing here at"—I glance at my phone—"two fifty-two in the morning?"

"I live here," she retorts. "What are *you* doing here?"

"I live here."

Mikey moved out eighteen months ago when she signed a record deal. I may have been living in Pittsburgh at the time, but I was so fucking proud when Sawyer told me the news. For months, I listened for her songs to be played on the radio before my own world imploded.

"Why are you living with my parents?"

"I just moved back. Ashley and I split up." Good riddance. "That doesn't explain why you're here—why the hell are you making coffee at three in the morning?"

"You moved back?"

I rub a hand down my face. I need to wake up some more if we're going to hold a coherent conversation. "Yes, about two months ago."

"You're living with my parents?"

Failure is a bitter pill that sticks in my throat.

"Yeah."

"Why?"

"I—" The thought of telling her the truth—that I can't afford an apartment on my salary when she's a famous rock star—burns. But I'd rather suffer through that than tell her some bullshit story. "Apartments here are expensive. I need to save some money. Your parents wanted some work done. So they offered to let me stay here in exchange."

"Work?"

With a sigh, I lean against the counter, crossing my arms over my chest. "I redid their bathroom. Now that they're gone on a cruise—"

"They went on a cruise?"

Her question pisses me off. Sawyer said Mikey was busy with a tour, but does she talk to her family at all? Dan and Kelly have been planning this anniversary cruise for the last six months.

"Jesus, don't you talk to your family?"

Her shoulders tense. Dammit, that didn't come out right.

"Shit, Mikey, I'm sorry—"

"I do. But only a few minutes here or there," she says, nibbling on her plump bottom lip.

My attention snags on the motion, my body realizing this isn't the same Mikey I remember from her sophomore year in high school—the last time I saw her before moving to Pittsburgh. The gangly fifteen-year-old with braces and hair that couldn't be contained unless it was scraped back into a tight ponytail is gone. The girl is now a woman. Mikey is now Michaela. Caramel colored hair in smooth waves, wide blue eyes the color of the autumn sky, and light pink lips that beg to be sampled.

Oh, hell no.

I slam the lid on those thoughts. Even if I was ready to date again, Mikey is off limits. She's like a little sister to me. She *is* the younger sister of my best friend. I've known this family since Sawyer and I were seven and she was a baby. Sleep deprivation is causing temporary insanity.

"Why aren't you staying with your parents?" Her words interrupt my internal lecture.

"They moved to California last year, closer to Whit and her family. She earned my parents' undying devotion by gifting them their first grandchild," I say with a smile and roll of my eyes.

Her lips tilt at the corners, but not into the smile I remember. Dark shadows mar the skin under her eyes, and she's so pale she's practically transparent.

"Are you okay, Mike?" I take a step toward her, stopping when she shudders.

"Me? I'm fine. Just tired. Thankful to be home now that the tour is done."

"A tour, huh? What's it like to be a big-time rock star?" I ask.

"Oh, um…" She fidgets with the frayed cuff of her sweatshirt, reminding me of the girl she used to be. "It's great. Everything I ever hoped for."

The smile she gives me doesn't quite reach her eyes.

Maybe she's tired. Fuck, *I'm* tired.

"How long are you staying?"

"Oh, um, I guess a few weeks…" She spins back to the coffeemaker and turns it off. "I'm really tired. I think I'll try coffee in a few hours. Sorry I woke you up."

I wave away her apology. "Don't worry about it."

She grabs her guitar case and shoulders the duffel from the counter.

"Here," I say, gesturing to her bag.

The duffel is surprisingly light when she hands it over. Don't all girls pack thirty pounds of shit for their face and hair? Ashley always did. It was a miracle if we could leave for the weekend with only two suitcases.

I follow Mike out of the kitchen, flipping off the lights as I do. I also try not to stare at the way her jeans hug the curves of her ass as she walks upstairs. Temporary insanity is a bitch.

She stops in front of the closed door to her room. It's still decorated with a carved sign spelling her name, along with a "Girls Only" decal that kept both of her brothers and me out of her room.

"H-how long are you staying?" She meets my gaze, and my breath catches in my lungs.

Her eyes have always dominated her face—it was creepy when she was little. They were so big compared to her tiny stature. But now they're...captivating.

Dude, you need more sleep.

"Until I have enough for a deposit for an apartment and a little bit of savings. In return, I'm helping with the remodels your mom wants."

"Remodels for what?"

I shrug. "Not sure. Just got the list from your mom and dad when I got here."

"I thought you were a teacher."

"Worked construction every summer through college. It might surprise you what I can do with my hands." The innuendo hangs between us. What the hell is wrong with me?

"Oh."

"Well, I'm gonna get back to sleep. First day of school tomorrow—today," I correct. "So, if I don't see you in the morning, I'll see you after school."

I reach up, passing the strap of the bag back to her. An electrical current zips from her hand to mine at the accidental brush of our fingers. I'm too aware of the way her lips part and the light breath that escapes between us.

"Good night, Mikey." I use her childhood nickname to remind myself of who she is. What she is.

Off limits.

"'Night, West," she says quietly.

I shuffle to my bedroom at the other end of the hall and glance back to find her leaning against her door, watching me. I give her a little wave, and she jumps, disappearing into her room.

Her bedroom door shuts a fraction of a second after mine does, and I release the breath I was holding.

Sleep. I need sleep.

"Good morning, everyone. How about we all grab a seat and get started?" The chorus of groans at my announcement is followed by the shuffle of bodies and bags as twenty-five teenagers move at a snail's pace.

The first bell of the day has rung, and summer is officially over. I should be happy to be here. It's a new school, a clean slate. But exhaustion still tugs at my muscles with stiff fingers, and a fuzzy haze hovers around the edges of my brain despite the three cups of coffee I mainlined before rushing out of the house.

My plan as I first drifted off to sleep had been to get to school early. But that plan had not included a middle-of-the-night wake-up call by a sexy blonde.

We talked about this.

Not sexy. Mike is like a little sister to me.

Get it through your head. No, not that head.

I would fit right in with one of the hormone-driven teenagers staring at me sleepily.

Pull it together, dude. You have a job to do.

I'd stumbled into the kitchen after the sun came up. Once more, she was in front of the coffeepot, the edges of a t-shirt grazing her thighs. I'm ashamed—okay, not really—that my gaze had lingered a little longer on the tan, toned legs under the t-shirt that was shorter than was good for my sanity.

Job. Kids. Teach. Say something.

"Good morning," I repeat. "For those of you who don't know me—and since I'm new to the school, that would be all of you—" I laugh at my own joke, and the kids groan. "My name is Mr. Abbott. Welcome to American History."

The routine takes over and thoughts of Mikey fade to the back of my mind, though they don't leave my brain completely. She haunts me in second period World History with a group of gangly freshmen who remind me of the Mikey I used to know. During my third hour planning period, the noticeable absence of Axe body spray allows my thoughts to easily drift to her.

Finally, lunch lets me interact with other adults. My department head introduces me to the other teacher in the history department.

"Welcome to Ridgeview," my coworker Mary says with a warm smile. She teaches World History and the honors program classes while Phil takes on AP classes and Pennsylvania Past, Present, and Future.

"Thank you. Have you been here long?"

"Fifteen years," she shares. "But Phil's been here for twenty-five."

I turn to my department head. "Twenty-five?"

He nods. "As of today."

"Congratulations."

I spend the rest of lunch learning about my coworkers—both in and out of the department—before heading back for fourth period American History again. I'd like to say a certain blonde isn't on my mind at all, but who am I kidding?

By the time the release bell rings at the end of the seventh period, my missed sleep is catching up with me. Even the extra cup of coffee I grabbed last period isn't touching the exhaustion dragging at my eyelids. Maybe physical exercise this afternoon will keep me awake for a few more hours. Driving home with the windows down and the wind whipping through the car doesn't help.

"Mike, you home?" I call, opening the front door and dropping my keys on the table next to it.

There's no answer—she's probably out catching up with

friends. It's probably better she isn't here when I'm trying to get her off my mind anyway.

According to the remodel plan I drafted, I'm right on track to meet the three-week self-imposed deadline, and I don't want to fall behind. Dan and I did the framing and drywall in the guest room before he left for the cruise, so tonight only calls for me to texture those walls.

An hour tops.

I head upstairs to change my clothes, unbuttoning my shirt as I go. Each of my legs has to weigh fifty pounds right now. A nap sounds like heaven, but I promised Dan and Kelly the basement would be finished by the time they got home.

"Come on, Abbott, wake up and get it done."

Mike's door flies open as I step in front of it, and I jump back.

"Jesus Christ, Mike, slow down."

She stares at me silently for a second before her gaze drops and seems to snag where my fingers are still undoing the buttons of my shirt. Her tongue peeks out, licking along her plush lips, and I close my eyes, unable to erase the image from my brain as easily as I can block the sight in front of me in real-time.

"Did you say something?" she asks, her voice husky. She blinks and rubs at her face, and I get the impression she just woke up.

The circles under her eyes are lighter, but still too dark for my liking.

"What? About you scaring the hell out of me?"

"Ha-ha," she deadpans. "No. Earlier."

"Just called your name when I walked in. I expected you to be out with friends or hanging out somewhere."

She shakes her head, sending her wild mass of hair moving. "No. I slept for most of the day."

Under normal circumstances, I might give her shit, but considering how pale she was when she got home last night, it was probably the right choice.

"Feel free to go back to sleep. I'm going to change and work on some texture in the basement."

"Do you want any help?" Her expression is so hopeful that my automatic refusal instantly dies.

"Sure. Meet you in the basement in five?"

She nods, and ten minutes later, my attention is riveted to the strip of skin revealed where her t-shirt has ridden up.

Quit ogling your best friend's little sister like a creeper and work.

Swallowing my sudden curiosity about the woman she's become, I spend a few minutes demonstrating what needs to be done and set her up on the wall opposite me. Where I can't see her.

My shoulders relax in the quiet, and I take a deep breath. The chemical smell of the texture spray and the new drywall linger in the air and remind me of my college summers. I clear my mind, knowing I don't need to concentrate since this is all muscle memory. I'm not focused on anything when my ears perk at the low hum coming from the other side of the room.

I pause, barely daring to breathe as the sound continues for several breaths before the faint strains of a song whisper in my ears. She was ten the first time she sang in front of her family—Sawyer and I had been playing video games in the living room, and she'd wanted to practice a song she was learning for school. Her voice was amazing then, and it's only gotten better with time.

The notes continue, not a song I recognize—either by her or by any other artist I listen to—but the sound wraps around me, infusing me with the sadness of the low tones and the heartbreak of the upper.

The sound stops and she turns to me, her eyes widening when she catches me staring.

"Um, how's this?" She gestures to the wall behind her.

Reluctantly, I shift my attention to the area she's textured, impressed by how well she did, given this is her first time.

"Great," I say with a smile. "You're a natural."

Her smile is bigger than it was last night, but still not the one I want to see. The question hovers on my tongue. I want to ask her what's wrong, but something tells me I'd get the same answer I got yesterday—she's tired. There's more though. I don't know how I know that, but there is. She won't react well if I keep pushing her for answers she doesn't want to give.

"This whole wall like this?" she asks, and I move my attention to what she's been doing.

"Yep."

She turns back to her wall, and I wait for the humming to begin again, but it doesn't. Finally, I restart the wall I'm working on, embarrassed to realize I need to redo the section I textured after she first started humming. Soon enough I fix it, and the silence continues.

Silence between Ashley and I had been tense the last couple of years we were together. Usually because of something I said or did to piss her off. But with Mikey, it isn't.

It's comfortable, but I still find myself breaking the quiet.

"Happy to be home?"

I keep my back to her as I turn to the next wall.

"You have no idea." She snorts.

"You said a few weeks, right?"

"More or less." Her vague answer piques my curiosity.

"Any plans while you're home?"

"A cheesesteak somewhere with my name on it." The smile is clear in her voice.

"Oh yeah? You and your friends going to hit up Pat's?"

"Pat's?" She glances over her shoulder at me, her face a mask of mischievous horror. "I'm a Geno's girl, Abbott."

"Pat's invented the sandwich," I argue.

She shrugs and sticks her tongue out at me. "I like what I like."

"You're crazy." Despite my words, I love the way her eyes have lit up. Who'd have thought a cheesesteak had that kind of power? "Geno's...what's next? Swiss cheese?"

A giggle bursts from her lips.

"Have you ever had Geno's?" she asks, hip canted out in a sassy pose.

"No, I'm a purist."

"So how do you know you like Pat's better?"

I shrug. "I guess I don't."

"We could always do a taste test. Hit up both places," she suggests.

"Name the time, Mikey."

"Friday night?"

Friday. Shit.

"Back-to-school night is on Friday," I apologize. "We won't be done until late, but what about Saturday? And maybe we could grab a drink when I'm done on Friday. A welcome-back-to-Philly night. You can invite your friends too."

The smile fades from her face. "My only friend is on location shooting a movie."

"Didn't you used to have a whole group of girlfriends?"

I vaguely remember Sawyer complaining about her friends when he came home before his last deployment.

She shrugs, the movement is stiff. "We just...we lost touch."

That hesitation creates uncertainty in the pit of my stomach.

"So only the two of us?" I ask.

She nods. "Is that okay? You can always invite your friends."

"Sawyer lives in California, so that would be a long drive for him."

"You don't have friends here?"

"Only been back two months," I remind her.

"Oh. Well, I guess it'll just be the two of us."

"Yep."

Why do I like the idea of that so much?

CHAPTER 3

MICHAELA

I'm glad—now—that West was here when I got home. I wasn't at first. He had scared the shit out of me—not hard, given how that night had gone. I had expected to leave a note on the kitchen counter that I was here and that I'd have a run-in with Mom or Dad the next morning. Mom had mentioned something about a cruise, but I guess I didn't pay attention to the dates she gave me.

While West teaches—more power to him for wanting to spend more time in school than he has to—I spend each day thinking about my next steps. My dream hasn't changed. I want to be a successful singer, but I'm not willing to compromise where Brad is concerned. I've blocked his number and left several messages with the receptionist at Reverb, hoping to speak to Randa Miller, the owner. I think she's Brad's boss.

"Are you sure I can't speak to the person in charge of the label reps?" I ask, attempting for the third time in as many days to reach someone I can report Brad's behavior to.

"I'm sorry, hon, but that person is unavailable."

That person. Obviously that information is some big secret.

"I'm a current artist with Reverb," I tell her.

"I'll make sure to pass along your message." She sounds ready to disconnect my call with an indifferent press of her finger.

"I've left a few messages already." The urge to scream bubbles in my chest, the frustration at the lack of response finally overwhelming me.

"I'll pass along your message. Thank you for calling Reverb Records."

Click.

"*Shit*!" I scream to the empty living room. The only response is the muffled sound of the TV. Since the silence stresses me out, I leave either the radio or TV on for the background noise.

Pacing the length of the living room and back, I struggle with the need to act now that I have a plan. Report Brad. Keep working toward my dream of being a famous singer.

The lack of response from my label is stopping that before it's even begun.

My phone rings, distracting me from my pacing.

"Hey, Mia."

My friendship with Mia Maddox formed under the most bizarre circumstances. I'd contacted her after her ex, Tucker Winston, released a sex video and claimed it was her. He lied. It was me. And I had finally proven it to the media when I showed them my tattoo—a perfect match to the one visible in the video.

"You sound like shit, Kay."

Her directness surprises a laugh from me. "Well, thanks. Tell me how you really feel."

"That's all I have for now. What's going on?"

I flop onto the couch with a sigh.

"Another call to Reverb. Another message."

Mia is aware that I'm home after my tour, but not exactly why I'm in Pennsylvania instead of LA. The only thing I shared with her is that I can't work with Brad anymore. Since she knows he's a jerk based on some of my other stories, it's not necessarily a surprise. But I'm not ready to tell her everything that happened when I'm still trying to process how I feel about it. So far, the two major responses are relief that I managed to avoid him when I left and embarrassment for putting myself in that situation to begin with.

But now frustration has joined the mix.

"Have you thought about getting out of your contract?" she asks.

"How would I even do that?"

"I'd start with an attorney. There are plenty in LA that specialize in entertainment law. There must be some way though. Come to LA."

"You're not in LA," I remind her, mulling over the idea. Maybe I can find an attorney here since I'm not ready to head back to California just yet. "Speaking of, how's Washington?"

"Wet," she says with a laugh. "It's rained here nonstop for the last two weeks. Now the director is rethinking the location."

"Isn't the story set in the Pacific Northwest though?"

"I wouldn't be surprised if he tells the writer to change it. But for now, we can't shoot until it lets up a bit, so I get to spend my time talking to you."

"Wouldn't you rather talk to your husband?" I tease.

She and Garrett are freaking adorable. They've been friends since childhood and have tons of inside jokes and stories, but their chemistry is still hot enough to set the world on fire.

"I'll talk to him later. I feel like I haven't talked to you in months."

"You've been busy kicking Hollywood's ass," I say.

"You've been busy on your tour too."

Two different levels. But I don't want to debate with her right now. Mia is a successful movie star. I sing to disinterested drunks at smoky bars.

"I'm not going to argue with you. But you know what I think."

She sighs but doesn't push. "Fine. How's Pennsylvania?"

Good question. I haven't stopped to think about it, too focused on trying to keep my career from dying completely.

"Meh." I shrug. "It's home."

Sort of. It's like a shirt that's a little too small—it doesn't quite fit, but I'm not willing to stop trying it on.

"You should come stay with me. I'll see if Garrett knows any entertainment attorneys."

Her interruption pulls me out of my thoughts. "Maybe."

"Maybe? C'mon, it'll be fun. We have a whole guest house you can use."

"I doubt you want a third wheel hanging around all the time."

"You're welcome anytime," she assures me.

I snort. "You say that now. Aren't you still a newlywed?"

"So what if I am?"

"Mi, don't you want to be alone with your new husband?"

"You'll have your own space," she says again. "I'm heading home in three weeks—hopefully. Once I know for sure, we'll set everything up."

"I'm fine. I'm enjoying my break for now and helping West with the basement."

"West? Sawyer's friend?"

"Yeah. Long story short, he's living here and finishing the basement while my parents are out of town."

"Ohhh. Is he cute?" she asks.

"Aren't you married?" I tease.

"Not for me, goof. For you."

"I dunno." I *do* know.

Cute is the wrong word. As the college guy I had a crush on when he came to see my brother, he was cute. Longish blond hair, green eyes sparkling with laughter over something he and Sawyer were talking about. He was the perfect specimen for my thirteen-year-old heart to fall in love with.

As a man? He is lethal to my libido. He still has the green eyes, but they're more watchful, more observant than they were when he was younger. Gone is the baby face of youth—his jaw is sharp and angular, and by the time I see him each afternoon, it's covered in a layer of scruff I want to catalog with my palms.

Other places too. It's surprising how strongly I'm attracted to him, given what happened with Brad. But my body and mind have decided it's safe to lust after him.

"Who are you kidding? Tell me!"

"He..." How to describe the experience of just being in the same room with him? "Cute isn't the right word, Mi."

"No?"

"Nope." I pop the *P* and squirm against the couch as my heart rate picks up its pace.

"Gonna live out a boy next door love story?"

I laugh at Mia's absurd question. "He's my brother's best friend."

"So?"

"He just broke up with his fiancée."

"Why?"

"I'm not sure. I haven't asked."

"Well, ask him. If there's a chance they might get back together, run far away," she says, and my snort of laughter is self-deprecating.

She says that *now*, but where was the advice before Tucker?

"There isn't anything between us. I'm just this annoying kid sister type to him."

"Remind him you're not *his* sister," she says. A loud noise in the background interrupts her, and she sighs. "Shoot. The rain stopped. Back to work."

"You love it," I remind her.

"I do. Don't forget, look into that attorney and let me know if you want to do any checking around LA. I can talk to Garrett," she offers.

"I will."

If I don't, she'll pester me until I do. But I would anyway. If someone from Reverb finally calls me, great. But I'm not going to wait around for that to happen when I have no idea if it will solve the problem or not.

"Later, lovey."

"Bye."

I barely put my phone down before it pings again. But this time it's a text from West. We exchanged numbers earlier this week.

WEST

Parent night runs until 8. Is that too late for you?

No.

Is it too late for you? Isn't that your bedtime? *laughing emoji*

As old as I am, I think I'll survive.

Roaring Revolution work? I'll meet you there at 8:30.

Where?

It's a speakeasy. On 18th street.

There's a door next to the all-night diner there.

I can head home, pick you up?

That's not me getting butterflies from reading the word "home" in his text messages. Nope. It's another Michaela. But I don't want him to think I can't do anything on my own.

That's okay.

I'll find it.

You sure?

Yep. 8:30. Roaring Revolution.

See you then.

𝄞 𝄞 𝄞

My Uber drops me off next to the all-night diner on 18th Street at eight twenty-five. An old weathered door is under a single old-fashioned lamp. This must be the place.

Rolling my shoulders back, I put on my confidence the same way I donned the rest of my clothes before I left the house. And finding an outfit had been a research project all on its own. Google didn't give me much to work with since I don't need a costume and can't afford anything new. My closet is in a sad state —I didn't leave much behind when I relocated to LA. But I managed to find a white floral mini-wrap dress hiding between the prom dresses in the back corner. It doesn't scream 1920s, but it was nicer than a tank top and cut-off shorts.

The door opens as I reach for the handle, and a bouncer dressed all in black and wearing white suspenders stares at me.

"Can I help you?"

I clear my throat. "I'm…um…I'm looking for Roaring Revolution?"

Maybe this isn't the right door.

Then why is he dressed like a mobster from the twenties?

"Password," is all he says.

Password? West didn't give me a password.

"I'm, um, meeting a friend here. He didn't give me a password—"

"Velvet." The word is breathed behind me, so close I shiver as West's breath caresses the back of my neck.

I want to lean into the arm West wraps around my waist with a squeeze. Nerves jump in my belly at the innocent brush of his fingers.

No, not nerves. Butterflies.

Calm down, this isn't a date.

"Sorry, forgot about the password," he whispers.

"N-no problem," I stutter, dragging my tongue across lips that suddenly feel like they've been baking in the sun all day.

The bouncer motions for us to walk past him, and West grabs my hand, yanking me toward a dark-stained wooden banister leading down. I'm so focused on watching the way his pants cup his ass, I nearly run into him when he stops and turns to face me, a grin stretching across his face and lighting up his eyes.

"Ready for this?" He's like a kid on Christmas Eve, practically bouncing in place, and I can't fight the laugh bubbling up at his expression.

"Excited?"

"To enjoy history while I have a drink? Absolutely." He grins, his eyes traveling from the top of my head down to my wedge sandals, leaving a trail of heat in their wake. "You look nice."

The warmth of my body settles in my cheeks at the combination of his compliment and the fire banked in his eyes.

"Thanks. You do too."

His white shirt is tucked into gray slacks, and the top few buttons are undone.

"Parent night. Sorry, but I ditched the tie in my car."

"How could you?" I tease.

He laughs and reaches out to lace his fingers with mine. "Let's have a drink."

CHAPTER 4

MICHAELA

The stairs are steep in the old building, and by the time we reach the bottom of the two flights, I'm gripping his hand and one arm for dear life.

"Ta-da," he says, pulling me next to him. His breath tickles my ear, and goosebumps lift along my neck and shoulder.

The dim lighting of the long, narrow room glows from the top of the exposed brick walls. Dark wooden tables and chairs are scattered with large leather sofas, while the well-lit bar is the sparkling focal point.

The whole scene lends an illicit atmosphere to where we are, what we're doing, and excitement thrums through my blood. Low music plays through hidden speakers, and even though the bar is quiet, West stays close, keeping his voice low.

"You want a drink?" His teeth gleam in the shadowy entrance.

I nod, loving the heat of his hand where it rests against the small of my back. "Okay."

He leads us through the few patrons to two open barstools, holding my hand until I sit down.

"What'll it be?"

I'm so caught up in West, I didn't even see the bartender step in front of us.

"Whiskey sour for me," West says before turning to me.

I frantically scan for a menu, but the pressure of his hand squeezing mine brings my gaze back to his.

"No menus."

The last part is murmured so only I can hear him.

"What should I order?" I whisper back.

I don't know what they serve in a speakeasy. Is it different from another bar?

"Trust me?" he asks, and I nod before he turns back to the patient bartender. "Mary Pickford for the lady."

The bartender taps the bar once and disappears to make our drinks, leaving West and me alone again.

"What's a Mary Pickford?" I wrinkle my nose. "It sounds like a librarian's name."

West throws back his head and laughs, drawing my attention to the strong tendons in his neck.

"God, I missed your sense of humor," he says. "It's a rum drink with pineapple juice and grenadine."

"That sounds really good," I admit. "Why isn't it busier in here? It's Friday night."

He shrugs. "I heard about this place through a Philadelphia history group on Facebook. I don't think a lot of people know what it is or how to find it."

"How sad. Won't it shut down if people can't find it?"

"I hope not. I've been here twice so far and love it."

The bartender returns, and West hands me the rose-colored drink while he holds another the shade of amber with a cherry on the top for himself.

"A toast?" he asks, arching his eyebrow as he watches me.

"Sure." I hold my glass next to his and try to resist the hypnotic draw of his eyes. "What are we toasting to?"

"History?" he asks, and I shake my head.

"No. Not history." Nothing in my history is worth toasting. "Old friends?"

Because despite my attraction to him, he only sees me the way Sawyer does.

We're both silent for a moment, glasses held up awkwardly, when he snaps his fingers.

"I've got it. To new beginnings."

The way he's studying me as he says the words has my thighs squeezing together. Stupid body can't get on board with the friends concept.

Can you blame me? He's the smartest guy I've ever met and hotter than a grill on the fourth of July.

"T-to new beginnings," I echo, tapping his glass with mine.

The liquid is cool and fruity, and I take several swallows before I put the glass down.

"You like?"

"It's yummy." I lick the residual sugar off my lips. "What about you?"

"My whiskey sour? You want a taste?" He offers me the glass, and I take it from him for a sip.

"It's okay. I like mine better."

"Good. I didn't want to share anyway," he teases, surprising another smile from me. He motions to a nearby open couch, and I grab my drink to follow him.

The heat of his leg against mine as we sit side by side is a vacation in the Caribbean after spending a winter in Greenland. I've spent the last year in a deep freeze, burying my thoughts and emotions deep, but his touch thaws me little by little. I feel more like myself than I have in the last eighteen months.

The smooth jazz piping through the speakers flows into my body, and I relax farther into the couch. Music is the only thing that has ever made sense to me. There's something there, a connection that doesn't exist for me with anything else.

"This place is missing a dance floor." West's words bring me back to the present.

"What?"

"You," he says simply. "Your body has been moving to the rhythm of the song for the last few minutes."

"It has?" I didn't realize I had moved at all.

He nods, his gaze never leaving my face as he studies me.

"I was thinking about how I always felt connected to music in a way I never felt with anything else. The rest of the world is chaos, but music makes sense to me. It's the only thing that ever has," I admit.

"What do you mean?" He turns his body, curving toward me. His arm rests along the back of the couch and his fingers brush along my shoulder.

"I hated school. Words, numbers, all of it. Sawyer didn't tell you?"

Why would he and West talk about my struggles with school?

"No. Tell me what?"

"I was nearly held back my sophomore year. Up until then, Mom and Dad always figured I didn't like school. I didn't, but no one knew why. Finally, one of my teachers asked to evaluate me for dyslexia. She had it and noticed some of the same symptoms she struggled with."

"Dyslexia?"

I nod. "Dysgraphia too."

"How did no one catch it sooner?"

I shrug. "I'm not sure. But I was good at hiding the symptoms. I just figured I was the stupid one in our family."

"You're not fucking stupid," he grits out. "Jesus, did someone tell you that?"

"Kids can be mean. It was a long time ago."

"Not that long ago. It shouldn't have gone undiagnosed for so long. Someone should have caught it. One of your teachers along the way should have noticed something sooner and asked questions. Something." He breathes deeply, his words bitten out with more passion than when he talks about teaching—and he's usually very passionate about teaching.

"West, it's okay. I was only trying to explain my connection with music. I don't want you to be upset."

I squeeze his knee in comfort. He brings his hand up, covering mine until he fully interlaces my fingers with his.

"Sorry." His embarrassment is clear, and I tighten my fingers around his.

"You don't need to be sorry. I just wanted to tell you."

"Thank you for sharing that with me," he murmurs. "Your voice is incredible."

I huff and try to pull my hand back, embarrassed by his earnestness, but he holds on.

"You don't need to flatter me. My voice is okay, but nothing spectacular."

"You don't think so? You got a record contract," he responds. "What's it like being a famous rock star?"

"I'm not—" I nearly tell him that I'm not famous, but the way he's looking at me—with pride, wonder—locks the words in my throat.

"You're not...?"

"I'm not *that* famous," I tell him quickly, taking a drink to hide my discomfort. I should have just told him the truth. "Besides, lots of people get record contracts and never make it."

"Never make it? You were just on tour." His eyebrows knit in confusion, and my stomach nosedives.

"Yeah, but—" Yet again, the words push at my lips, ready to admit how not-famous I really am.

"But what?"

"They...they weren't that big. Small venues."

Can I call those bar floors venues?

He opens his mouth with a reply, but a server interrupts.

"Refills?"

West turns to me, and I nod before he orders a second drink for us.

"Why history?" I ask after the server leaves, desperate to change the subject from my fabricated fame.

He finishes what's left of his whiskey before answering.

"I've always loved it. We grew up in this city where all this history happened—"

"I've seen *National Treasure* many times thanks to you," I say seriously, teasing him.

He pokes me in the side, and I squirm away. "Funny girl. Yes, *National Treasure* is still my favorite movie. But Philadelphia is almost four hundred years old. A lot of history exists in our hometown."

"But you moved away." I remember when Sawyer told Mom and Dad about West moving. He hadn't been back long from a deployment in Afghanistan—his last one. "You broke Sawyer's heart."

"Pittsburgh was not my choice," he says with a grimace. "Ashley is from there and wanted to move back."

"Your fiancée. You moved for her?"

"Yep." His lips form a thin line before he leans forward, resting his elbows on his knees. The silence, so comfortable with him before, is awkward. "I wouldn't have chosen to move away on my own."

"Sorry."

"Why are you sorry?" He blinks several times, and the awkwardness fades. "You weren't the one who lied to me."

"What?"

The server drops off our new drinks, and West takes a sip before nodding. "Ashley was a liar. And when I found that out, I could no longer trust anything I knew about her. Anything I knew about us."

His face shows a mix of anger, pain, and exhaustion. He and

Ashley broke up because she lied to him. And here I am doing the same thing.

It doesn't matter. You're not dating him.

That thought doesn't stop guilt from swimming uneasily in my stomach.

"Sounds like we've both made some bad decisions in the past."

"Why? What bad decisions have you made lately?"

I take another sip instead of answering. I'm not interested in disappointing him by telling him about my bad choices.

"Nope. No more of the conversation downers. We came out to enjoy ourselves and our drinks—"

"Don't forget the history."

"And the history." I roll my eyes with an indulgent smile. "Let's talk about something else. Anything else. There's only one rule."

"What's that?" He leans in closer, the scent of his cologne encompassing me in a bubble of bergamot, citrus, and beach.

My breath catches. What do his lips feel like through the layer of scruff?

"Mikey?"

I snap back into focus.

"Oh. One rule. We need to have fun."

A smirk tilts his lips, and my skin singes where he locks his pinky around mine.

"Deal."

CHAPTER 5

MICHAELA

"Tonight was fun. Thanks for inviting me." I smile, even though I'm sad our night out is coming to an end.

"Tonight was because of you. Welcome home, Mike." He glances over at me with a quick grin before refocusing on the road. "As for the fun, it was more fun once we followed your rule."

I laugh, pulling on the fabric stuffed into his cup holder, unexplainably fidgety in the comfortable seat of his Subaru. The fabric is smooth and cool as I slide it through my fingertips. "What is this?"

He glances over again and groans. "My tie. I wore it for back-to-school night."

I didn't see him this morning before he left for school. Probably a good thing. The white button-down and gray slacks were distracting enough. Add the tie in, and I might as well be a puddle on the floor.

"Do you wear a lot of ties?"

"Not if I can help it," he says. "I don't mind occasionally. On nights like tonight."

"It's still looped." The silk threads through my fingers until it hooks on the knot at the center.

He lifts a shoulder and lets it drop. "I didn't think about untying it, just getting it off."

"I bet you look cute in a tie," I tease him and he huffs.

"Cute? Puppies are cute. Kittens are cute. Cute is the kiss of death," he complains.

"You don't want to be cute?"

"No." He pouts.

I laugh at his over-the-top reaction. "Well, what other word do you want me to use?"

"Handsome?"

"I don't know. I haven't seen you in a tie except for when you went to prom, and then it was a bow tie," I tell him. "Not that I would mind seeing you in one. You could always model this one for me. Then I can make an informed decision."

Flirting with him is dangerous. But I can't help it.

"I could show you what I can do with it instead," he murmurs, and my body temperature increases by a thousand degrees.

"What?" I didn't hear him right. He'll correct me, and I'll realize I nearly embarrassed myself by combusting on the spot.

"What?"

"I don't think I heard you correctly," I say as he eases the car to a stop at a traffic light.

He looks at me, and I forget to breathe. His face is cast in light and shadow from the road around us, the other cars, but there is no mistaking the spark of heat in his eyes as he captures my gaze.

"You did. But if you need me to repeat it, I will. I could show you what I can do with that tie. If you want."

My breathing shallows, and my heart thumps loudly in my chest. Desire surges through my body, flooding me with heat until my toes curl against the bottoms of my wedge sandals.

"I-I-I—" My brain has short-circuited, and I have no idea how to respond. Releasing my death grip on the silk material, I cradle it carefully in my hands.

The light turns green, and he turns his attention back to the road. I lick my lips and try to regain control of my body. When he doesn't say anything else, I consider his words in the silence. It's not comfortable, not awkward, but...charged, crackling around us and ready to ignite at any second.

Time speeds up, and it feels like four seconds later he's pulling into the driveway and shutting off the car, still without a word. Is he second-guessing what he said?

The heated glance he sends my direction tells me he doesn't regret anything. But if I tell him no, I have zero doubt he'll accept my decision and forget this conversation ever happened. I'm in control.

My passenger door clicks open, and I jump before settling my hand into his. The innocent slide of my palm on his creates an electric arc from my fingers to my core, and my knees buckle.

"Careful." His fingers tighten around mine.

Yes, he would be careful with me. The smooth tie is still clutched in the fingers of my other hand as I let him lead us up the sidewalk to the front door. I flipped the porch light on before I left, and it provides a glow around us as he turns to face me.

"Do I need to apologize?" he asks quietly. "What I said in the car..."

Anxiety underlies his words, calling to the uncertainty in me. I want to reassure him. But what does that look like?

"Did you mean it?" I murmur, fidgeting with the tie in my hands.

"Michaela. Look at me." The way he says my name makes my heart pound almost painfully. Two fingers lift my chin until his eyes lock with mine. "You've known me for as long as you can remember. I wouldn't say it unless I meant it."

"Oh." Every other thought disappears at the intensity of his gaze, the green nearly eclipsed by the darkness of his pupils.

My breath leaves my body on a gust as desire obliterates every emotion I've struggled with all week—failure, sadness, anger.

The only thing left in this moment is how he makes me feel—safe, confident…desired.

"This is your decision. If you say you'd rather forget I said anything, okay. But—"

I'm in control and that knowledge makes me powerful.

"What if I say yes?" My voice is only a whisper between us, but he's so close, he hears me clearly.

"Are you saying yes?" He tugs slightly at the tie between my fingers, reeling in my body inch by slow inch.

I relax my fingers, letting the silky material slide along my skin in a different caress. My nipples pebble in my bra at the sensation, and I close the last of the distance between us, bringing my body flush with his and meet his hungry gaze.

"Yes."

The word is barely past my lips when his mouth claims mine. The sparks from the car, from the moment before, ignite into a white-hot inferno as his tongue teases my lips. He grips my hips, each finger another connection of pleasure feeding whatever this is between us. I've known him for nearly my whole life and crushed on him for half of it. But never in a million years could I imagine the reality created by the skillful combination of his lips, his tongue, and his hands.

My back connects with the door behind me, and I gasp in surprise.

I lift my hands to trace my fingers from his wrists to his biceps. The bulge against my stomach lights a path to my core with thigh-clenching clarity.

He's as turned on as I am. Just from a kiss.

No, not merely a kiss.

A toe-curling, firework-sparking, mouth-gasm.

Is that a word? Who cares? If not, it should be. And the definition would be the way he's kissing me right now.

His fingers twist in the fabric of my dress at my waist, but he doesn't let go, doesn't try to grope me on the front porch. His restraint, the knowledge of something more coming, shivers along my spine to pulse in my core.

He shifts his mouth to nip along my jaw, and my head falls back against the solid surface, granting him better access he makes good use of. Hot open-mouthed caresses move south, settling at the pulse in my throat before he sinks his teeth roughly into the spot, then soothes it with his tongue.

"*West.*" This is what it means to be consumed.

Because what he's doing with every glide of his lips, every brush of his fingers? With the rasp of his voice as he growls against the tendon he just tasted?

All-consuming.

"We should take this inside. The neighbors don't need to see what I'm imagining."

If my panties were damp before, now they're drenched.

Yes. Yes, to all of it. Even if I have no idea what it is. There is no doubt what he's thinking is beyond anything I can imagine.

"Keys?" I murmur, running my fingernails along the short hair at the back of his neck.

His fingers tighten almost painfully, and I suck in a breath. He rubs his hands against my hips before releasing me and stepping back.

Immediately, I miss the warmth of his body against mine, his weight pressing me against the door.

"Michaela?"

His use of my real name snaps my attention back to the keys he's dangling in front of my face.

"Sorry, what?" I shake the haze away in time to notice the left side of his mouth curl in a smirk.

"Still with me?" he asks.

"Yes." Darting my tongue along my lips, I savor the flavor of him left there.

"I need to unlock the door."

"What's stopping you?" I tease without moving away from the door.

His eyes darken, the lust blazing back to life. Before I can shift, his arm burrows beneath me, lifting me until my feet dangle several inches off the ground and my body presses to his from shoulders to hips.

Oh. My. God.

I can't lift my legs to lock around his hips, given the position of our bodies, but the overwhelming desire to do so has my teeth sinking into my lip on a whimper.

"What's the matter?" he asks, nuzzling my jaw until his lips graze the shell of my ear.

"I want—"

"I know exactly what you want," he interrupts, sliding the key into the lock. "And I intend to deliver. But someone must be into delayed gratification."

The way his lips wrap around the word *gratification* creates another level of awareness. The heat of him, the way his muscles shift under my fingers as his arm bunches to twist the knob. I'm ready to pick up where we left off when he pauses on the threshold, part of us cast in the shadows of the dark entryway and the other caught in the warm glow of the porch light.

I open my mouth, ready to beg for more, but close it under the intensity of his stare.

"Last chance, Michaela," he warns, and I shiver at the tone of his voice as he says my name. "If I cross this threshold with you in my arms, it tells me you still want this. That you're ready for what's about to happen."

I gulp as nerves flutter in my tummy with the butterflies.

"W-what if I want to stop?"

He presses a chaste kiss against my lips.

"Tell me," he whispers. "No matter how much I want you, I want you to want this more."

"Okay." I nod, tightening my hold around his neck. "I want this. I want you, West."

My words release his feet, and he moves forward at an agonizing pace until we're shrouded in darkness. Once we're inside, he steps back against the door, pushing it closed with a quiet snick in the stretched silence between us. He releases his arm, and I slide down his body while my own quivers with anticipation.

His attention doesn't leave my face as one hand disappears behind him to turn the lock. Every other one of my sexual experiences has been all about flash—quick heat. If I expect the same with West, he turns my expectations one hundred and eighty degrees on its head. He brings his hand back into view, and I hold my breath, ready for the flash to consume us. Instead, the smolder continues to build as he uses one finger to trace a line of heat along my jaw.

How can one touch—and such an innocent one—create a flood of desire so strong that I'm ready to strip naked right here, right now? I want to throw myself against him. I want his lips to annihilate any reality other than one centered around the sensations he's creating. But there's something about the way he holds himself, limits his touch to only his finger against my jaw, that locks me in place, centering all my focus to where his skin grazes mine.

"Kiss me?" I ask.

He shakes his head, and the sting of rejection pinches my stomach. I step back in retreat, ready to go hide in my room when his other hand shoots out and holds me in place.

"Where are you going?"

"I—you—if you changed your mind..."

"I haven't," he replies, stepping closer, wrapping his heat

around me again. "But if I kiss you now, I won't stop. And then our plans for this"—he holds up the tie that started this whole thing—"are forgotten."

"Oh." My breathing shallows as his eyes move down my body, leaving frissons of heat in their wake. A half smile tilts his lips, and I'm surprised a fire doesn't spark around us.

"Now that we're both clear on what's going to happen when I kiss you again, I want you to go upstairs. Take this." He hands me the tie, and my heart gallops in my chest, desperate to let the fire consume me. Aching to ignite the torturous smolder burning through my body. "Get undressed. Wait for me."

His expression tells me he expects obedience. Without question.

But I've never been much of a rule follower.

"W-wait for you to do what?" My breasts, heavy in the confines of my clothes, ache to feel his touch.

"That's for me to know," he murmurs, his voice dropping lower and eliciting a deep tug of desire in my center, "and you to find out."

Oh. My. God. Is it possible for panties to incinerate? Because mine just did.

I don't waste any time, snagging the tie from his fingers and hurrying up the stairs, only to freeze when I reach the top.

His room? Or mine?

The thought of invading his room without him there holds zero appeal, so I turn into the first doorway, into my room. The familiarity—the purple and teal bedspread, the concert posters from high school still tacked to the wall—lends a sense of security. Stuffed animals still line the top shelf of the bookcase filled with everything except books.

What will West think of seventeen-year-old Michaela's decorations?

Doubt creeps in, pushing out the sparks he had stoked to a glowing fire. He's one of the smartest people I've ever met, successful, kind, generous. Case in point? What he's doing for my parents while they're gone. And when I think about how insanely gorgeous he is, how much of the total package is wrapped into one person, my confidence plummets. What does he see in me?

What do you think he sees? What does everyone *see?*

The snarky voice fuels the doubt, and I turn around, prepared to stop this before it can go any further, but come up short when I find him in the doorway, arms up along the jamb as he watches me with glittering eyes.

"I thought I told you to undress." He steps into the room, and the desire thumps to life again. It wars with insecurity, paralyzing me between the two emotions. He studies me for a minute, his face shifting from lust to concern. "What's wrong?"

"I—nothing."

He steps closer, and he lifts his hands to curl around my arms.

"Something's wrong." It's all he says, but it's enough to remind me of how well West knows me.

"You—what do you see when you look at me?" I brace myself. Does he see the girl in the sex tape with Tucker? The girl who broke up America's Sweetheart Couple, no matter that he was single when I went out with him?

"What do I see? Michaela, when I look at you, I see a beautiful woman on the outside," he says, and I sigh in disappointment. "But on the inside, you're still the girl I used to know. The funny one who told enough knock-knock jokes to make anyone groan, the sweet one who rescued ladybugs from the house to take them outside. Beauty, inside and out."

His words unleash something in me, the anxiety scattering in a thousand directions. Closing the distance, I wrap my arms around his neck. Lifting to my toes, I simultaneously tug his lips to mine. I may have surprised him at first, but between one breath and the next, he takes control of the kiss, his hands caging my hips.

My legs hit the bed, and I fall backward with a cry of surprise.

When I open my eyes, he looms above me, an easy grin curving his lips. His face sobers, the lust reigniting in his gaze the longer he stares at me. It's like his eyes have a direct connection to my core, and it tightens with anticipation.

"You were told to get undressed," he says, his fingers shifting to the bow on the side of my dress. With one tug, it unknots.

"Sorry?" My voice is meek, overwhelmed by the hunger building between us.

"Unfortunately, sorry isn't going to cut it." He moves one edge of the dress aside, groaning at the tie on the other side. His fingers yank impatiently at it, and my breath breaks as that knot comes loose too. Dragging the fabric away, he sinks his teeth into his lower lip, reminding me of the way they claimed mine. The way I want them to master me again. "Beautiful."

I lift my arms to pull him to me, and he grips both my wrists in one hand. Snagging the tie from beside the bed, he arches an eyebrow, and I squirm as heat streams through my body.

"Let me help you," he murmurs. Lifting me slightly, he tugs the dress over my head and down my arms, only breaking his grip long enough to toss it behind him. He pulls the tie from where he hung it over his shoulder and loops it around my wrists, tightening it until the silk presses snugly against my skin. It looks odd, the tail hanging long, but he grabs it and yanks, pulling my arms above my head, stealing my breath in the process. "Perfect."

"Now what?" I ask, my voice husky with the need for him to continue.

He smirks. "Depends on you."

"On me?"

He nods. "Should I punish you for not doing what you were told?"

"P-p-punish?" The word both scares and excites me.

"Mmm." Dropping his head, he drags his nose along my neck.

His lips settle on my galloping pulse, and my hips shift restlessly on the bed.

I need more, but he straightens again, breaking the connection between us. I can't stop the whimper that escapes as need overwhelms me. He unbuttons his cuffs, rolling the cotton up his forearms as he rotates and searches my room.

"This'll work."

He grabs the scarf threaded around the door handle of my closet and steps closer.

"W-w-what are you going to do with that?" I drag my tongue across my lips, hoping to relieve the Sahara-like sensation overwhelming them.

"Trust me," he promises. Lifting the scarf, he wraps it around my eyes until I can't see anything.

"West?" Without my ability to see, I pick up the tremors of uncertainty in my voice.

He wouldn't leave me like this, right?

"I'm here."

The bed dips, forcing me closer to him, and the callouses along his fingers drag up my arms to rest at the straps of my bra. Had I imagined in a million years something like this happening, I would have chosen more carefully than a basic white bra and panties.

"No frowning."

His lips brush against mine, once, twice, before settling more firmly against me, his tongue licking along the seam until I part them, moaning at the taste of him—slightly spicy like the whiskey and citrusy from the orange garnish, but there's something else. Something uniquely him.

He coasts his hands along my shoulders, burrowing under me to flick the clasp of my bra and drag it down my arms. Cool air washes along my nipples, tightening them almost painfully as my bra tangles with the tie at my wrists.

He groans, the sound deep and sexy, heightening my arousal further.

"You. Are. Stunning." His words are bitten out, like he's in pain, but his fingers keep their unhurried pace, gliding along my sides in a caress that would be ticklish if I wasn't turned on to the brink of combustion.

He traces along the undersides of my breasts, and I shift to try to move him where I want him. I don't get very far before the length of the tie holds me in position.

"Touch me," I beg.

He chuckles. "I am." To prove his point, he lifts his fingers high, circling my nipples without touching them.

I'm going to die. This is torture, having his hands on me but not exactly where I want them. Where I need them. My panties are soaked, and my breasts ache with the need for him to touch me. Completely. Everywhere.

"*West*," I moan.

"Why touch when you can taste?"

His question registers in the split second before his mouth claims my nipple, and I arch up, immobilized by the tie forcing my arms in place. Pure, unfiltered desire crashes over me as his lips, tongue, and teeth tease the tight bud. My thighs squeeze, seeking friction I can't give myself since my fingers are trapped above my head.

"Delicious," he murmurs, moving from one breast to the next. The scruff on his cheek drags across my breasts, heightening the soft sensation of his mouth as it surrounds my other nipple.

"Please," I beg, although I'm not sure whether I'm pleading for more or to be released from this torture. Every part of me aches, desperate for his touch, but at the same time, pleasure buffets my body in waves.

"Please, hmm?" His hum resounds against my neck. How is it possible for those vibrations to travel to settle in my core? "Please, what, I wonder? Less?" He leans back, cool air rushing across my breasts, and I whimper. "More?" His hand settles on my hip before he runs a finger along the edge of my panties.

"More. Definitely more," I answer.

"More, huh?" he asks, the smile evident in his voice.

"*Yes,*" I plead, hips surging off the bed. I need his touch lower.

"Greedy girl." His weight shifts, and suddenly the pressure on the tie is different. I tug—there's more movement, but I'm held in place by something more solid than before.

"What did you do?"

"I need both of my hands for what I have planned next. Your headboard works pretty well to keep you where I want you."

His growl controls my hips, lifting them to beg for his touch. I need more or I'm going to explode.

His fingers tug at the elastic edge of my panties, and I shift to help him. Once the fabric clears my ankles, he pushes both my knees up and back, exposing me to him.

"Hello there," he murmurs, and I want to combust at the tone of his voice. He drags a finger through my folds, and I hold my breath, forcing back a scream of desperate pleasure. "You're so wet. For me? Or do you like being tied up?"

He tweaks a nipple, and I moan as pleasure lights up my core.

"Answer me," he demands.

"B-both," I murmur, biting my lip as he pinches the other nipple.

"Don't hide your pleasure from me, Michaela." One finger brushes against where my teeth sink into my lip, and I release the injured flesh. "Let me hear you."

He moves, the crisp fabric of his slacks rubbing against my leg. Is he still fully dressed? I suddenly get the mental picture of me tied up and begging on my bed while he looms over me, still clothed.

Oh god.

"If I get undressed, this will be over before it begins," he tells me.

Holy shit, did I have that whole conversation out loud?

"You tensed when you felt my pants. I'm clearing up any misconceptions. Right now is all about you. Just feel."

And I do.

His lips brush my inner thigh, the muscle jumping at the movement.

"Oh god."

"Only me," he chuckles. "Just a taste."

His tongue drags through my folds, back to front, and I yank at my hands, desperate to touch him. But the fabric holds. My moan doesn't quite sound human, but it must be enough to encourage him to keep going. His tongue circles my clit, pulsing against the bundle of nerves in a rhythm my body recognizes.

"*West,* West, please. Oh my god. Please." I twist my hands against the tie, no way to move my arms other than the small window he's given me. My heels are thrown over his shoulders, my toes curling in the fabric of his shirt, but without any other purchase, I'm at his mercy.

The orgasm shimmers at the edges in all its terrifying, awesome glory. I want to run away from it as much as I want to run toward it.

One of his hands traces up along my skin, caressing my breast, his fingers pinching at the peak, while his lips close around my clit, sucking and nibbling slightly until I'm writhing against him. My breath comes in gasps I can't control. Nothing is under my control. It's all him. I want to beg, but the only sounds leaving my lips are unintelligible words interspersed with his name.

"Come for me, Michaela." That's the last push I need, permission to shatter apart in fireworks of pleasure that explode behind my eyes.

No, not fireworks. Stars. I'm flying, lost in the sensation his mouth and fingers pull from me. The orgasm keeps going on and on until the pleasure morphs again, my fingernails digging into my palms as I finally come down from the high. The light of my lamp is bright as West tugs the blindfold free, his eyes the only thing I can focus on. They glitter as if lit by firelight as he stares at me in wonder.

"Now it begins," he says before his lips claim mine in a kiss that fuses itself to my soul.

CHAPTER 6

WEST

Slowly, I open my eyes, sure my alarm is going to go off any minute for school.

It's Saturday.

Mmm. Good. I'm so relaxed, I don't want to get up. The benefit of recognizing it's Saturday morning and I can sleep in settles over me, and I burrow farther against the soft mattress and sheets, squeezing my arms around—

Holy shit. From relaxed to frozen in an instant. My breath stalls in my lungs as Michaela nuzzles against my chest.

My cock stirs against her hip, ready for another round, and I recite battle dates of the Revolution to calm down.

Storming of Fort William and Mary. Battles of Lexington and Concord. Siege of Boston.

Who am I kidding? So long as her breath still whispers across my chest and the silk of her hair wraps around my fingers, I'm going to want to wake her up the way we went to sleep—with me buried so far inside her that I forget where I end and she begins.

No, moron, quit thinking with your dick. He got you into this mess to begin with.

She'd looked gorgeous in a dress that hit her mid-thigh when

I found her outside the speakeasy. Like a Christmas present meant just for me. And I enjoyed the fuck out of unwrapping her.

What would Sawyer say? Remember him? Your best friend? Her older brother?

Shit. Fuck. Damn.

If that's not enough to deflate my hard-on, my next thought is.

She's a famous rock star. What would she want with a broke as fuck high school history teacher?

I attempt to slide out from under her, but her arm tightens, her hand brushing my nipple and creating a painful rush of blood to my groin.

"West," she murmurs, freezing me in place.

One breath, two, and she relaxes against me again. Breathing a sigh of relief, I slide to the edge of the bed and replace my body with a long pillow we knocked to the floor last night.

She instinctively curls against the pillow, and my eyes catch on the smooth expanse of skin exposed from her shoulder to her calves, her breast peeking through her hair. A siren begging me to lie back down and pull her into my arms. I can still taste the tight bud in my mouth, and it waters for another sample.

Dude, quit ogling her like a pervert and retreat!

She tightens her hold on the pillow, her brow furrowing, and I tuck the covers around her, watching until she relaxes fully once more.

I feel like a dick, sneaking out in the middle of the night like this. But my guilt doesn't stop me from leaning over and snagging my clothes where they lie scattered on the floor. I move slowly, both reluctant to leave as well as careful to not make a sound. I don't want a witness to my cowardice.

The door squeaks open as I turn the knob, and I freeze, whipping my head back to her and releasing a sigh of relief when she doesn't move. With a sigh, I step into the hall, pulling the door closed behind me and vowing to spray some WD-40 on the squeaky hinge.

Why? Planning another sneak out? What about sneaking in?

I silence *that* bad idea and take the ten paces to my room, not daring to breathe until my door is closed and locked behind me.

"Because I need to lock her out," I say and undo the lock with a roll of my eyes, then crawl into my own bed. "You're an idiot, Abbott."

I should never have slept with my best friend's baby sister, no matter how beautiful she is.

Staring at my ceiling, I miss the warm weight of her on my chest, and I swear the scent of her jasmine and apple perfume still tickles my nose. Her scent must be on me since she hasn't been in here. I flop to my other side as I consider taking a shower. Maybe I should. Clean slate.

But the other part of me argues that I'll need to shower later, and I should enjoy the way her scent wraps around me as long as I can. Because eventually I'll need to get my head on straight.

By the time the sun comes up, I'm committed. Last night may have been one of the hottest experiences of my life, but it can't happen again.

It's a mantra I repeat to myself as I stumble down the hall to wash the scent of her down the drain. When my dick twitches with the hope of her catching me in the hallway in only a thin towel.

It finally starts to sink in once I'm dressed in faded jeans and a t-shirt, determined to work in the basement until I'm too tired to move today.

Or tonight.

I need a jolt of caffeine to kick-start my brain, so the coffeepot is my next logical choice. Mug in hand, I stand at the counter and wait for the coffeepot to finish brewing, tensing as warm arms circle me, soft breath teasing me through the thin cotton of my t-shirt.

"Good morning." Her voice is husky as she nuzzles against my back. "You're up early."

"Morning." I clear my throat and set the mug down on the counter, dreading what comes next.

Lacing my hands with hers, I tug them away from my body so I can spin around to face her. A small smile plays on her face, and her eyes are a combination of sleepy and happy as she meets my gaze. Her hair is a mass of rumpled curls I want to run my fingers through, and I squeeze her hands to fight the urge.

Fuck, I'm an asshole.

I open my mouth to say something—anything—but come up blank, my mouth snapping shut again, and the light in her eyes dims, her smile fading shortly after.

"W-what's the matter?" She swallows slowly, and if possible, I feel worse than I did when I first came up with this plan.

"I—" It's the only thing that comes out, and I want to groan in frustration.

"You?"

"Last night was amazing."

It's the wrong thing to say, given the way her eyes brighten again. I want to kick my own ass for leading her on, if only for a moment.

"I thought so too," she breathes out, attempting to step closer.

I lock my muscles, keeping her at arm's length figuratively as well as literally.

"I've been thinking, Mikey. As great as last night was, we shouldn't have done that. I shouldn't have." The flinch when I use her nickname is telling. As is the way she curls into herself.

"Oh."

"Oh?"

She nods, her tongue dragging along her lips. My attention fastens to the movement almost involuntarily. I want to kiss her again so badly my lips tingle with the need.

Don't even think about it.

"You're r-right," she whispers, yanking her hands away from mine. "It shouldn't have."

"Yeah. Yeah, I'm glad we're in agreement. Last night was a mi —" I can't bring myself to use the word *mistake*. "Well, we shouldn't have. You're Sawyer's sister."

"Is that why?"

It's one of the reasons, and it sounds a lot better than *you're too good for a homeless history teacher*.

"Why what?"

"Don't play dumb. We both know you're smarter than that. Why last night shouldn't have happened?"

"Well, yeah, kind of. You might be his little sister, but I always felt like you were my little sister too. Last night—"

"Shouldn't have happened. I heard you the first time. K-kid sister status." She rocks back on her heels, eyes shuttering. "Yep, that's me. Sawyer's sister, Mikey. Hey, is there any chocolate milk? Maybe some Lucky Charms? It's Saturday, right? Ohhh, cartoons."

I shake my head, darting out a hand to wrap around her elbow when she starts to retreat. "Michaela."

"*Mikey*, remember?" The smile she gives me doesn't reach her eyes. And since I've seen the real one since she's been back, I can tell the difference. And I fucking hate it. "What's the big deal, West? We had too much to drink."

"We didn't," I argue. "Two drinks aren't enough for either one of us to get drunk."

"Why are you so wrapped up in what did and didn't happen? It was just a mistake."

Her use of the word has me grinding my molars in frustration.

"Well, yeah, but..." What else am I going to say? We both agree. Last night was a mi—nope, still can't say the word, even in my own head.

She waves away my statement, like she couldn't care less about what I'm saying.

"Already forgotten. It's not like it was very memorable anyway."

Excuse me? What in the actual fuck?

"What?" I manage to spit out.

She shrugs. "It's okay, bro. Some people simply don't have chemistry."

Chemistry? I had her coming so hard we exploded the goddamned lab.

"Anything else?" she asks, sidestepping until my hand falls uselessly back to my side.

"What? Oh, um, no."

She nods. "Okay."

She turns around to leave the kitchen without another word, only turning back at the last second. "Listen, I know we had plans to check out cheesesteaks, but I'm not feeling so hot. Can we do a raincheck?"

Fuck.

Suddenly the consequences of my actions are starting to pile on, one right after another.

Why are you upset? Weren't you planning to avoid her anyway?

Our competitive taste test had slipped my mind.

"Yeah, sure, of course," I assure her. "I need to work on the basement anyway."

My mouth opens again to invite her, but I close it just as quickly. I need some time alone.

"Okay. I'm going to head back to bed. Let me know if you need any help, I guess."

"Okay. Feel better, Mikey."

Mikey. Your best friend's younger sister.

I can't forget again.

I drag my ass up the basement stairs eight hours later, exhausted. It wasn't even physically taxing work, but I've never liked painting, and I especially don't like it after spending the week with a helper who makes whatever we're doing fun.

When I hit the top tread and enter the kitchen, all the lights are off, the room cool. It's like no one has been here all day, but since I came up around one for a sandwich, that's not true. And Mikey must have been down here at some point, right?

But other than my plate from earlier, there aren't any dishes in the sink or in the dishwasher. Her presence usually leaves its mark. Lights are left on, music playing on a radio, there's movement—life—around her that doesn't exist when she's gone.

She said she wasn't feeling well.

Maybe it wasn't merely an excuse to avoid me. Maybe she really *is* sick. I don't bother with any lights, my legs protesting as I take the stairs up to the second floor. It's just as quiet as the main level. The symbolism of her closed bedroom door isn't lost on me. My arm weighs a million pounds, but I manage to push through the sensation and tap on her door.

"Mikey? You there?" I call out. She doesn't answer, and I drop my hand to the knob and twist.

Locked.

"Mike?" I try knocking again. "Everything okay?"

"Huh?" Her voice sounds muffled, like I woke her up. Shit.

"You feeling any better?" I call through the door, cursing the thick wood between us.

"What?"

"Can you let me in?" I turn the knob again like it will magically open.

"Not tonight, West. I'm going back to bed."

"Do you want any medicine? Soup or something?" I bet Kelly has a can of chicken noodle in the kitchen.

"Not hungry."

"Medicine?" I try again.

"No."

"You're sure?"

"Yes."

"Okay, if you're sure. Good night." I hold my breath, waiting next to the door, but no response comes, and I finally retreat to my room.

Helplessness overwhelms me—knowing I can't go in there and check on her, take care of her—grates.

She wouldn't want you to take care of her anyway, asshole. You hurt her feelings.

I'd figured that out after I replayed our conversation in the kitchen for the fifteenth time while I was painting. Even if she had called our night together a mistake—fuck, I was beginning to hate the word—she'd originally come into the kitchen and wrapped her arms around me.

But nothing can happen between us. She's a musician. I'm a teacher. She's my best friend's little sister. And I recently broke up with my fiancée. If all of that isn't enough, she's seven years younger than me, for Christ's sake.

Still doesn't mean I like how she said she could so easily forget our night together—it's an acid that has eaten at me all goddamned day.

But I want to apologize—I'd been a dick before she lashed out. Figured she used the "not feeling well" as an excuse to leave the kitchen. Only now I feel worse. Because maybe she really is sick if she's spent the entire day in her room.

I sleep like shit and hang around the kitchen for most of the morning, waiting for her to come downstairs. It's been twenty-four hours since I saw her last. I've knocked a few times since I came back upstairs yesterday afternoon, and each time she's mumbled that she's resting. I'm beyond concerned. When noon hits and she still hasn't made an appearance, I decide enough is enough.

I pop the lock on her door with a paperclip. Those damn

hinges squeak as I push it open, but she doesn't move within her pile of blankets on the bed.

"Mike?" I whisper.

The room is dark, stuffy, and she lies facing away from me. I step forward slowly, starting to sweat in the heat of the room. But she's wrapped under a mountain of blankets like we're in the middle of a winter blizzard.

"Mike?" I cup her shoulder through the blanket, and she tenses before rolling onto her back.

Even with the lack of light in her room, I can see how pale her skin is, the way her blond hair mats to her face. She finally peels her eyelids open, revealing her glazed and lifeless blue eyes.

"West?" Her throat sounds raw, and my own throbs in sympathy. "I locked my door." She starts to lift her head but groans and closes her eyes before making much progress.

I sit gingerly on the bed. "Shh. I was worried about you, so I picked your lock."

"Worried..." Her brow furrows.

I lift my hand to brush a finger across her forehead, and before I even make contact, I know. Heat radiates from her skin when I finally rest the back of my hand against her cheek.

"Sweetheart, you're burning up. Have you had any medicine?"

I glance around, even though I know better. She hasn't been out of her room to grab water, let alone medicine.

"C-c-cold." She flinches away from my touch and tries to bring her covers back up.

"I know. I'm sorry." I tuck the covers around her. "Let me get you something to help it."

"Don't need..."

"You do," I argue. "You're running a fever. You need meds and water. Some food too."

"Mmm."

Leaving her on the bed, I grab Tylenol and a glass of water from the kitchen, tucking a Gatorade in my pocket for later. The food will need to wait until her fever comes down. Despite being open for a few minutes, her room is still stuffy, so I make a decision she'd never let me get away with if she wasn't sick. Putting the glass and bottle of acetaminophen on my dresser, I go back into her room and grab a pair of clean pajamas before I turn back to the bed where she's fallen asleep again.

"Come on, baby." I burrow an arm under her knees and one under her shoulders and lift. It doesn't take much since she's so fucking tiny.

Her personality is what makes her seem larger than life.

She shivers in my arms but otherwise doesn't move until I rest her on top of the covers of my bed, making quick work of changing her clothes for fresh pajamas. I press two pills into her hand and watch her swallow them with a sip of water. Once she's finished with that, I tuck her into my bed, brushing a kiss on her too-warm temple.

Satisfied that she's resting, I head back to her room, stripping the bed and pulling the blanket off the floor where it covers her vent. Hopefully this will air the room out—the smell of sickness is strong enough to clench my stomach in sympathy.

Why didn't she tell me?

I already know the answer—she hadn't talked to me because of what I said to her in the kitchen.

Avoiding the guilt threatening to wash over me, I plug her phone in to the charger and head to the laundry room with her sheets. When I get upstairs to check on her again, she hasn't moved, but the deep grooves in her forehead have eased, and her breathing is deep and even.

I should have checked on her earlier. *Actually* checked on her. Not just asked questions through a thick door. Did she think I would ignore her if she asked for help?

"Don't answer that," I mumble to myself.

Why would she think I wouldn't help her?

I'm her friend. Shouldn't that count? I'm good at taking care of people. I'd done it with Ashley. If I were alone, I'd probably do what Mikey had done—hole up in my room and pray for death while I slept. But when Ashley or I had been sick, we trusted each other to help.

The misplaced trust in my ex-fiancée is another gaping wound, and I shove all thoughts related to her into the box they escaped from.

Mikey kicks the covers off, her body battling the fever as she tosses and turns. I rinse a washcloth in cool water and place it on her forehead. She settles for a little while before shivering again, and I tuck her back into the covers. An hour later, I take a break and grab a sandwich for myself before returning. She's cooler to the touch, but the flush of the fever still covers her cheeks.

I rest against the headboard, dozing between doses, and ignore the question pinging around my brain. But the thought is harder to avoid the next time I wake up to check on her, and yet again, for the last dose of meds I give her around two in the morning.

Would I do this for Sawyer, too?

CHAPTER 7

MICHAELA

I hate getting sick.

It was fine when I was little and Mom would take care of me. I got to watch TV and eat on the couch, plus everyone else took care of my chores.

After leaving my parents' house, no one cared if I was sick. There was still a job to do—a show or expensive studio time or any other grown-up responsibility.

I might be at home now, but Mom is gone and...wait a minute. I pop my eyes open, coming face to face with a sleeping West. His jaw is relaxed, mouth slightly parted as he breathes deeply. What time is it?

How about what day *is it?*

I remember being both pissed and hurt when he called us a mistake. Being so tired, I only wanted to lie down but hating that my bed still held traces of his spicy bergamot scent. And, no, I didn't burrow my face into his pillow.

Yeah, sure, we can go with that.

So what happened between then and now? Better question—and more important at the moment—why am I in his bed?

"You're going to get a wrinkle right here," he murmurs, reaching up and running a finger between my brows.

I flinch and pull away from his touch.

"Wh-what happened?" My mouth feels like Death Valley, my lips cracking as I move them.

He rolls slightly and grabs a bottle of Gatorade from the nightstand beside him.

"It's already open," he says, handing it to me.

I twist the cap, lifting onto one elbow to sip at the liquid. It's warm, but I don't care since it tastes amazing to my parched mouth. A dribble escapes and slides down my chin. He catches it before it can drip anywhere else, his calloused touch reminding me of the other night. The one I told him was so forgettable.

Ha. Yeah, right. If forgettable means you'll remember it forever.

Memorable or not, it doesn't explain the gap in my memory from our conversation in the kitchen until now.

"Thank you." The drink eases some of the dryness, and I try to sit up. He stops me with his hand on my shoulder.

"Wait…stay here with me a minute, okay? I'll explain." His eyes are so earnest, I can't help but relax back against the cool pillow.

"I'm listening," I murmur.

If he doesn't start talking, I can think of something better to do with our lips.

No. Remember. Mistake. Not happening again. No more impulsive choices. Also, you probably look and smell like death. Cool it, girlfriend.

"West?" I prompt when he stares at me without saying anything.

"You were really sick," he finally says. "I didn't know at first. But when I didn't see you yesterday morning either—"

"Yesterday?" I ask. "What day is it?"

"Monday."

"Monday?" I sit up quickly, only for him to gently pull me back down. "You should be at work."

"I called out sick today."

"Why?"

"Why?" His tone says that's a dumb question, but I don't understand.

"Yeah."

"You're sick—were sick. You don't feel like you have a fever anymore." He rests his palm against my cheek, and the desire to lean into his touch is powerful. I fight the urge, intent on staying strong. "Your eyes aren't glassy anymore either."

"I feel better," I admit.

"Why didn't you tell me you were sick? Come get me or text me or something? I feel like shit. You were suffering and—"

"Don't worry about it. I'm a big girl, I can, and have, taken care of myself when I get sick."

"But I was here. I could have gotten you medicine sooner. I don't run away at the first sign of trouble."

No, you just call it a mistake.

I bite the words back. The other night shouldn't have happened. I can admit that. Even if I don't want to. He's being mature. Responsible. I need to be more like him. It was nice to be wanted though. Especially by someone like him.

"Well, thank you for taking care—hey, wait a minute. Wasn't my door locked?"

His cheeks pinken, and he grins sheepishly. "I picked it."

"What? West—"

"I was worried about you. I'm glad I did too. Your fever was insane."

"I would have been fine, eventually," I argue.

"Tylenol helped you get there faster," he counters.

"Why am I in your room?"

"I wanted to keep an eye on you," he says, like his response is reason enough.

"Still doesn't explain anything."

He sighs. "I washed your sheets, aired out your room a bit. Changed your clothes. I—"

"You changed my clothes?" I lift the covers and, sure enough, different pajamas than the ones I lay down in two days ago. "*All* of them?"

He rolls his eyes at my high-pitched squeak. But after our conversation in the kitchen, I didn't anticipate him seeing me naked again.

"Not a big deal. You were sick."

"West!"

"What? You have to admit you feel better than you would if you had woken up in clothes you'd been wearing for several days." He shrugs like it's no big deal.

"I do, but—"

"You'd have done the same thing for me."

I would, but I might also have ogled him a little. Maybe. The thought of him seeing me naked again—even if I was sick—still has heat crawling up my cheeks.

"Is your fever back?" He lifts his arm again, and I scoot out of reach, nearly falling out of bed.

Graceful, thy name is Michaela.

I swat his hand away. "No."

"Then wh—oh. Why are you embarrassed?"

"You saw—"

"I didn't look," he says. "I closed my eyes."

"Are you lying?" I can't say one way or the other, unsure of what his tells are. Does he ever lie, considering what he told me the other night?

"Yes. But would it make you feel better if I didn't?"

"A little," I grumble.

"Then pretend I had my eyes closed." He stretches, moving his arms overhead and revealing a sliver of toned stomach between his t-shirt and lounge pants. "Now that you're awake, we should probably feed you."

"I'm not hungry."

"Your body will want food once it's reminded what it tastes like."

"Okay, Mr. Know-It-All." I stick my tongue out at him, and he smirks.

His expression does crazy things—that don't involve hunger—to my stomach. Not that particular kind of hunger anyway.

"Don't you forget it." He shifts from the bed and looms over me, and again, I'm reminded of the other night, my traitorous body responding predictably. "I'll get something started. Want to head down? Or should I bring something up?"

"Down," I say automatically.

Staying in bed—in West's bed—is too confusing, muddling my brain even more after being sick for the last few days.

"Okay."

"I'm going to shower first, then I'll be down," I tell him, trying to ignore the way the fire sparks to life in his eyes.

"I'd offer to help, but—"

The end of the sentence hangs between us, and I swallow, knowing exactly why we can't. Why we shouldn't.

"I'll be down soon."

He nods but doesn't say another word before he leaves the room. I collapse against the pillows on a sigh. Maybe staying here is a bad idea now since West and I have slept together. But what other options are there?

My legs are shaky when I stand, and I sway like I'm on a ship the entire walk down the hall to my room for fresh clothes and my phone. West must have plugged it in since it's on the charger, and I remember having it in bed with me. A handful of texts from Mia are waiting and grow more concerned with each new thread.

MIA

Remind me again why I left my hot AF husband to come shoot a movie where all it does is rain?

I'm never going to complain about no rain again.

Kayla?

I hope the reason you're not answering is because you're enjoying your time off. *wink emoji*

And by enjoying time off I mean climbing your roommate like a tree.

Okay, I need some sign you're alive, please.

Michaela?

You didn't answer your phone.

Where are you?

MIA: If I don't hear from you by this afternoon, I'm calling the cops.

The last one is from this morning, and I breathe a sigh of relief while keying in my response.

Sorry. Been super sick. Like out of it for two days.

My phone immediately pings with a response.

I was about to call in the SWAT team, Kayla.

Don't scare me like that!

Are you feeling better?

Sorry.

Lost the whole weekend.

Even Friday? Weren't you supposed to go out?

I went out on Friday. Got sick Saturday morning.

No fun.

Did you convince West you're not his sister? *laughing emoji*

Ha.

Ha? Is that a yes?

That's a long story.

Is it still okay for me to stay with you after the shoot?

That bad, huh?

Of course!

You can head to my place now if you want. Or I can text you when I'm on my way home?

I'll be fine here until you get home.

Wouldn't want the press to think I'm breaking up your marriage too.

Kayla. *sad emoji*

Who cares what they think?

I do. Despite everything. I still care about the name they called me. Home-wrecker. Even though Jax and Charlie weren't together. It bothers me how much they talked about my video—one I didn't consensually make—with Tucker.

I'm not going to give them anything more to talk about.

So what are you going to do until I get home?

I can stay with Sawyer.

You're sure?

Yep. I'll go be the bratty baby sister to him for a few weeks. *wink emoji*

Then I'll come hang out with you.

It'll be fun!

The director is glaring at me since I'm on my phone and should be filming. Gotta go. Love you!

Have fun!

The longer my plan percolates, the more I like it. Sawyer is a workaholic. I'll have his apartment to myself.

West works all day. You have the house to yourself here too.

But here, I can easily remember the two of us in this room, the light low but bright enough to show off the way the muscle in his jaw had pulsed as he'd come the other night. His cologne lingers in the air long after he leaves the room. Temptation incarnate. And given my track record, I don't do so great saying no when faced with something I crave.

I shoot a quick text to Sawyer and head for the shower. I could spend all day under the hot water after the last few days. But a knock on the bathroom door after twenty minutes shoots that idea down.

"Mikey, you almost done? Breakfast is ready."

"Yeah," I say reluctantly. "Be out in a minute."

I check my phone as I head downstairs, hoping for a response from Sawyer. Nothing. And patience isn't my strong suit. It's fine though. I'll leave Sawyer alone until after breakfast.

"Hey, feeling better?" West notices me hovering in the door and motions me forward with a smile.

"Definitely more human."

Is this as awkward for him as it is for me?

"Good." He points at the table. "I kept it light since I wasn't sure how much you could actually eat. Toast and fruit."

I shrug. "This is more than I normally eat for breakfast."

He pins me with a stare, and I swallow roughly as I hover over my seat.

"What do you normally eat for breakfast?" His voice is deceptively casual.

"Coffee," I tell him, lifting my cup for a drink. My stomach rebels slightly, but I don't care.

Damn him. He even made my coffee the way I like.

Sawyer, please text me back.

"Coffee isn't food," he lectures.

"Yes, *Dad*. Last time I checked, I was old enough to look after myself."

"If you're only having coffee for breakfast, that's not really looking after yourself," he says.

I open my mouth to argue but snap it shut again. His statement reinforces exactly how he sees me. Little sister. Why am I going to argue with him? Instead, I spread jelly on my toast and take a bite. My stomach growls as the sweet berry flavor bursts on my tongue, and I'm nearly finished with the whole piece before he speaks up again.

"Slow down there, turbo. You don't want to make yourself sick."

I roll my eyes but do as he says. I don't want him to think I'm a slob.

"Thanks for breakfast," I mumble.

"Sure." He shrugs. "Why do you keep checking your phone?"

Busted.

"No reason." I try to play it off. "Just texted Sawyer, and I'm waiting to hear back."

"Sawyer's on a job right now."

"What? How do you know?"

"He called me last week to tell me he was going to be hard to get a hold of. Otherwise, we talk a few times a week."

I deflate as my plan to avoid West-sized temptation goes up in smoke. Shit. But maybe—

"Any chance you have a key to his apartment?"

Sawyer wouldn't mind if I showed up and let myself in, right?

Sawyer, who still has a "Keep Out" sign on his bedroom door here. Sawyer, who is the most private person I've ever met. It's great for his security job. Not so much for a little sister who could use a place to crash for a few weeks.

"No, why would I? He lives in California. I live here."

"Just figured I would ask."

"Why?" The intensity of his stare makes me feel like I'm sitting in an interrogation room under a bright spotlight. I want to confess all my crimes.

"If you did, I was going to borrow it," I say, and he arches a brow. "I thought about staying with him while I wait for a friend to get back from location."

"What friend?" His nostrils flare, and his chest expands. I shouldn't love that his reaction smacks of jealousy.

But I do.

"Jealous?" I ask, hope stupidly building in my chest.

"Concerned."

"Oh."

"What friend?" he repeats.

"My friend Mia. She said I could stay with her in California, but she's filming a movie right now."

"You need to go back out to California already?" I must be imagining the disappointment in his voice too.

"I don't need to. But I thought it would be a good idea." If the kitchen was awkward before, it has nothing on the discomfort created by the confusion on his face.

"Why?"

"You like that question a lot," I retort.

He shrugs. "Intellectual curiosity. Why do you think it would be a good idea?"

I look everywhere but at him, finally fixing my stare on the lone blueberry left on my plate.

"Michaela?"

A shiver runs down my spine. The way his tongue wraps around my full name reminds me of the other night. When I was Michaela, not Mikey.

"Michaela."

Looking up, I'm immediately held in the intensity of his gaze.

"Why do you think it would be a good idea?" he asks.

"I haven't forgotten the question," I snap.

"You just haven't answered it."

"I don't need to."

"I would appreciate it if you did. If I made you uncomfortable—"

"Why would I be uncomfortable, West?"

"Because of the other night," he says.

"What about the other night?" I want to goad him to admit it. To say it out loud.

We had sex.

"That I—you—we..."

"We?"

"God dammit, Michaela. You and I had sex, and I'm concerned about how you seem uncomfortable around me now. That you want to run to California. Happy?" His words come in a rush.

"No," I whisper, clearing my throat. "I'm not happy. I *am* uncomfortable. But it has nothing to do with you. And everything to do with how I feel about the other night. You're a temptation, West. And I have no faith in my self-control. I'm afraid I'll throw myself at you for a repeat. I want to avoid that rejection if I can."

"I don't want you to leave," he admits. "I liked hanging out with you last week. Before Friday. Not that I didn't like Friday either, but..."

"But what?"

"You're my best friend's little sister. I've known you since you were in diapers. I shouldn't have let Friday night happen."

"You weren't the only one making decisions that night."

"No, but I am the one who should have put a stop to it. And not only because of who you are. I have no business getting involved with anyone."

He scrapes a hand through his hair and stands, walking his plate to the sink.

"Why?"

His shoulders tense, but he doesn't turn around, and he doesn't acknowledge my question.

"Is it because of Ashley? You're still in love with her?" They'd been together for almost ten years.

He spins around, the disgust so strong on his face, I suck in a breath.

"Love? Fuck no. Any feelings I had for her were obliterated when I discovered she had been lying to me," he spits out.

I've never heard West talk the way he is now, and the surprise must register on my face because his expression changes to resignation and his tone loses its malice.

"Ashley lied to me for years. And I only just found out. I'm not in the right headspace for anyone at this point. I have some shit to work through."

"I-I'm sorry, West. I didn't know."

"Most people don't. Only Sawyer. Now you." He turns and focuses on rinsing his plate, the water running long after his plate is clean.

Standing, I approach him slowly, a déjà vu feeling hitting me from the other morning. Only there was no hesitation before. Will he welcome my touch?

Only one way to find out.

I slide both arms around him, leaning my cheek against the warmth of his back. He tenses, and I prepare to step away before his hands come up and lock my arms where they are.

"I'm sorry," he whispers.

"Me too."

"Can we start over on this friends thing? Forget everything else?"

We could both use a friend.

"Okay," I agree, squeezing my arms around his waist. "Friends."

CHAPTER 8

WEST

"Wait." Mikey's whine comes from several feet below us, and I glance at my best friend in time to see him roll his eyes. "Sawyer, Mom said you had to."

He scoffs and jerks his head in the direction of a large branch overhanging the roof.

"I thought we were heading for the treehouse." I release one hand and point up another four branches.

"Dude. Not anymore. I don't wanna talk about what I did with Kelsie last week with little ears who will just go tattle to Mommy. C'mon."

Sawyer starts across the large branch, and I follow, trying to ignore the plaintive whines from the seven-year-old with the platinum blond pigtails.

"Sawyer." She huffs and puffs, stretching for the next branch up, not letting her short stature stop her when she has to reach up on tiptoes to scratch her fingers around the branch too wide for her grip.

"If your mom sees her, your ass is going to be grounded," I warn him.

He shrugs. "Mom went to the store, and Dad's at work for another thirty minutes."

I glance down again, meeting blue eyes that are both determined and frightened. My heart squeezes in my chest, and I consider ignoring him and waiting for Mikey. He can tell me about his date with Kelsie later.

"Don't be such a pussy. Mike's climbed plenty of trees. She'll be fine."

I flip him the bird but make my way across the branch. Sawyer's already on the roof, motioning at me to hurry up.

"Dude, slow your roll. Not all of us bench two twenty-five," I say.

"You could if you'd work out with me in the morning."

"Get up at five to lift weights?" I fake a shudder. "Hard pass."

My feet scrape the roof, and I let go of the branch and walk to where he's waiting by his bedroom window.

"Sawyer."

Why does Mikey's voice sound so close? I turn, half expecting to see her leaning over the railing of the old tree house. Instead, she's hanging on the part of the branch between the tree and house.

"Dude!" I rush back to the edge of the roof, Sawyer hot on my heels.

"Michaela Grace, what the hell are you doing? Mom's going to kill both of us if she catches you on that branch," he growls, and I watch the little face with the almost-too-big eyes pale.

"Shut up, dickhead. You're going to make her fall."

"It would serve her right," he mumbles, and I spin enough to punch him in the stomach.

"W-W-West." Her lip quivers, her eyes filling with tears.

"It's okay, Mikey. I'm going to come get you, okay?" I wait for her nod before easing my hands back up. I don't want to shake the branch and cause her to fall. "Can you start heading back the way you came?"

"I'm scared."

"Okay, okay. You just hang tight. I'm coming." Hand over hand, I shimmy out to where she's clinging to the branch, her little legs dangling way too fucking high for my liking. "Can you climb on my shoulders? Like a piggyback ride."

"Uh-huh." She wraps one arm around my neck, followed by another. I want to breathe a sigh of relief, but my oxygen is a little low given the grip she has on me.

"Mikey, can't breathe," I wheeze, and her grip loosens fractionally. "Thanks, kiddo."

Every shift of the branch has my heart racing, worried I'm going to drop her. When we're close enough to the tree, I help her find her footing again.

"Back down now, okay, Mike?"

She nods and starts to lower herself. The sickening crack of a branch has my heart stopping. I reach for her half a second too late, and she hurtles down with a scream. But the face looking up at me in terror as she plummets to the ground doesn't belong to seven-year-old Mikey. No, this is the grown-up Michaela I can't get out of my head.

"Jesus H. Christ." I shoot up in bed, heart racing, palms sweaty. My biceps burn like I was just hanging from that tree branch again instead of dreaming about it.

But it wasn't Mikey who fell that day. It was me. After dropping her back at the tree, I started back toward Sawyer while keeping an eye on Mikey and lost my grip. It had taken almost a month for my collarbone to heal. By the time I was back to one hundred percent, the branch was gone.

And what was that shit about it being Michaela's face looking up at me? The memory of that image causes goosebumps to shiver down my spine, despite the late August heat. I pick up my phone to check the time and lie back with a groan. At this point, I'm simply waiting for my alarm to go off since I only have a few more minutes. I won't be falling back to sleep after that dream.

I haven't seen much of Mikey since our conversation in the kitchen a few days ago. Not that I'm surprised, given the shit I dropped on her about Ashley. But I couldn't stop it from breaking loose when she asked me if I was still in love with my ex-fiancée. The hug she gave me afterward was unexpected, the softness of her arms around me easing some of the anger that still coursed through me at the memory of Ashley's betrayal.

Since that innocent touch in the kitchen, I've avoided touching her whenever possible. Yeah, we agreed we could be friends. And her hug had some sort of magical healing power over the gaping wound Ashley left, but considering the sparks that innocent contact created? Better to avoid touching altogether.

Instead, I've spent as many hours at school as I can, and returned home to either work in the basement or grade papers in my room. The nights I work in the basement are an exercise in self-control since she always offers to help. And either I put her to work or she sits on an overturned bucket and peppers me with questions.

My favorite nights are when we both work. It's in those moments that her voice whispers across the room and wraps itself around me with songs I don't understand but can't help but feel. Curiosity pushes at my lips each time, begging to ask her questions about her life, how much longer she's staying, what's next.

But outside of our first conversation about her career, she ignores questions about her career and switches the subject. She's cagier than Sawyer. And considering he was special ops while in the military, that's saying something.

I haven't asked her again how much longer she's staying. I'm too afraid of the answer.

Occasionally, I've glanced up to find her watching me, desire clear on her face. Those moments are eroding my control look by look.

My alarm finally goes off, and I silence the annoying blare. If only it were so easy to silence my Michaela-centered thoughts.

Truth is, she probably knows more about me than I do about her. Maybe if I can convince her to do our cheesesteak taste test, I can get her to open up. Even the playing field a bit.

The light streaming from beneath her bedroom door as I pass is bright enough to make me pause and tap lightly.

"Mikey, are you up?" She doesn't answer, and I try the knob, twisting it easily, and poke my head in. "Mikey?"

She's curled up, her brow furrowed while small whimpers escape her parted lips.

Stepping into the room, I close the distance to lower myself onto the bed next to her.

"Mike," I whisper, bringing my hand up to cup her shoulder and shaking her gently. "Mike, wake up. You're having a bad dream."

The whimpers are now joined by tears tracking down her cheeks. Almost of their own volition, my hands shift, wiping away the moisture with my thumbs.

"Mikey, you're having a nightmare. Wake up, baby."

Baby? Where the hell did that *come from?*

She pops up as fast as I did earlier. Her eyes clear as she blinks and focuses on me, a wrinkle forming between her brows. The urge to smooth it is so strong I've already lifted my hand before I stop, frozen between the desire to touch her and the need to keep my distance.

"West?"

I offer her a small smile.

"Sorry, I didn't mean to barge in, but at first I thought you were awake. Then it seemed like you were having a bad dream."

I watch a shudder rack her body, and my protective instincts rise to the surface. And they're not necessarily the big brother kind.

"I..." She shakes her head. "I guess I must have."

"You guess?"

"I don't remember," she says quickly. Too quickly. Normally I would call out the lie, but I have my own secrets to keep. Namely how badly I want a repeat of the other night, but she'll never know that.

"Oh. I guess I'll let you go back to sleep then." I stand from the bed, immediately missing the heat radiating from her, her coconut shampoo wrapping around me like an old friend.

"Yeah." She keeps watching me. Eyes so big and so blue I could drown in the indigo abyss.

God, this is awkward.

"I'll see you later." I give a stupid little wave and retreat from her room to the safety of the bathroom and a shower. And the fact that it's colder than I had originally planned?

I refuse to think about why.

I'm back in my room getting dressed when I pick up my watch and notice how late it is. Might be related to my reluctance to leave Mikey's bedroom this morning, but no excuses. I usually try to be at work about an hour before the students show up on campus, but today, I'll be lucky if I'm there thirty minutes early. I rush out the door to my car, relegating Mikey's nightmare and my confusing reaction to the back of my mind.

It isn't until nearly lunchtime that I realize I left the house without grabbing my lunch bag. Cafeteria food will be an unsatisfying substitute. The class before lunch is almost over—the juniors paired off to work on a partner project I assigned them—and I'm debating the merits of spending several dollars in the vending machine in the teacher's lounge when I glance up and notice a familiar blonde hovering in the doorway.

My eyebrows lift in question, and she holds up my lunch bag with a smile.

The bell rings, and my students rush to pack up. I follow, meeting Mikey in the doorway after the last teen files out.

"Hey."

"Hi," she responds, handing me my bag. "You forgot this, and I figured you might need it."

Letting out a small laugh, I usher her inside the now empty classroom, closing the door to mute the noise in the hallway. "You're right. I was just debating a lunch of Doritos and a Snickers bar."

"There's always the cafeteria," she offers, trailing around the classroom to take in the different displays I set up on the walls.

I grimace and rub at the imaginary ache in my stomach.

"Umm..."

Her eyes meet mine over her shoulder, and her beauty in this moment—blond hair waving down her back, her lips and cheeks a light shade of pink—hits me in the solar plexus. Beautiful. Inside and out.

"You don't like cafeteria food?"

I shrug. "Not a fan of it when I was in school. Still not a fan. But you didn't need to drive thirty minutes here just for this."

"It's okay. I have an appointment in a bit downtown."

"What's downtown?"

"Oh, umm..." She nods toward the bag clutched in my hands. The one I'd almost forgotten. "What's for lunch today, teach?"

"Mikey. Is everything okay?"

"Why wouldn't it be?"

Fuck, I hate the non-answer. The question for a question. Ashley was really fucking good at both of those.

I step closer to her, lowering my voice.

"It's not okay because you're being evasive. It feels like you're lying to me. And we've never lied to each other before. I'd rather we didn't start now."

With a sigh, her shoulders drop, and a wall I didn't see before crumbles.

"I'm meeting with an attorney."

"An attorney? Are you in trouble?"

She snorts. "Not like that. I want them to review my contract with Reverb."

"Are they taking advantage of you?" My voice comes out more like a growl than a question.

"I—I'm just not happy. I want to know what my options are." Her hesitation still makes me wonder what she's not telling me, but I know more than I did a few minutes ago, and I'll take that trust and build upon it to get the whole story.

"Do you need my help?"

She shakes her head. "I don't think so."

"Would you tell me if you did?"

"Of course," she says.

"Promise me."

"What?"

"Promise me, Mikey. I'll be here to help you if you need me."

"I know that."

"Promise me," I demand for the third time.

"Okay, fine, I promise." Her eyes meet mine, and it's clear—she's telling me the truth. "I guess I should let you eat your lunch."

"Please stay. Keep me company. As for lunch, nothing fancy. A sandwich. Some carrots. A yogurt for my planning period this afternoon if I'm hungry."

"Sounds very sensible," she teases. "No dessert?"

Her question creates all sorts of images in my mind. Her spread out on my desk, my name breaking on her lips.

What the fuck is wrong with me?

I would say I need to get laid, but that's never been my style. I didn't have a serious girlfriend in high school and dated Ashley all through college. But suddenly sex is the only thing I can think about. No, not just sex. Sex with Michaela. I'm in so much fucking trouble. How do I shake this? I'd ask Sawyer, but something tells me I wouldn't get further than telling him I can't forget the night I spent with his sister before he'd catch me with a right hook. My jaw aches as I picture the encounter.

"I have a bag of M&Ms in my desk," I finally choke out.

"What kind?" Her eyes light up and she moves closer to my desk, giving away her plan, and I cut her off before she can open a drawer.

"Peanut butter."

"Ohhh. Gimme."

She lunges for my desk, and I put myself between her and my prized chocolate. The way she presses against me when she tries to reach around me gets a response from my body. A predictable, inappropriate response.

Best friend's sister, I tell my dick.

Not like he's listening to anything but the friction of her body against mine.

I clear my throat and sidestep, letting her have the candy she lifts in triumph over her head.

"Lunch," she says happily.

"Mikey, candy isn't lunch." Why the hell am I lecturing her like a child? If she wants to eat candy, who cares?

I do. I want her to take care of herself. But if she's not going to, then I will.

"Here," I continue, pulling out a spare chair from a table and sliding it next to my desk. "We'll share mine."

I split my PB&J sandwich with her, ripping it apart since I don't have a knife to cut it with.

"Thanks," she says quietly before nibbling a bite off one of the ends. "I didn't mean to steal your lunch."

"You're not stealing if I offer. And I have plenty."

Between us, we make quick work of the sandwich and carrots. I set the yogurt aside for later.

"Dessert." She upends the open bag of M&Ms, and the candies bounce across the napkin spread on the desk between us.

She grabs one, and I mimic the action, pinching my finger and thumb together and lifting the candy slowly to my mouth, popping it inside and letting the hard shell dissolve on my tongue.

"What are you doing?" she asks, picking up another one and popping it into her mouth as well.

I let the chocolate mostly finish before crunching it between my teeth.

"Savoring." My attention is caught on her lips, the way they purse around the candy, my voice husky with the unasked question of what she would taste like if I kissed her now.

That plush pink cupid's bow parts, her breath catching.

"S-savoring?"

Her question has me lifting my gaze to meet hers. Dark pupils nearly eclipse the blue, leaving only a small ring of color.

"Some things you eat fast. Get them out of the way. Other things are slower. More intentional. Tasted." My eyes drift to her lips again in time to see her tongue peek out and drag a sheen of moisture across.

It would be so easy to lean forward the foot or so separating us. To graze her lips with mine. To partake.

"Mikey," I whisper, despite recognizing the complications of kissing her again the way I want to.

"West."

It's only my name. Merely a breath between us. But enough to knock down every barrier I've been building all week. Lifting in my chair, I close the distance, my mouth a hair's breadth away from hers, ready to savor her the way she was meant to be, fuck the consequences.

"Mr. Abbott—ohhh, sorry."

Michaela and I jump apart, my attention shifting to the student in the doorway. Her cheeks are bright red with embarrassment. Relief courses through me that the universe gave me the interruption I needed when I no longer had the willpower to stay away from the greatest temptation I've ever faced.

"Hey, Sara, what can I do for you?"

"I, uh, I had a question on the homework assignment and was hoping to talk to you about it. I can come back though." She starts to back away, intent on escaping the awkward situation.

"No, no, that's okay. We were done having lunch." I glance at the clock above my door. "And since lunch period is almost over, let's talk about it."

I turn to Mikey, who stands next to me, her hands gripping the keys to Kelly's Volkswagen. "You don't mind, do you?"

"No, you're fine—I mean, it's good. I should get going." She gestures to the door, her movements exaggerated and flustered. "My appointment."

Even after she leaves, I can't put the almost-kiss in the back of my mind like everything else. It refuses to stay there, cropping up in moments when I think I've finally succeeded in putting Mikey firmly in the friend's little sister box in my brain. Again.

I'm in big trouble. The thing is?

I'm finding it hard to care.

CHAPTER 9

WEST

"West, may I speak with you?" The history department head steps into my classroom and closes the door.

Did I do something wrong inviting Mikey to stay for lunch? My planning period has been filled with thoughts of that almost kiss, but now worry overrides the attraction I've been struggling with.

And denial isn't helping. Not in the wake of the memory that plays on repeat. The moment I almost kissed her that continues to plague me with blood-pumping clarity.

Well, what about this?

Another image. This one of Michaela on her bed, naked except for the silk of my tie around her wrists.

Kill. Me. Now.

Clearing my throat, I don't stand, preferring the camouflage my desk provides.

"Er, sure, Phil, come on in." I gesture to the chair Mikey used earlier, trying to push thoughts of her away. Now isn't the time or the place. "If this is about having a friend on campus for lunch—"

"Friend?" he interrupts. "Not at all. We've all had our spouses join us from time to time for lunch."

"She's not my spouse," I explain. "I just forgot my lunch."

"Ahh." He gives me a look that says he doesn't quite believe the explanation. "Regardless, not what I'm here to talk about."

"Okay. What can I do for you?"

He gives a weary sigh. "The district announced budget cuts for next fall. Given the enrollment numbers at Grant this year, they are considering closing the school and redistributing staff and students."

"Closing?"

He nods. "I'm afraid so. There's been a steady decline as the neighborhood funneling into Grant has gotten older. It's at about half capacity at the moment."

I can't imagine being in a high school that was closing. Sawyer and I had both attended school here at Ridgeview. He was involved in sports, and I was on the debate team.

"That's terrible. The students will be split up?"

"And the staff," he says. "The board is reviewing proposals now to redraw district lines without Grant to see what the impact on student population will be."

One thing nobody ever tells you when you're going to school to be a teacher? How little control you have, and how much control the board has.

"What does that mean for the teachers already in these schools?" Like me.

He sighs. "Teachers with tenure will be given priority over those without. If positions are still available, they will be competed."

"I don't have tenure." An obvious statement since I've been here less than a month.

"You do not," he confirms. "But Grant's history department head and I have both announced our intent to retire at the end of this school year. Any of the history teachers at either Grant or here at Ridgeview will be given top consideration, tenure or not."

"How many history teachers are there at Grant?"

"Two, besides the department head."

"Do they both have tenure?"

"I'm not at liberty to disclose those details." But his expression is telling—I'm on the chopping block.

"When will the district reach a decision?"

"The board meeting to confirm details to communicate to parents will be next month. They're aware something is being discussed, but not what exactly. I'm sure you can imagine the number of calls the administration office has received."

"May I ask when they plan on recruiting for the new department head?"

"Are you interested in it?" he asks.

I nod slowly. "I am. It's something I thought about for the future, but if the opportunity is available, I'd like to at least try for it."

"I'll keep that in mind and let Principal Jenson know as well."

"Please do."

The bell signaling the end of the current period echoes through my empty classroom. An omen? I hope not.

"I'll let you prepare for your next class." He stands stiffly, moving slowly toward the door.

"Thanks, Phil. I appreciate you telling me," I call after him.

He gives a wave of his hand, greeting several students already trickling into the classroom.

I wish he'd come at the beginning of the period and not the end. I have zero time to process the information now, and my head is spinning. More than likely, my job as a history teacher at Ridgeview is ending.

But maybe the next step is beginning.

I'm new to this school, but it doesn't mean I don't have the experience to at least apply for Phil's job. What's the worst that can happen?

They tell you "no," and you're out of a job and have to find a new one?

Grimacing, I rub a hand over my churning stomach. According to my clock, there are five more minutes before next period starts, and the bathroom is between my classroom and the next on the opposite wall.

"I'll be right back," I tell a student in the front row.

"Sure thing, Mr. A."

Mr. A. Fuck, I like that. I like these kids. I don't want to start over. Especially not for the second time in as many years.

The bathroom is deserted, and I stare at my reflection in the mirror. A muscle ticks in my jaw and anxiety flashes in my eyes. With a sigh, I splash cold water on my face, closing my eyes and taking several deep breaths.

"There's nothing you can do about it now," I murmur to myself.

"Huh?" The kid walking into the bathroom freezes. "You talking to me?"

"Myself, actually."

"Okay..." The look he gives me says he thinks I'm a few fries short of a Happy Meal.

No, not crazy. Just ready for the universe to give me a break.

"Don't worry about it," I tell him as the bell rings, signaling one minute left of the passing period. "Worry about that instead."

"Sh—" He stops, eyes widening as he catches himself. "Shoot. Gotta go."

I follow him out of the bathroom, but he heads to the right while I go left, falling in behind two of the girls in my class.

"Did you see her?" one girl asks her friend.

"Who?"

"What's her name? The singer," she says, catching my attention.

Are they talking about—

"Michaela. I remember now."

"Michaela? Michaela King? Here?"

A smile tugs at the corners of my mouth as I pretend not to eavesdrop. They don't see me behind them, and I can't wait to tell Michaela she has a couple of fans in the school.

"Yep." The *P* pops loudly in the emptying halls.

"Ew," the other one says, disgust evident on her face even in profile. "You'd think after filming a porn with Tucker Winston she'd hide out forever. What was she doing here?"

Her friend shrugs. "No idea. I only saw her by the office earlier."

"Gross."

The two girls walk through the doorway, and I lose track of the conversation. But one word burns itself into my brain.

Porn.

No, I shake my head. Not possible.

Is that why she's been so hesitant to share details of her life? No, she had. She had just gotten back from a tour.

She's been slow to open up, but she wouldn't outright lie. Right?

But isn't a lie by omission still a lie?

"West? Everything okay?" Mary is standing outside her classroom, studying me with concern.

I blink myself back to reality, back to the hallway, now empty of students since the final bell for the period has rung. "Fine. Sorry, I'm fine."

I give her a smile, and she returns it before stepping into her classroom. Following her lead, I walk into mine. Whispers come to a stop, and I'm suddenly reminded of why I would never want to be a teenager again. The level of scrutiny from twenty-four pairs of eyes is unnerving, and sweat builds between my shoulder blades as I make my way to the front of the room.

What class am I even supposed to teach now?

A book catches my eye.

American History: Colonial Revolution – Industrial Revolution.

Thank god, something I could teach in my sleep. I manage to make it through the lesson, pairing them off much the same way I did the juniors. With over-the-top groans, the students scrape the chairs and desks into pairs, and I drop to my seat. Pulling open my laptop, I open a browser window, hesitating for a moment before clicking out of it and into the lesson plans I built. I've always prided myself on being a patient person, but the fact that I can't Google Michaela right now eats at me.

By the time the final bell rings, I'm anxious, raw. Sick to my stomach. But a thought did occur to me while in the last class. Not to use my work computer. So when the last student leaves and silence surrounds me, I close the lid of my laptop, powering it down. My phone rests heavily in my hand.

Don't do it. Just ask her.

Because she's been so open and transparent?

She told you about the lawyer.

Only after I pressed her.

I swallow slowly, unlocking my phone, my finger hovering indecisively over the Safari icon before I finally press down, bringing up a fresh search window.

Better to find out now.

Last chance.

I ignore the final warning my conscience gives me, pausing as I consider what search words to use.

Michaela King. Tucker Winston.

I scroll past the first few hyperlinks until I see one I can't help but click on.

The video is all in shadow, but still light enough to show a couple kissing passionately on the screen. My attention stays locked on the woman, waiting to see some sign the man is undressing Michaela. But the video stays in shadow except for the few seconds where a light highlights the tattoo on the woman's right shoulder.

Sighing in relief, I close the video. It's not her, thank fucking Christ. Michaela doesn't have a tattoo. I would have seen it the other night.

I'm ready to close out of the app when another link catches my attention.

Michaela King and Tucker Winston - The Details Behind the Dirty Deed

Michaela to Tucker: I love you!

Mia Maddox confronts Michaela...Stay Away from My Man

Michaela spotted on the east coast. Is that a baby bump we see?

Anxiety and self-loathing squeeze my chest in a vise. Breathing is difficult.

Did we have sex while she was in a relationship with another man? While she was carrying another man's baby? Fuck, but the question strikes a little too close to a wound still raw from Ashley. Would she have slept with me if she was dating Tucker? If she was pregnant with his child?

Call me crazy, but my cynicism rears its ugly head.

Fool me once, shame on you. Fool me twice...yeah, the rest of the saying is familiar. And it may have been a different woman between the once and the twice, but I'm not interested in lusting after another man's girlfriend.

I need to know. I could text her, but it's easier to conceal things through a screen. I need to see her reaction when I ask her about Tucker.

Pulling up in the driveway a little while later, I have no idea how I got here. My laptop bag sits on the seat next to me, like it all happened in the background since all I'm actively thinking about is what I just saw online.

"Mikey, you home?" I call out as I walk through the front door.

"Hey! You're home earlier than normal." A smile lights her face as she pads down the stairs. Dressed in cut-offs and a massive t-shirt that looks like it once belonged to Sawyer, she could still pass for a high schooler. Her hair is pulled up in a messy bun, locks escaping everywhere, and her bare feet show off light purple toenail polish.

As she comes closer, her smile fades until she's standing on the second step, eye level with me.

"What's the matter?" she asks.

"Are you dating Tucker Winston?"

She flinches when I say his name. "What? Where did you hear something like that?"

"Are you?" Why is she avoiding the question?

"I wouldn't have slept with you if I was dating someone else," she spits out. "But I'm so glad you think so highly of me."

Anger tightens her features. God, this is so fucking familiar I want to puke. Any time I asked Ashley a question, it was always an evasive answer.

"You're still not answering my question."

"Oh my god, no. Okay? *No*. I am not dating Tucker Winston. That guy is a world-class asshole." She steps down, heading into the kitchen.

"Are you pregnant with his baby?" The words are out of my mouth faster than I can process them.

She rounds on me so fast I blink in surprise. Her cheeks are bright red, her nostrils flaring, eyes wide.

"What. Did. You. Just. Ask. Me?" Unlike the emotion playing on her face, her voice is calm. Eerily so.

Shit…but I've already come this far.

"Are you pregnant with his baby?"

She lifts her shirt enough to reveal her stomach. "Does this *look* like I'm pregnant with his baby? With any baby?"

"Umm—"

"Just so we're clear, *Weston*—" The emphasis on my full name has my balls shriveling up like I'm a kid in the middle of a lecture.

"I slept with Fucker one time. One." She holds up her index finger to demonstrate her point. "Almost a year ago. I had no idea I was being filmed. I had zero clue he was such an asshole, and the only reason I came forward to admit it was me in the video was because it was ruining the life of a person I now consider my best friend. You remember? The girl I was telling you about. The one I'm going to stay with. Mia."

"Uhh—" All my words desert me as quickly as the anxiety dissipates.

She stomps off to the kitchen, and cupboard doors slam before the faucet whooshes on.

Apologize, you idiot!

My conscience has decided to rejoin my body after I kicked him out earlier. And he has some good advice. Like a man walking to his execution, I head for the kitchen, stopping in the doorway to see what I'm up against.

The anger I expected. The tears I didn't.

"Mikey..." I start, but I'm unsure of how to continue.

"Go away."

I don't listen, not only stepping into the kitchen, but into her path when she tries to leave.

"I'm sorry." My apology is a whisper when my anger was a scream. Putting more power into my voice, I try again. "I'm sorry. I heard something at school. Someone saw you, and they were talking about you and Tucker—wait, did you call him Fucker?"

She's looking down, but I see the left side of her smile quirk up. "Nickname Mia's husband gave him."

I huff a laugh but keep going with my apology. "I'm really sorry."

She shrugs. "Not the first time. Probably won't be the last."

"It will be from me. I shouldn't have put any stock into what I heard earlier."

"Who did you hear it from?"

Her question has the tips of my ears flaming in embarrassment.

"I overheard two students talking and assumed the worst. And before you say it, I know better than to take anything a teenager says as gospel, but around you, about you, I'm finding it hard to use my head."

There are too many emotions tied to her to be rational. Another sign I'm in big trouble.

"Do you want to know what really happened?" she asks, meeting my gaze head on.

I hate that her eyes are red and glassy, that her cheeks are still damp from tears I caused.

"Yes."

"Come here."

She walks to the living room and sits on the couch, patting the cushion next to her. Once I'm seated, she hands me her phone with a video all cued up.

Michaela King delivers press conference after leaked sex tape.

The video takes forever to load. But finally, there she is, sitting at a table in a conference room, a paper trembling in her hand where it rests against the table.

"Good morning. You, ah, you may not know me, or maybe some of you do." Her smile is self-deprecating. "I called you here to clear up the rumors that the woman in the video with Tucker Winston is Mia Maddox."

Several questions get lobbed her way, but I hear one clearly.

"If not Mia, then who is it?"

"The woman in the video with Tucker is me."

A jumble of voices and questions.

"Tucker says the woman with him is Mia Maddox. You're saying he was wrong?"

I can't turn away, can't turn off this train wreck of a video, even though the urge to throw up is nearly overpowering. Watching her take on the bloodthirsty reporters, watching the light in her eyes dim the longer she listens to the comments from the crowd, it fucking sucks.

"Not only is he wr-wrong, but he, uh, he knows he was. Sh-shortly after the video came out and he released his statement, I reached out to him. W-when I first saw the video, I knew when it was and where it was and who it was."

"Where?"

"When?"

Michaela's head jumps as her attention is captured by different voices.

"I-I-I went out on a date with Tucker about six months ago. At the time, I understood that he and Mia were broken up—"

"Did Tucker indicate the two were planning to get back together?"

How the fuck would she have known that? I lock my jaw at the asinine question, ready to deck the asshole who asked it.

"He didn't." This time her smile is sad, her eyes filled with regret. "During our date, he never once brought up Mia. We went to dinner at a restaurant in Virginia where he was filming. We—I—he—we had some good conversation, and at the end of the date, he kissed me in the lobby of the hotel we were both staying at."

"Did you knowingly book a room at the same hotel as Tucker?"

Who the fuck asks questions like this?

"I didn't book my room. My label did. I-I'm not sure if it was on purpose or not." She turns to the side of the room—searching for help?—before turning back to the crowd of reporters again. "O-one thing led to a-another and you know what happened. It's on the video."

"Did you and Tucker create the sex tape in hopes of making Mia jealous?"

"I-I-I didn't know T-Tucker was recording the v-v-v"—She closes her eyes and takes a deep breath—"the video."

Why is she alone facing these assholes? Is this why she's unhappy with Reverb?

"If you didn't know, why should we believe it was you? The video could have been recorded anywhere. How do we know this isn't you trying to get your fifteen minutes of fame?"

She takes another deep breath, letting it out, but she's still wearing her anxiety like another piece of clothing. "In the video, a tattoo is clearly visible."

"A compass," a reporter shouts.

"With a quote," another adds.

She nods.

"On her right shoulder," she confirms. "The quote is one I heard a friend of mine say once—'not all who wander are lost.'"

Tolkien. When *The Hobbit* movies had come out, I became obsessed. I read all of Tolkien's books, studied him. Learned that quote. Shared it with Sawyer when I was at the King house for dinner one night.

In the video, Michaela scrapes her hair over her left shoulder and turns before gently tugging on the sleeve of her dress to reveal a beautifully etched compass with words too small to read on the screen—words I memorized years ago.

The noise level grows deafening, lights flashing as picture after picture is taken. The tension in Michaela's shoulders and neck is visible over several moments until she pulls the shoulder of her dress back up and slowly turns forward again.

"Thank you all for coming today."

The video stops, leaving a blurred image of her standing as her announcement ends. I pass her phone back to her.

"You didn't know?" I ask.

"I didn't. I-I might be a performer, West, but I'm not an exhibitionist. I don't want other people to see me like that. Do you know how many times people have viewed the sex tape? Twenty-five million. It makes me sick."

"Can't you get the video taken down?"

"I tried. The record label tried. But the main sites were already downloaded. It's out there on ones I've never even heard of."

"Mikey—" I wrap an arm around her shoulders, cursing myself when she tenses before relaxing.

"You know the most important lesson I've learned since I started doing this, West?"

"What?"

"There are very few people you can trust in your life. Including yourself."

Fuck, her truth hits a little too close to home. Only I hate the way it sounds on her lips.

CHAPTER 10

MICHAELA

West is silent.

"How are you surprised by all of this? It was all over the internet a few months ago." I was sure everyone in my family knew. That everyone I had ever met must know based on some of the messages I got after the video from people who were supposedly my "friends" during high school. But no one in my family has been brave enough or callous enough to bring it up.

"You know I don't pay attention to that tr—" He cuts himself off before he can utter the word.

"Trash," I finish for him.

"Mikey—" The regret is clear in his voice. If anything, it only makes my humiliation burn hotter.

"I'm not proud of being out there like that, but I am happy that I told the truth. Mia didn't deserve what Tucker was trying to do."

"You didn't deserve it either," he says. His arm tightens around my shoulders, and I desperately want to lean into his warmth, into the support he's willing to give me. Now. But he questioned me earlier, and that holds me back. "I acted like an asshole coming in here the way I did."

"I'm not going to argue with you," I retort. He *did* act like an asshole. It was completely out of character for him. I didn't think he was capable of that kind of behavior.

"I should probably explain." He seems so uncomfortable. Is this what it's going to be like now? This awkwardness interspersed with moments where I think we're friends? One step forward and two steps back?

"You don't have to." So much has happened since I left home. So many changes and assumptions and consequences that I've never gotten an explanation for. I'm used to doing my own thing and dealing with the fallout by myself.

"I want to." His voice is quiet but determined.

"Okay. I'm listening."

But he remains silent for a long moment. I'm ready to tell him to forget it—for the second time—when he drags a hand through his hair, surging off the couch. His sudden movement startles me, and I watch him pace.

"I can't—I need to walk. Walk with me?"

"Where?"

"Around the block?"

It's unexpected, but not an odd request, and I stand next to him. Physically, he's inches away, but in every other way that matters, he might as well be on the moon.

"Sure."

I grab a pair of flip-flops, and we leave the house, turning right. The heat of the day is starting to ease, and the summer evening is quiet—idyllic except for the knots of uncertainty tightening my stomach.

"You know when I met Ashley, right?" He breaks the silence while his left hand brushes against mine between us.

"College."

"I met her the first weekend I moved into my dorm room. I literally bumped into her when I was leaving the building and she was coming in. Her stuff went everywhere. By the time we picked it all up, I had her phone number and a date for Friday night."

"Sounds pretty cute."

Picture perfect. But I understand that pictures don't always tell the full story.

The side of his mouth quirks in a shadow of a smile, but he doesn't stop walking, and his focus remains on the sidewalk in front of him.

"It felt like it. One date led to another and another, and before I knew it, we were graduating, and I accepted a job in Pittsburgh since she was moving back home."

"I remember." I hadn't been able to explain why I was so sad about his move. Going to college while Sawyer joined the Army, West wasn't at our house much anyway. But his move meant I would never see him.

"I moved. Fuck. I even proposed," he groans to the sky, clenching his fingers around tufts of hair.

"When did you propose?"

"Not right away. About three years ago. So we'd been living there what, two or three years?"

"Did you guys live together?"

"Yep. Neither of us saw any issues with it. Everything would be official eventually."

"What happened?"

"We set a date for a year after the engagement, but nothing ever got planned. She'd gotten a promotion and was working anywhere from seventy to eighty hours a week."

"What did she do?" I ask. If she attended Temple with West, she must be smart.

"She's an actuarial scientist for an insurance group."

Called it!

"Ah," I say, pretending like I understand what that is while making a mental note to Google it later.

"She was put on some big project at work. We hardly saw

each other."

"That must have sucked."

He shrugs. "It should have, right? But I ignored the fact that I wasn't as upset as I thought I should be. Ashley was...she was... well, for lack of a better term, she was high maintenance."

"High maintenance?"

"We needed a house in Shadyside. She had to wear designer clothes to work. She wouldn't dare be seen in any car more than a year old." He lists each offense with the tick of a finger. "It was expensive, but she made good money, and it was hers, so I figured, why not? Only it wasn't just her money. She'd spend hers, and I'd need to cover the mortgage. Or the groceries. Or you name it. And the savings account I had spent years building dwindled to nothing."

I can't picture him being very happy with someone like that but keep my comment to myself. "What about the wedding?"

His laugh is devoid of humor. "The project ended, and her hours went back to normal, but she kept finding excuses to put off planning. She wanted to relax after working so hard. She didn't see why it mattered since we already lived together. She didn't want to rain on her sister's parade when her sister got married."

"So, no wedding?"

He shakes his head. "Nope. But she made some good points, so I assumed we'd get married at some point when life started to slow down a little. I never pictured my fiancée coming to tell me she was pregnant before she was my wife."

"P-pregnant?" I sputter. "You have a kid?"

So much pain and anger is etched on his face, it makes my heart thump in my chest.

"If I had a kid, I wouldn't be here."

"Not what I meant," I defend. "I didn't realize you—"

"She's still pregnant, as far as I know. She came to me with the news three months ago. Only the timing didn't add up. She got pregnant the weekend I met up with Sawyer for a camping trip. And it had been over a month since we'd had sex prior to that."

"Oh, shit," I whisper, fully understanding what he's saying.

"She had been cheating on me for over a year. With a client."

"A year?" My stomach bottoms out. "How did you find out?"

"I waited until we got home after the doctor's appointment and confronted her about the timing before I stormed out of the house. By the time I got back, he was there."

"What happened?"

"She'd called and told him she was pregnant. With his kid."

"Holy shit. How did she explain you? You guys were living together!"

"He didn't know. They were always together when I thought she was out with girlfriends. Always went back to his place, but she never stayed the night. She always came home."

"Jesus, West." I throw my arms around him, giving him the strongest hug I can manage.

His arms curl around me, the heat of his hands branding me through my shirt.

"I'm so sorry." My voice is muffled against the cotton stretching across his chest.

We stay wrapped together for several moments before he clears his throat and steps back, gesturing for us to keep walking.

"When I heard those girls talking earlier, when I read what I did online, I—I don't know. Thinking you were with someone when we slept together, pregnant with his baby—"

All the pieces click into place for me. I may not agree with how he questioned me earlier, but at least I understand why.

"It brought it all back," I murmur.

If I thought I had trust issues, they pale in comparison to the betrayal West has lived through.

"I guess so. I didn't even stop to think about why I felt the way I did. My only thought was to talk to you."

"Because you thought I was like Ashley." Bitterness coats my words. I didn't do anything wrong. I'm not only paying for my supposed crimes, but hers as well.

This time he stops, his fingers wrapping around my bicep to halt my progress.

"No. You're nothing like her."

"Then why did you come home so upset?" Anger and hurt mix equally inside me. He can't say I'm nothing like her and then accuse me of doing exactly what she did to him.

"I..." He is so adorably confused I can't help but smile at the picture he makes, releasing some of my anger and hurt.

"You?"

"I don't know."

"That's not an answer. It's a cop-out. Just tell me. Be honest with me."

His eyes flare at the word I used unintentionally.

"I *am* being honest with you."

"Then you're not being honest with yourself." Frustrated because he still won't tell me why he was so upset, I throw my hands up, dislodging his fingers from my arm. "To hell with this. I'm going home."

I don't get farther than about five feet before he's in front of me, stopping my progress.

"Mikey." His eyes are begging me to let him off the hook on this one. But I'm not interested in letting his behavior slide.

"You don't get a free pass to treat me like shit, West."

"I said I was sorry."

"I want to know why."

"I told you already."

"No. You didn't. First"—I wave my index finger in his face—"you accuse me of doing what Ashley did to you." A second finger joins the first. "Then you tell me I'm nothing like her." A third. "And now you 'don't know' when I know that you do. Thank you for sharing, but I'm going home."

I step around him and march toward the house.

"Mikey." He groans my name, and I'm reminded of a different name, a different groan, and my traitorous body responds, my nipples pebbling against my bra.

If nothing else, the attraction I feel for him is honest. Even when he's being a bonehead.

"Would you please stop calling me that ridiculous nickname?" I growl, spinning around and crossing my arms over my chest to hide my body's natural response to him. "It's not my name."

"I've called you that since we were kids," he defends.

"I'm no longer a child, West. I grew up a long time ago."

"But—"

"You know, for being so smart, you sure are pretty stupid."

"What the hell does that mean?"

I close the distance between us again. "It means I'm attracted to you, dummy. And for you to ignore it, pretending it doesn't exist by calling me by a nickname I had as a kid? It's either your way of telling me you don't feel the same attraction, or your way of telling me I'm somehow beneath you."

"How do you figure that?"

I hold up a hand in response. "It's not about thinking, West, it's about feeling. And I'm tired of ramming my head against the brick wall you've erected between us. You wanna be friends? Fine. We're friends. But I'm going to go inside, *pal*, and try to stuff all my feelings down, because I'm tired of them biting me in the ass every damn day."

Spinning back toward the house, I ignore my name when he calls after me. I can't keep fighting my attraction to him, and I refuse to defend myself over crimes I didn't commit. Using my code for the garage, I let myself into the house and trudge up the stairs to my room. No sign of West, so he must have kept walking.

Good. Let him. Maybe then he'll figure out the truth he needs to tell me.

Boys are dumb.

MIA

Not Garrett.

Mi! I need you on my side here, please.

Sorry, sorry.

Agreed, boys are dumb.

Better?

Much.

Which boy is being the dumbest?

West.

Uh-oh. What happened?

He saw the video. And a bunch of other shit articles on the internet.

Oh, honey, I'm sorry.

Then instead of asking me about it like a friend, he accuses me of being pregnant with Fucker's kid.

That article was the worst! *eye-roll emoji*

I hate it.

Do you ever feel like you're fighting a never-ending battle?

Not only does the general public not believe me, but apparently a person I've known most of my life doesn't either.

Do you think he could have been jealous?

LOL. No.

Why would he be jealous over me?

Why wouldn't he?

Because he thinks he's my third pain in the ass big brother?

Are you sure about that?

I don't know. Not after our lunch today. He nearly kissed me. But tonight's questions color that interaction.

Yes!

Maybe?

My money's on jealousy.

You'd lose that bet.

Thanks for letting me vent.

Anytime!

<3 U!

lip emoji

"Dumb. They're all dumb," I say to the empty room.

All my high school boyfriends.

Fucker.

Brad.

West.

One of these things is not like the other.

The only common aspect about any of those experiences? Me. Maybe it's something wrong with me. Maybe I put out some sort of weird vibe that only attracts assholes.

West isn't an asshole.

But he could definitely act like one. Jealousy, according to Mia. I snort a laugh.

No way.

Mia doesn't know the whole story. She isn't aware that there was even a night with West, let alone that he called it a mistake. And I've tried to be on board with his opinion, I really have. I've told myself the same thing repeatedly. But it's had zero impact on my attraction to him. I'm a cliché—the best friend's little sister crushing on her older brother's best friend. Again.

Only now feels so much more real than it had when I was a teenager.

I have to stop. Stop thinking about him that way, stop thinking about the other night. Lying here, replaying the other night in my head like some viral TikTok video, isn't doing me any favors.

"Nope. Not happening," I mutter.

Maybe a shower would scrub the phantom sensations from my body since nothing else is helping the images in my brain.

CHAPTER 11

WEST

Well, fuck, that went well.

A part of me considers going after her, but the other part realizes I need some time to process what she said.

The garage door goes up, and I make sure she's inside and the door is closed before walking in the other direction, tucking my hands in my pockets as I ruminate over the events of the day.

Lunch. The news about my job. The gossip about Mikey.

Fuck. I do it even when she's not around.

I was nine the first time I went home with Sawyer after school and met Mikey. It's what everyone called her—Mike or Mikey. According to Kelly, she had given up trying to convince people to call her Michaela.

Mikey was a toddler at the time, blond hair so light it looked like white dandelion fluff around her head.

From that day forward, she has been cemented as Mikey in my brain. Until a few weeks ago when I saw her bent over the counter at the coffeepot in the middle of the night. Since then, my thoughts about the girl I'd watched grow up haven't been so brotherly.

Do I deliberately use Mikey as a nickname?

Yes.

Is it for the reasons she listed? Not returning the attraction? Thinking she's beneath me? No. Hell no. I want her beneath me all right, preferably on a soft surface, but I'm not picky about comfort. As for the attraction? Without a doubt, she's sexy as hell when she's fired up about something, including when she was passionately telling me what an idiot I am.

She isn't like Ashley. At all. The two couldn't be more different if they tried. My emotions today had nothing to do with what Ashley did. And unlike what I told Michaela, I know exactly why I was angry.

Watching the video. Realizing it *was* Michaela with another man. The knowledge still has my molars changing each other's surface area.

Michaela is mine.

Mine.

And that possessiveness as an automatic response confused the hell out of me.

Forty-five minutes and several blocks later, I let myself back into the house with the keys jangling in my pocket.

"Mikey—shit—Michaela?"

I have to start thinking before I speak, especially since she's told me why she doesn't want me using the nickname. It's not that I find her unattractive or beneath me. Neither of those could be further from the truth. I've been using it to control my attraction to her.

If she's attracted to me, then why do I need to control my attraction to her?

Good question. And not one I have an answer for, despite thinking about nothing else for my entire solo walk.

She's not in the kitchen when I check there first and I head upstairs. Her bedroom door is open, so I turn in there, hoping to find her.

Empty.

"What are you doing in my room?"

I turn around, ready to defend myself—I wasn't in her room, only in the doorway—and the words die in my throat. I didn't hear the bathroom door open, but she's framed by it, towel wrapped around her, skin rosy as coconut-scented steam fills the hallway between us.

"Well?" she asks, raising her eyebrows.

"You took a shower?"

For being so smart, you can be pretty stupid.

She rolls her eyes at the obvious answer to my question.

"Why?" I ask.

"Why what? Why'd I take a shower?"

My attention fastens to a drop of water that grazes her collarbone before being absorbed into the towel covering her breasts. Blood rushes to my groin, the desire to lean forward and sample the dewy texture of her skin almost overpowering.

"Why do you think I don't feel the same way about you?" I meet her eyes, waiting for her to process my question before she opens her mouth to respond.

"You told me the other night was a mistake."

I take a step toward her, closing the gap between us, loving the way her chest lifts with her breath, thrusting her breasts forward.

"I never called it a mistake. I said it shouldn't have happened," I correct. "And you agreed with me."

"Only after you said it first."

I close the distance another foot, and she retreats a half step, her hands gripping the knot of the towel in the center of her chest. But the whiteness of her knuckles against the towel isn't caused by fear. Just like the way her breath hitches isn't. I understand what she's experiencing because I'm in this too, because of how well I know her.

"What if I wasn't being honest when I said it?" I ask, backing her up against the bathroom counter until she can't go any farther.

She releases the towel to press her hands on my chest, where my heart pounds wildly.

"What if the only thing I've thought about since the other night was you? What if the only thing I've wanted to do since then is worship you over and over and over again?"

Her pupils dilate, and her tongue peeks out along the seam of her lips.

"Worship?" The breathy quality of her voice makes me smile.

She's as turned on as I am.

"Have you thought about that night too, Michaela?" I lift a hand, running my finger from her shoulder to her elbow, enjoying the shudder that racks her body at my caress.

"Yes." She tilts her chin to look at me, and desire that mirrors my own fills her gaze.

"What have you thought about?" I align my hips with hers, letting my erection press against her stomach, loving the small moan that works its way out of her throat.

"The tie," she admits, the color of her cheeks deepening.

I lean closer, my lips grazing her ear. "The tie, huh? Did you like that?"

Her breathing shallows, her breasts rising and falling rapidly. Her body is already giving me an answer, but she gives me the word too.

"Yes."

"Anything else?" Dragging my nose along her jaw, I follow the line down her neck, placing my lips against the pulse fluttering at the base.

She tilts her head to give me better access, and I take what's so sweetly offered to me, sinking my teeth into the tendon, relishing the jerk of her hips against mine. The friction stokes the fire coursing through my veins.

"You," she whimpers.

On a scale of one to ten of how badly I want Michaela, I'm at a hundred. And I haven't even gotten my hands on her yet.

Time to remedy that.

"Me?" I coast my lips to her shoulder while I lift my hands to her hips. "What about me?"

"I—everything. I can't get that night out of my head, no matter how hard I try." Her eyes blaze open, and I see the truth of her struggle in the cerulean depths.

"I thought you said our experience was 'forgettable'?" I tease, flexing my fingers against the fabric of the towel that barely covers the top of her thighs.

"I lied," she confesses.

"You lied. Do you know what happens now?"

"No?"

"I remind you that nothing between us is forgettable."

I lift her to the counter, spreading her thighs. She grasps my arms in surprise, but I'm not finished with her yet. Not by a fucking long shot.

"Nothing," I repeat.

I've denied myself long enough, locked every ounce of lust behind a gate obliterated by the vision of her standing in the bathroom doorway, steam billowing around her. I lift my hands to the knot of her towel, wrapping my fingers in the cotton, and pause.

She arches her back, pressing her chest against me, and my control snarls at the leash I still have it locked to.

"Do you know my favorite holiday?" I ask.

"H-h-holiday?" Her brow furrows, and I don't deny the desire to brush the wrinkle with my lips.

"Christmas." Extending my index finger, I run the tip along the line of the towel. "Want to know why?"

"Yes." She wraps her legs around my thighs, holding me to her.

"I love to unwrap my presents. To discover what's waiting for me." I make quick work of the knot until the towel drops to pool around her hips.

Fuck. Her breasts are a work of art, her nipples tightening the longer I stare at them. Every part of my body vies for the opportunity to touch her first. But my hands win the battle, lifting almost without thought to cup her breasts, my thumbs brushing over the dusky pink tips.

"*West*." Her head falls back on her shoulders, and she thrusts her breasts farther into my hands. She's so fucking responsive.

"Yes?" I pinch both nipples, twisting slightly.

"I..." She squirms against the counter.

"You?" I prompt, still teasing, still twisting.

Her next response is a moan. I lean over, drawing one of the buds into my mouth while my hand continues to play with the other. She digs her fingers into my scalp, pulling me closer. Like I'm going anywhere. The taste of her, the feel of her, shackle me to her in chains I don't want to break.

I move my free hand to her hip, tracing the crease between it and her thigh until I find the apex. My finger slides easily along her folds, intent on my sole mission. To worship her body the way I've wanted to every night since the last time. As much as I want to bind her hands again, I'll need to save that exploration for later. There's another need racing down my spine. Releasing her nipple with a pop, I drop to my haunches, pressing her thighs farther apart and exposing her to my gaze.

"Beautiful." My thumbs rub lightly along her inner thighs.

"West," she whimpers as I press her legs wider, the touch of my fingers not quite what she needs.

"Is this what you want, baby?" I lean forward and drag a slow lick from back to front.

"God, *yes*." Her thighs tense in my grasp, and the way she moans makes my dick twitch against the zipper of my pants. "More, please."

"Your wish is my command."

I repeat the caress, back to front, before swirling my tongue around her clit. She tastes incredible. And like a gourmet meal, I devour her, sucking her clit into my mouth, nibbling slightly at the hard nub before releasing it to tap my tongue in a rhythm that has her panting for more. Her words are now a mix of moans, whimpers, and my name, filling me with animalistic pride. I've brought her to this point. I've made her muscles tense, curled her toes, and locked her body in stillness. She's close. I stand and claim her mouth in a deep kiss, tangling my tongue with hers and absorbing the whimper of her interrupted orgasm.

"West." She breaks the kiss, her eyes opening to stare at me.

The vision she makes—lips pink and swollen from my kisses, hooded eyes and tangled curls falling down her back. I'm never going to forget this moment.

"Yes?"

"I didn't—" She gestures to her pussy, and I bite my cheek to hold back the threat of a smile.

"You didn't what?"

"You know exactly what I didn't do," she whines. "I was so close."

I lift my hands to her breasts, my fingers closing over a nipple while I drag open-mouthed kisses along her jaw, then rim her ear with my tongue.

"You have two choices, Michaela."

"West." Her hips grind against the counter, seeking friction as my fingers twist and pinch at the tip of her breast.

"Two choices," I repeat. "Are you paying attention?"

I snag her earlobe between my teeth.

She cries out. "*Yes*. Two."

"Correct," I say, shifting my attention to her other breast. Fuck, my dick is a steel pipe against the front of my pants. "Choice number one. I use my fingers and my tongue to bring you to the brink of orgasm—"

"Yes, please. That option," she says quickly.

"Let me finish."

"That's my line," she quips. Only she could make me laugh at a time like this with her quick wit and sassy tongue.

I claim her feisty mouth in another kiss that almost makes me forget what I'm doing. Almost.

"Where was I?" I pretend to think for a minute, drawing out the speed as my fingers feather along her folds. "Oh, I remember. I'll bring you to the brink of orgasm over and over again. But you won't come until I allow you to."

Her eyes flutter open, blazing at the image I've given her.

"You said that's my first choice?"

"Mm-hmm." I apply pressure with my thumb against her clit, rotating slowly until her eyes close again. "Do you want to know option two?"

"Y-yes."

"You lied to me," I say, and her eyes fly open to meet mine. "Calling us, calling this"—my thumb holds a steady pressure while I use my index finger to trace her opening before pressing forward, her walls spasming around me—"forgettable."

"I know, and I sh—"

I silence her with another kiss before pulling back again.

"Do you remember what I said the other night?" I ask.

She nibbles her lip, and her breasts swell with her breath. She remembers.

"What did I say?"

"It was my choice."

I flex my fingers into her hips, relishing the way she arches her back to press her breasts against my chest.

"What was?"

"P-p-punish."

"So, I can either make you wait for your pleasure—" I draw out the choice, waiting for her whimper to fade before I give her the second option. "Or I spank you."

She tenses, her pupils dilating, and her lips part on a quick intake of breath.

"W-will it hurt?" she asks.

That she's even asking me the question tells me what I said intrigues her.

"A little," I admit. "But it will also feel good. *Very* good."

"Oh."

"What are you thinking right now?"

"I—" Her tongue slicks over her lips, and I want to follow the path. But I wait. For her. "Have you ever done this before?"

I nod. "I have."

"With Ashley?"

"No."

Ashley was only interested in missionary style sex. But after she and I broke up, I headed to a bar I'd read about. One where people are open to experiences—a wide variety of them. And over the course of several weeks, I picked up a few women and learned about the experiences I liked. When I got home to Philadelphia, I found a place here like the one in Pittsburgh. It's one I haven't visited since Michaela returned.

I won't hide what I'm thinking from her, opening myself up to her just as surely as she is to me.

"I—I want that one."

Everything—my heartbeat, my breathing, my need—stills as I study her. "Which one?"

I'm not making assumptions, even though my muscles are poised, ready for her answer.

"Option two. I trust you."

At that admission, another emotion overwhelms all the lust coursing through my body.

Protection.

"If you want to stop, all you need to do is tell me."

"I remember."

I don't say anything else, claiming her mouth as my hands

claim her body, lifting her against me and carrying her out of the bathroom, heading for my room. Seeing her the other day, her blond curls spread out over my dark sheets, had left me rock hard. The heat of her pussy against my stomach is another kind of torture, but I can't give in. Not yet.

I lower myself to the bed with her still in my arms, her hips grinding against me as her hands delve into my hair. Cuffing her wrists, I tug her hands down, shifting both into one hand. I break our kiss and wait for her eyes to open.

"Ready?"

"Y-yes." The slight hesitation reflects her anxiety, and I press another chaste kiss against her lips.

"Stand up." With some shifting and help from me, she's soon standing next to me, wrists still wrapped in my grasp. My mouth waters for her pussy, now at eye level, and I close my eyes to ward off the need.

Later.

I wait for several breaths, letting the moment drag out. Waiting until she least expects it to yank her forward across my lap, her ass dead center. She cries out, and I dip a hand between her legs, dragging my fingers through her folds until she writhes against me, my name falling from her lips as her release hovers at the edges.

"Now, the question is how many," I muse, moving my fingers as if absentmindedly, but knowing exactly how to touch her, to tease her, to build the ache.

"How many?" She peeks over her shoulder, eyes wide.

"I'm going to say five."

"Five?"

"Mmm." I make a non-committal sound and drop my free hand to her spine. "Lean down."

For a moment, I think I'll need to up the count since she studies me before finally dropping her head back down. My fingers graze the cheeks of her ass, dipping to play in her folds before moving back up.

Smack.

She jerks and cries out as my hand connects sharply against her left ass cheek.

"One." I glide my fingers between her thighs again. "God, you're fucking soaked."

Finding her clit, I circle it with my index finger.

"*West,*" she moans.

Smack. Smack.

"Two, three."

I don't need to touch her to recognize how turned on she is as her hips squirm in my lap. Instead, I rub at her pinkened cheeks, loving my handprint on her ass more than I want to admit. This time I trace her spine all the way up her neck, watching goosebumps follow as I drag my fingertips back down.

Smack.

"Four."

My thumb finds her clit this time as I pump two fingers into her.

"God, please. Please, West. Please."

"Beg for me, baby."

"Please. I can't...I need..." She tries to lift her hips to ride my fingers, even as I withdraw them.

Ignoring her whimper, I lower my fingers to her mouth.

"Taste."

The way her lips latch around my fingers has my cock weeping, ready to join the action.

I pull my fingers away, and she follows until she can't anymore and lowers her head again without the reminder.

"Good girl," I tell her. I rotate my palm along her cheeks, tracing the marks already left by me, before lifting and lowering it with a resounding *smack*. "Five."

The word is barely out of my mouth before I'm moving,

lifting her to the bed and dropping between her knees. My hands press her thighs apart while my lips fuse to her clit, my tongue dipping in to taste her repeatedly.

All I can hear is the word "please" and my name on her lips, her fingers tightening in my hair while her hips lift off the bed. Confident she'll keep her thighs open, I lower one hand, placing my index finger against the tight hole of her backside. Between one breath and the next, I'm a knuckle deep, my other hand burying itself in her pussy.

All sounds cease to exist as her hips and back lift off the bed, her body driven by pleasure as her climax crests. I keep going, working her through it until she collapses on the bed, spent.

CHAPTER 12

MICHAELA

Oh. My. God.

All I can feel is West. He's in me, around me, everywhere.

I've never experienced anything like this. The nerves when I made my choice, waiting for him to follow through, all of it dulls in comparison to the overwhelming pleasure coursing through my body as his tongue swipes one final time against my clit. I shudder, drawing my shaky knees together when he scrambles from the bed and undresses.

I turn my head to watch him. Sculpted shoulders taper down to his toned chest and abs. His dick juts out from his body toward me.

He grabs a foil packet from his drawer, and he turns to face me as he rolls it on, a hot smirk firmly set on his mouth.

"On your knees, baby."

I don't think, don't question, just shift to my hands and knees on the bed.

The bed dips as he lowers one knee and then the next, his body heat radiating as he drapes himself over me. His hands find my breasts, kneading, before his fingers pluck at the nipples. I bump my hips back, searching for him.

"Are you ready for me?" One of his hands cups my pussy, and he growls his approval. "Fuck, yes, you are."

He shifts, nudging my entrance, moving inch by inch until his hips tap mine.

"You feel so fucking good." Each word is broken with the press of his lips against my spine, even as his hips retreat. I can't stop my whimper at his absence.

"*West.*" I need him. Need to be filled by him.

With a snap of his hips, he buries himself to the hilt, building a rhythm as he repeats the motion. He reaches, tracing my clit with a finger once more, and the pressure builds as he speeds up. The sound of skin slapping against skin mixes with our moans.

"I need you to come for me," he growls before sinking his teeth into the tattoo on my shoulder, driving his hips forward and pressing against my clit.

Every single nerve lights in a flurry of fireworks behind my eyes as the orgasm rushes over me, pulling me under or untethering me from the earth, I don't know which. All I'm aware of, all I recognize, is the man who stills inside me, pouring himself into the condom as he works through his own release.

Exhausted, we collapse on the bed, his arms tugging me to his chest as soon as he rids himself of the condom. His lips find my shoulder again, pressing several kisses against the skin there before he speaks.

"I'm done."

"I should hope so." I smile sleepily, and he squeezes me.

"Brat. I meant I don't want to fight how attracted I am to you."

"Why do you have to?" I ask, craning my neck to meet his eyes over my shoulder.

"I'm seven years older than you."

"So?"

"So, people will talk."

"Not the first time for me. Besides, seven years isn't a lot."

"Sawyer's going to kick my ass."

I wrinkle my nose. "We don't need to tell Sawyer. You said yourself he's on a job right now."

"I'm going to tell him, Michaela. You're not some dirty little secret for me. I want the world to know you're mine."

Rotating slightly, I bring my hand up to his head, pulling down to claim his lips with mine.

"How do you know exactly what to say when I need to hear it?"

"I'm psychic," he teases, pressing a kiss against my nose. "Not really. I'm not saying it because you need to hear it, I'm saying it because I mean it. I'm not giving you up again."

𝄞 𝄞 𝄞

The ringing of my phone has me nearly slicing a finger instead of the carrot I'm cutting. It's a Philadelphia number, and I bobble the phone in my haste to answer it.

The attorney. Finally.

"Hello?"

"Ms. King?" The man's voice is clipped, like he's in a hurry. So am I, considering what he charges per hour.

"This is she."

"This is Curtis Rawlins from Lloyd, Rawlins, and Smith. We met to discuss your current record contract."

"Yes, Mr. Rawlins, I was concerned when I didn't hear from you last week."

"Yes, I received your messages. *All* of them." He makes it sound like I've left more than three.

"Were you able to review the contract?" I try to keep the defensiveness from creeping into my tone. What a jerk.

"I did. I had both of my colleagues review it as well." He sighs.

"Unfortunately, I don't believe there is anything we can do to help you terminate it."

My stomach rolls. Up until now, I've been hoping for a loophole in the contract since I haven't been able to connect with anyone who matters at Reverb.

"Oh." Tears burn behind my eyes, and I nibble on my lower lip as the reality becomes clear—I'm stuck at Reverb or I need to quit.

"The contract is very well written."

I want to snort out a laugh at his less than helpful comment.

"Okay. Well, thank you for looking."

"Of course. Sorry we couldn't be of further assistance. My office manager will run the card you gave us and will send you the receipt."

Great.

He can't help, but he can easily charge the emergency card I found in my guitar case. Mom and Dad are going to have a fit.

"Thank you for calling me back, Mr. Rawlins."

"Goodbye, Ms. King."

The phone beeps in my ear, and I shakily lower it to the counter, putting the knife down and taking several breaths.

I can't go back to Reverb. The thought of spending any more time with Brad has bile rising in my throat.

I can't.

But I have to go back or quit. Either way, I fail. Because apparently that noncompete is rock solid.

"What am I going to do?" I whisper to the empty kitchen.

West is still at work for another hour or so. And since he doesn't know the full story, he wouldn't understand why I'm so upset anyway.

You could tell him.

As quickly as I have the thought, I shake it loose. No way. I remember his face when he found out about Tucker. I don't even want to imagine if he found out about Brad too.

Sniffling, I grab my phone, tapping out a text message to Mia.

FINALLY heard from the attorney.

MIA

And???

There's no way out.

Yeah, right. Who said?

The one I talked to and BOTH his partners.

Do any of them specialize in entertainment law?

Well, no.

Why don't you reach out to an attorney in LA?
One who knows what they're talking about.

Well, for one, I don't know any.

For two, I'm broke.

I've already used the credit card more than I'm comfortable with. I have no idea what the limit is, and I don't want to find out.

MIA

I could pay for it!

That's a generous offer, Mi, but I can't accept it.

What? Why?

Because I don't want to be a charity case.

You're not a charity case. You're my friend.

And I want to stay your friend.

Thank you anyway, though.

So what are you going to do now? Go back to Reverb?

I don't know. I haven't decided yet.

Well, think about it. Call me if you want to talk it out.

I will.

What I told Mia was right. I have no idea what I'll do. But I need to decide sooner rather than later since the people at Reverb have never been very patient.

I'm still trying to decide what to do an hour later as I rinse tomatoes at the sink. Red roses fill my vision, and a strong arm encircles my waist, pulling me back against a body I've gotten to know intimately over the last two weeks. *Very* intimately.

"For you," he murmurs. He brushes the back of my neck with his lips, inciting a riot of goosebumps along my spine.

"You brought me flowers?"

I want to lift them, bury my nose in them, and sigh happily at the unexpected gesture. The last two weeks with him have been a dream. True to his word, West's behavior toward me has been like nothing I've ever experienced before. He is kind, attentive, affectionate. The total package. I don't understand why Ashley cheated on him, but I'm selfishly glad she did because it means he's here with me now.

"Mmm." His affirmation is a vibration of sound against my neck, where his lips trail kisses along my hairline.

He tosses the bouquet on the counter next to the cutting board and runs his hands under my shirt, then along the band of my shorts. My thighs squeeze together as desire pools at the simple touch. I lean my head back against him, reaching my arms up and back to thread my fingers through his hair.

More. I want more.

Until three weeks ago, I could honestly say I wasn't a fan of sex—I had better luck getting an orgasm from my vibrator than a partner. Until West. Since that first night in my room, the smallest touch, the briefest of looks, is all it takes. And I don't think it's one-sided. If he and I are in the same room together, he usually finds some way to touch me. The touching leads to kissing, and the kissing leads to orgasm after mind-blowing orgasm.

If an orgasm delivered by him is a drug, I am an addict who doesn't want to surface.

He spins me suddenly, pressing me back against the counter, his hands landing on either side of my hips. As big as he is, his strength doesn't scare me. The opposite. It makes me eager about what might be next.

He claims my lips, immediately deepening the kiss as his hands cup my jaw. The heat builds between us, and I press myself tighter against him, groaning at the friction of my breasts flattening against his chest, the way my body softens against his hardness. He tempers the kiss, teasing me with chaste brushes and a smile when I finally flutter my eyes open.

My hands are clasped around his neck, while his rest on my hips. Right now, in this moment, this is what happiness is. And it's worth the last six shitty months—hell, the last eighteen months—to be in *this* moment with him.

"Hi," he whispers, dropping his forehead against mine. "What's the matter?"

"Matter?" I look up at him. His face is lined with concern as he studies me.

"You've been crying."

The problem with knowing West forever? He can tell that something's wrong just by looking at me.

I shrug, trying to play it off. "Nothing."

"Michaela," he murmurs, lifting his hands up to cup my shoulders. "You've been crying. I'd really like it if you told me why."

With a sigh, I drop my forehead to his chest, breathing deeply. "It's fine. I…I heard from the attorney earlier."

"He finally returned your messages?"

"Yeah."

"What did he say to make you cry?"

"It doesn't look like I can get out of my contract with Reverb," I whisper.

He hugs me tighter, his lips dropping to my hair. "Aww, baby, I'm sorry. I have total faith in you though. You can work out the rest of your contract with them and then do your own thing. I'll be here every step of the way."

I want so badly to tell him why I *can't* go back to Reverb. But I don't. Instead, I burrow against his chest.

"Thank you for my flowers."

"You're welcome. I didn't mean to distract you from your—" He peers over my shoulder at the cutting board. "Tomatoes?"

"Salad," I correct. "I woke up this morning and really wanted a salad."

"This morning, huh? The first or second time I woke you up?" His voice drops to a growl, and a throb pulses low in my stomach.

He's insatiable. It's not uncommon for him to wake me up in the middle of the night, or after his alarm goes off, his fingers or tongue bringing me to the brink of ecstasy. Waking up to an orgasm? That's a method I can get behind.

"Neither," I say, pushing against his shoulder. "When I actually woke up without you next to me in bed."

He smirks, his expression a patented way to make my panties damp. "You won't have to worry about that tomorrow."

"Lazy Saturday?" I'm ready to spend an entire day in bed with him and his talented fingers.

"If I can finish the basement tonight, absolutely." He drops a kiss to the end of my nose and steps back, heading for the stairs. "I'm going to go change. Will you come down and keep me company?"

"Of course. Eat first?"

"Only if you're the main course," he murmurs, and a blush heats my cheeks.

"What?"

He spins around. "What?"

"What did you say?" I ask, even though I heard it loud and clear.

"I said 'sure.' What else would I say?" he teases. "You all right? Your cheeks are all red."

His teasing makes me giggle, and I wave him back to his task before turning and finishing the prep on the salad that has been at the forefront of my mind all day.

I'm dishing up our dinner when he comes back into the kitchen, tugging down a faded t-shirt. I hand him one of the plates and follow him to the table.

"How was work?" I ask, taking a bite. I can't contain my moan at the fresh flavors of the greens and juicy tomatoes.

His eyes darken at my little noise of appreciation, and he shifts in his seat. "Good. I gave a pop quiz in my second period today."

I groan. "You're so mean! Pop quizzes are torture."

"Is it still torture if I let them use the notes I asked them to take for the twenty minutes before the quiz?" He quirks an eyebrow.

"Not as bad then, maybe."

"Tough crowd. They all survived," he promises.

He tells me about another class where a student came in dressed in a full colonial costume for an oral report, and I laugh when he explains that the report was all about Benjamin Franklin traveling to modern times and his fascination with cell phones.

By the time he's done, we're finished and taking our dishes to the sink, and I follow him to the basement stairs.

"When do you think you'll head back to LA?"

"Why?" I ask warily, pausing.

He glances up, stopping a few steps below me.

"Just a question." His tone may seem nonchalant, but the way his shoulders tense tells me he's not as indifferent to the answer as he wants to appear.

"I'm not sure."

"You're not?" He turns back to walk up a few steps until he's eye level with me.

"No?"

The way his expression shifts, the tension fading until all I can see is the desire I've become familiar with. It's there anytime he looks at me, and it creates enough heat to fry my brain.

Who am I kidding? I don't ever cool down when he's around…or when I think about him…about us.

"Umm…what was the question?" I ask dazedly.

He barks out a laugh, threading his fingers through mine and tugging me down the stairs with him.

"You ready to work?"

He doesn't wait for me to answer, instead he hands me a screwdriver for the light switch and electrical outlet plates while he preps the baseboards.

He crouches down, shorts riding low on his hips, t-shirt stretched across his back so snugly the shift of his muscles distracts me. I completely forget the task he's given me.

"I can feel your eyes on me," he says, startling me from my ogling.

"Sorry, not sorry?"

He looks over his shoulder, giving me a flirty wink, and butterflies take flight in my stomach. Simply from his expression.

"Look all you want, baby," he growls. "I don't mind."

"Y-you don't?" The heat in his gaze has stolen my breath.

"I like knowing your eyes are on me, Michaela."

"You do?"

He nods. "I'd rather you were touching me, but since I can't have my lazy Saturday without working tonight, we're going to work until we finish."

The way he says "finish" causes my thighs to clench with need.

"Delayed gratification," he says. "I can stand the heat, can let it build for later. Can you?"

"Foreplay," I murmur, and his eyes turn impossibly darker.

"Exactly. You okay with that?"

Am I okay with having several hours of innuendo and sexy, smoldering glances? Is "hell, yes" too over-the-top?

"More than okay."

"Then get to work." He points at the wall. "The sooner we're done, the sooner I can take you to bed."

Several hours later, I'm stretching a kink out of my neck when his arms wrap around me from behind.

"Are you done?"

"You tell me, Mr. Carpenter," I tease.

He yanks me back, nipping my neck before growling in my ear. "You have a sassy mouth."

"All the better to kiss you with."

"Then I guess you better kiss me," he answers, spinning me in his arms and backing me against the wall.

Lifting on my toes, I fasten my mouth to his, licking at the seam of his lips until he opens, letting my tongue tangle with his. My hands cuff his biceps while his make short work of the button and zipper on my shorts.

"We're not going to make it upstairs," he says against my lips, grabbing my ponytail and pulling my head where he wants it to deepen the kiss.

"Do you hear me complaining?" I pant. My hands yank at his belt, my body greedy for him.

"There's that mouth again." He rolls his eyes with a smile.

"Guess you need to find some other way to occupy it."

"Yeah, I guess maybe I do."

CHAPTER 13

WEST

"What is this about again?" Michaela lifts her head from my shoulder, giving me a curious look.

Our lazy Saturday was a success. The only time we left the bed was for food and a shower. Snuggling and watching TV—my choice—are the only things on the agenda today. I'm not ready to go back to work tomorrow.

I drop a kiss on her forehead.

"*The Blue Planet*? You've never seen it?"

"Not around TVs very much."

Sometimes I forget. Her life is so different from mine. She's only here temporarily. Once her record label tells her to, she'll be going back to California. In six months, I may or may not be unemployed...again. She could be with anyone. But she's here with me. My arm tightens around her almost automatically.

I don't want her to go.

She squirms next to me, and I relax my hold.

"Sorry."

"It's okay. It didn't hurt," she says.

"You were moving around."

She drops her hand to my thigh, tracing along the crease until she's palming me through my lounge pants. I go from apologetic to turned on in the space between two heartbeats.

"It didn't hurt," she repeats, curling her fingers slightly, and stars pop in my vision.

Now I fidget under her attention and understand.

"You keep it up and we won't be watching anything, and lazy Saturday will bleed into lazy Sunday." I grip her wrist, but can't make myself pull her away.

"I don't see the problem." The words are whispered against my neck as her lips trail up to my ear.

Squeezing my eyes shut, I try to ignore the urge to give in, determined to do something with her that does not involve a part of my body buried inside her. With a deep breath, I gently pry her hand loose, tangling my fingers with hers.

"I'm going to start the episode now," I murmur. But I can't help but drop my lips to the pulse point in her wrist first.

"Okay?" She studies me for a moment, then shifts away, and I tighten my arm again, holding her to me.

"There isn't a problem." I refer to her comment a few minutes ago. "I wouldn't mind it at all."

"So why—?"

"As much as I want to forget the movie and fuck you until you can't move"—her breath catches at my words, and I need to remind myself I have a *but* at the end of my statement—"I want you for more than your body, Michaela."

Her face softens at my words. After the last two weeks, I get the impression that the things I want—to learn about the adult version of her, to talk to her, make her laugh, bring her flowers—are all new experiences for her.

"Watch." I gesture to the screen in front of us as the familiar theme starts, followed by the beginning narration by David Attenborough.

I can't count the number of times I've seen it, but it has the same hypnotizing power over me every time, and I'm excited to share it with the woman cuddled against my side. I glance down once about halfway through and find her eyes are riveted to the screen. Her pale pink lips are parted, her eyelashes long as they sweep along her cheeks. With her messy bun and zero make-up, she's the most beautiful I've ever seen her.

She must feel my inspection, because she glances up, a small smile playing on her lips.

"What?" she asks.

"You're beautiful." I lift my hand to stroke my thumb down her cheek as it heats.

Time seems to stop, the sound of the TV fading until all that's left are the two of us as we stare at each other. She reaches for me as I dip, and our lips connect like we've been kissing for years instead of weeks. But it's brand new too. The heat is still there, but...*more*. Deeper somehow.

We shift until she straddles me, our tongues tangling while I lift the hem of her shirt, tugging it off impatiently. She's not wearing a bra, so her breasts thrust toward me, begging for my touch. I don't hesitate to pull her closer, pressing against her upper back and sucking one of her nipples into my mouth. Her head falls back, and I groan as her hips slide back and forth across my dick. Even through our clothes, her heat sears me, and my dick presses insistently against the fabric of my pants, desperate to be inside her.

"West."

My name on her lips is the sexiest sound, intensified when she whimpers as she drags her pussy against my erection.

"Please," she murmurs.

My hands fall to her ass, squeezing her through the cotton of her shorts before trailing down to run a finger along the center of her panties.

"You're soaked," I groan, pushing the fabric aside to slide one finger, then two, into her pussy, and grin when she grinds down and rides my hand.

I circle her clit with my thumb, and the walls surrounding my fingers spasm. Lifting my hips slightly, I stop touching her long enough to tug my pants down, my cock springing free and into her waiting hand.

"Fuck," I groan as she squeezes.

Thank god she's on birth control. The thought of stopping to grab a condom makes my head spin, and I grit my teeth while her hand and her hips work to line me up at her entrance. While I hold the fabric of her panties to the side, she lowers herself inch by agonizing inch until I'm fully seated inside her.

I flex my hips up, grinding my pelvic bone against her clit, loving the moan that works its way out of her throat. My orgasm is building in my spine, heightened by the way her breasts bounce in front of me as she seeks her own pleasure.

"Pinch your nipples," I demand, holding her against me.

"W-w-what?" Her eyes flutter open, dazed and glassy as her own orgasm builds.

"Now," I growl.

She lifts her hands, pinching at both nipples lightly.

"Harder."

She obeys, twisting at them, and her walls spasm again, but this time around my dick.

"Don't stop," I warn her.

My hand releases her hip, and I move my fingers to her clit.

Her pussy squeezes me like a vise, and my balls tighten with the need to come.

"West," she whimpers, her hips losing their rhythm as they lift up and down.

"I need you to come, baby. Right the fuck now. You hear me?"

"Mm-hmm." She nods, tendrils of her hair escaping her bun to slither along her neck.

Her mouth opens on her next moan, her pussy milking my orgasm out of me as I lose track of everything but her. Her walls tighten, and at the weight of her body against mine, the sight of her as her chin tilts up, exposing the tendons in her neck as she comes—I don't hold back. I can't. Pistoning my hips, I work both of us through our orgasms until we're spent. She drops her hands from her breasts before leaning against me, her forehead resting on my shoulder while her breath skates across my chest through my t-shirt.

I drop my lips to her hair and rub my hands along her back.

"I think I like *The Blue Planet*," she says, surprising a laugh from me.

"Me too, baby, me too." Although I've never experienced watching it like that.

"West? You here?"

Michaela and I both freeze at the voice coming from the front door. The ending credits of the first episode roll, and in about five seconds, Kelly will be in the room with us.

"Shit. My mom." Michaela squeaks, scrambling off my lap and tugging her sleep shorts back in to place while I hastily pull up my pants.

She puts her shirt back on, but I don't have time to warn her that it's inside out and backward, the tag facing out under her chin.

"Here you are—Oh, Kayla, honey, what are you doing home?"

Kelly rushes forward, wrapping her arms around Michaela and lifting her up off the couch in a hug.

"Hi, Mom. Surprise." Michaela's voice vibrates with awkward nerves. Three minutes earlier, and her parents would have found us with my dick buried inside their daughter.

Dan steps into the doorway, his glasses giving him an owlish appearance as his eyes move across us. Kelly has Michaela locked in a hug and doesn't seem to be letting go any time soon.

"Mikey, hey, kiddo, didn't expect to see you here. Kel, let me hug her too." Dan hip checks his wife, who passes their daughter to him.

Kelly steps around them to hug me, and I hope the smell of sex isn't as strong as I think it is.

"How was it?" she asks.

I panic for a moment, thinking she's talking about the hotter than sin sex I just had with her daughter on her living room couch. But no. She's asking about the house while they were gone.

"Great," I croak out and clear my throat. "Michaela even helped me finish the basement."

Kelly's eyebrow arches at my use of Michaela's full name, and heat burns in my face. Her gaze moves from me to her daughter, and when her shoulders tighten slightly, there is no doubt she's noticed the state of Michaela's shirt. Her attention whips back to me, and my shoulders hunch.

"She did, did she?"

I nod. "She's pretty good at painting."

"Painting, huh?"

Please, please don't call me out in front of Dan when I can still feel Michaela all over my deflating cock.

Her eyes search mine for a minute, and I stop hiding the feelings I've developed for Michaela over the last few weeks. Slowly, her eyebrows drop, and the tension eases from her shoulders. Her slight nod tells me what I was hoping to see. She's okay with whatever is going on between her daughter and me.

I return the motion, relaxing when a smile stretches her face.

That's one blessing received. I still need two others. Dan's. And Sawyer's.

I'm not sure which conversation I'm afraid of more.

"Basement looks great, son," Dan says, settling on the couch next to the one where I'm sitting.

I grabbed a shower while Dan and Kelly checked out the work

on the basement. Michaela had showered separately and, while I missed having her wet, naked body against mine—shower sex is fucking amazing for a reason—I didn't want to get caught until I had the chance to talk to her dad.

Son.

The word tightens my throat and makes it hard to speak.

"Thanks. Glad I could help. How was your cruise?"

He rolls his eyes with a smile. "Don't tell Kelly I said this, but I'm glad to be home. The first week was nice, and the second week was okay, but by the third, I wanted my own bed and a good cheesesteak."

We both chuckle. But when he moves to pick up the remote, I hold up my hand.

"Dan, can I talk to you?"

He puts the remote down and studies me before nodding.

"Yeah, of course, West, what's going on?"

The last time I asked to talk to him like this, I told him about breaking up with Ashley and asked if he and Kelly would mind if I stayed with them for a little while.

Shit. How do I start *this* conversation?

"Well, you know, Michaela came home right after you and Kelly left for your cruise."

"That must have been a surprise for you," he jokes.

"Yeah," I nod. "She showed up at about three in the morning on Monday."

Dan groans.

"Of course she did. And she's been here ever since?"

"Yeah, um, about that. Since she's been back, we've been hanging out and well..."

"Well, what?" he prompts.

"I—uh—well, we, I guess." I let out a deep breath. "What I'm trying to say is that I've developed feelings for her. And I think she has some for me too."

His eyebrows climb to his hairline.

"You and Mikey?" he asks, clearly surprised by my admission. "Aren't you a little old for her?"

I cringe, because the seven-year age gap has crossed my mind too.

"Dad!" Michaela groans from the doorway and rushes forward to sit next to me on the couch.

"What? It's a serious question, kiddo," he says.

"I'm not a kid anymore. And West is right."

"Right about what?" I ask.

"You're not the only one with feelings," she says, meeting my gaze.

I want nothing more than to claim her lips with mine, but I'm very conscious of her father watching the two of us closely. Instead, my pinky finds hers on the couch cushion, and I link the two together.

"So, what does this mean exactly?" Dan asks, interrupting the moment between us.

"I want to date Michaela. And I'd like your approval." I don't shift my attention away from her, and her eyes sparkle at my announcement.

"What does Sawyer have to say about all this?" Dan asks.

"He doesn't know yet." My stomach tightens at the thought of the conversation I still need to have with my best friend.

"Hmph. I'm sure that will be an interesting exchange," he says. With a sigh, he continues. "I've known you since you were nine years old, West. If anyone was going to date my daughter, I guess I'd be okay if it was you."

Relief washes through me, and Michaela smiles.

"Does Kel know?" he asks.

"Kelly does indeed," she says, walking into the room and sitting in a chair across from her husband. She gives me a wink but doesn't say anything about what she almost walked in on.

"What do you think?" he asks her.

"If the kids are happy, who cares?" She shrugs. "But"—she

levels a serious look at first me and then Michaela—"I'm not interested in seeing anything a mother should never see. Got it?"

Embarrassment fills me at what she *isn't* saying, and I nod.

"Yes, ma'am."

"Michaela Grace?"

"Jeez, Mom. You act like we're going to go at it like rabbits or something."

She rolls her eyes. She has no idea how much her mom caught on to when she found us in the living room earlier. And in all honesty, we've spent a lot of time horizontal. Or vertical. The direction doesn't matter to me, but we'll have to be more careful now with her parents home.

"I don't want to know," Dan mutters, wiping a hand down his face.

"Neither do I," Kelly echoes.

"We'll be respectful," I promise.

Respectful would mean not sleeping with their daughter under their roof while they're home.

I know myself well enough to recognize I won't be able to stay away from her. What I can promise is that I'll be aware of their presence and steer clear of awkward situations.

"More importantly, just be happy," Kelly says.

Happy.

With Dan and Kelly's blessing, I feel lighter. I'm the happiest I've been in a long time. I don't want to hide my relationship with Michaela. And now I don't have to.

CHAPTER 14

MICHAELA

Flipping to my other side, I grip my pillow and squeeze my eyes closed.

The universe hates me. I *should* be tired. I *am* tired. But can I sleep?

Nope.

"Sleep, Kayla," I mutter to myself.

After getting back from dinner at a little Italian place my parents love, they went to bed, and West dropped me at my bedroom door with a chaste kiss to the forehead, insisting that we didn't need to flaunt our relationship in my parents' faces by immediately sleeping in the same bed together.

For most of my adult life, I've slept alone. Now, after two weeks, I can't sleep without his arm draped around my waist, his soft breath against my neck.

"Ugh." Rolling onto my back, I blink my eyes open and stare at the dark ceiling.

To hell with this. Tossing my covers aside, I move quietly to the door and open it slowly, glad it doesn't squeak like it did when I was a teenager. The noisy hinges got me into trouble more times than I could count.

Tonight, unlike those nights years ago, Mom and her disapproving look aren't waiting when I step out. The house is quiet as I make my way down the hall, twisting the knob on West's door. Thank god he left it unlocked. It keeps my stealthy actions a secret. The room is pitch dark except for the red glow coming from the nightstand. It's adorable that he still uses a traditional alarm clock.

1:47.

West is on his back, an arm thrown over his eyes while his chest rises and falls evenly. His shoulders are bare, the muscles relaxed in sleep. Stepping out of my sleep shorts and panties, I drop them on the floor and pull my t-shirt over my head. The light whisper of sound as it falls barely makes it to my ears as my pulse thrums and desire coats my thighs.

Sleep. I came in here to sleep.

Lifting the covers, I slide next to him, tangling my leg with his as I lower my head to his chest. The steady sound of his heartbeat vibrates under my cheek, and I breathe a sigh, relaxing against him as my arm circles his waist. My fingers graze his dick, and desire pools in my belly at the realization that he's semi-hard. I brush against him again, deliberately this time, before closing my palm around his length.

Up and down slowly, I repeat the caress, my fingers dampening with the pre-cum leaking from his tip. He shifts against the bed, and I freeze until his movements stop. His hard length is smooth and warm in my palm, and I clench my thighs, trying to soothe my building need. But all the slight pressure does is make me want more, not less. I lean up, shifting the covers aside, and expose him to my gaze.

Long and thick, his dick pulses in my hand, the head shiny in the dim light. Almost without thought, I bend down and drag my tongue along the moisture, moaning at his unique flavor. Shifting, I tuck my knees under me as I angle better to pull him into my mouth, running my tongue around the tip and lowering myself a little more until he bumps the back of my throat.

My pussy begs to be touched, but I need both hands to hold myself up. I lower and lift against my calves, hoping for some sort of friction, moaning as I swallow around him. The last time I did this, I hadn't gotten this far before he pulled me away to bury himself inside me. But since he's asleep, I have more control over our interaction than normal.

He's woken me before with his tongue circling my clit, the orgasm already barreling down on me before I was fully awake, and I want to do the same for him. A warm hand lands on my ass, and I jump as he slides it to my hip. The other one joins in, lifting me to straddle him like I weigh nothing. My knees land on either side of his head, and his tongue licks along my slit as he groans against my folds.

"Mmm. Hello, beautiful." I barely make out his words before his tongue taps against my clit and then circles the hard nub.

Lights flicker behind my eyelids, and I moan as one finger and then two press into me, finding the spot that nearly buckles my knees. I double my efforts, focusing everything he's making me feel on how my lips wrap around his dick, hollowing out my cheeks while I rim the head with my tongue.

"Christ," he groans, burying his mouth against my pussy.

His lips circle the bundle of nerves, sucking and nibbling as his fingers move in and out.

"You're going to come before me." He shifts one of his hands to my ass, holding me steady.

I don't break the connection, but increase my efforts, refuting his promise. *He's* going to come first.

"Fuck, baby, your mouth." His hips lift, driving him a little farther.

He always takes control, but this time I want him to lose it. To experience what I can make him feel. I move my hand down, cupping his balls as I moan around him again. His groan echoes in the room, and his hips lift off the bed while he hardens further against my tongue. He's close.

"I don't think so," he grits out.

He buries his tongue in my pussy, his hand coming down against my ass in a gentle smack, and stars pulse faster behind my eyes.

"That's it," he says as he laps at the desire coating my folds.

I'm right on the edge, ready to come.

One of his arms circles my waist, holding me against his tongue. I can't squirm away, and the orgasm barrels down, ready to consume me. I fight the pleasure, desperate to make him come first. Sheathing my teeth with my lips, I apply a light pressure, and I'm rewarded when his thigh jumps under my hand.

In response, he presses against the tight pucker of my ass. I can't hold it off anymore. My toes curl into the mattress on either side of his head, and I moan, so overcome I don't release him, using his cock to muffle my cries as wave after wave of intense pleasure pummels me. Finally, I collapse against him, my mouth breaking the connection as air saws in and out of my lungs.

"I win," he says before lifting me and spinning me to face him.

He pulls me down, claiming my mouth even as his hips shift to impale me in one sure thrust.

Aftershocks pulse through me, and I whimper around his tongue.

Breaking the kiss, he trails his lips to my jaw before nipping down my neck.

"This is going to be fast, baby."

He holds me to him, a hand on each hip, as he drives up and down faster and faster until another orgasm shimmers at the edges.

"Oh god." I bury my face between his neck and his shoulder.

"Not god," he growls. "Just me."

He increases the tempo again, hips rocking, and I sink my teeth into his shoulder, this orgasm shattering me into a million pieces of white-hot heat and pleasure. He lifts once, twice more, and stills, emptying himself into me with a growl as he holds me close.

When he finally loosens his hold, he rubs his hands up and down my back in slow, soothing circles.

"Couldn't sleep?" he asks.

"I missed you," I admit and rub my cheek against the light dusting of hair on his chest.

His chuckle is more a vibration in his chest than a sound.

"I could tell," he teases.

"Don't make fun of me," I say in a pouty tone.

He squeezes me as his lips brush my hair. "I'm sorry. I wasn't making fun of you. I'm glad you're here."

"You are?" Glancing up, I meet his eyes in the mostly dark room.

"I am," he says. "I missed you too."

I lower my head back down, and he resumes making patterns on my back. His heart is a soft melody under my cheek, and my eyelids grow heavy.

"Good night, baby." His lips graze my hair once more.

"Night," I murmur, relaxing into the sleep waiting for me.

I barely hear his alarm go off a few hours later, but I wake with the warmth of his lips when he presses them to my temple

"You smell good."

He huffs a laugh. "Thanks, I think. I have to go to work."

"'Kay." I burrow into the pillow, not ready to leave the warmth of his bed.

"You want to stay here?" he asks.

"Mm-hmm."

"I'd love to tell you to stay exactly like this and wait for me to come home, but something tells me your parents wouldn't approve."

"Probably not." I smile sleepily.

"See you after work?"

"'Kay. Wait—" I sit up, the sheet pooling at my waist, and his eyes darken as he takes in my nakedness. "Kiss."

He smiles and leans down, grazing his lips with mine. I lock my arms around his neck, keeping him where he is, and I delve my tongue into his mouth, moaning when he leans closer, pressing me back against the mattress.

"I've got to go," he whispers against my lips. "Save this thought for later?"

"Later," I promise.

His bedroom door opens and closes, and a thud sounds from the front door. Closing my eyes, I inhale his scent from the pillow and drift.

When I open my eyes again, the clock reads 9:43. I stretch and groan, moving slowly and re-dressing in the pajamas I'd shed as soon as I got to his room last night. A pleasant ache throbs between my thighs, and my nipples are sensitive where they rub against the soft cotton of my shirt.

When I open the door, I nearly run into my mom.

"Good thing it was me and not your dad," she warns with an eye roll.

He definitely would say something if he caught me slipping from West's room to mine.

"I'm running to the store in a little while. Let me know if you need anything." She heads down the stairs, and I open the door to my room and collapse on my bed with a huff.

That was close.

My phone buzzes on my nightstand, distracting me from my wandering thoughts.

UNKNOWN

Enjoying your vacation?

Who is this?

You would know if you hadn't blocked my other number.

Brad.

The flash of recognition transports me back to that night, and a shudder racks my body.

I'm not on vacation.

Call it whatever you want, but it's time to put your ass back to work.

I'm not going anywhere near you. Or Reverb.

It's cute you think you have any control over that, sweetheart.

Reverb still owns you for two more records. Even those fancy east coast attorneys can't get you out of it.

No, no, no, no, no. Bile rises in my throat and I take a deep breath. How does he know that I met with an attorney?

Either you get your ass back to California or you're in breach. Our lawyers would love to hear that. They've been bored lately.

With shaky fingers, I try to type a response several times before giving up.

What can I say?

And you better have learned some manners in the last few weeks.

Either you do as I say or I'm going to make your life a living hell.

My life had already been hell when I left that nasty motel in the middle of the night. But somehow, I don't doubt he could make it worse.

Suddenly cold, I block him—again—without an answer, lie down, and pull the covers up to my chin.

I can't go back. I can't.

What choice do you have?

None. Brad's right. I should have read the contract more closely before I signed it. Or found someone to read through it for me. But I was so excited to get a record deal, I didn't think much beyond that.

The thought of being around him again, about what he could make me do, makes me sick to my stomach.

"Kay?" Mom's voice comes through my door, startling me. "I'm headed to the store, and your dad decided to go with me. You sure you don't need anything?"

"Nope. I'm good, Mom. Thanks," I call, hoping my voice sounds normal.

I wait for the garage door to open and close before stumbling out of my bed and into the bathroom. I turn the shower on as hot as it will go. My legs give out as I step into the tub, and I sink to the porcelain, letting the water rain down on me until my hair is soaked through. In a daze, I wash my hair, mesmerized by the suds as they swirl around the drain. I repeat the process with conditioner, and finally with body wash, numb by the time I shut the shower off.

I wrap one towel around my body and another in my hair before I head back to my bedroom, sinking down on my bed in exhaustion as anxiety swirls in my stomach.

West finds me there several hours later, burrowed under my blanket and hiding from the world.

"Hey, I wasn't serious this morning," he jokes, his smile fading when I don't return it. "What's the matter? Are you sick?"

I am, but not because of any illness.

I shake my head.

"What's wrong?" His eyes are so full of concern as he lies on the pillow next to mine, I can't stop the tears from overflowing. "Michaela?"

His thumb comes up to brush one tear and then another from my cheek.

"I can't go back," I whisper, more to myself than to him.

"What do you mean? You heard from Reverb?" My head jerks in a nod, but the tears don't stop. "I…I haven't been completely honest with you."

His fingers against my cheek tense, and I flinch before pulling away.

"What?" The warm concern is gone from his voice, and all that's left is a flat, emotionless copy.

"I—" Closing my eyes, I bite back the sob that wants to escape but meet his gaze with my next words. "I'm not famous, West. Not by a long shot. And it gets worse."

"Define worse."

I pull up Brad's text messages and hand him my phone. By the time he's done reading the short exchange, his knuckles are white, a muscle in his jaw ticking furiously.

"Who the hell is this?"

"M-m-my label rep," I stutter out.

"Baby." He tosses the phone to the side, drawing me into his arms and pulling me against his chest.

"He-he-he…" I close my eyes, more tears leaking out and onto West's shirt.

"Did he do something to you?" he asks me gently.

"He tried. The night I came home," I whisper. "I couldn't remember anything Sawyer taught me."

"Shh." He rubs a hand along my back, his tone soothing.

"He-he-he was going to-to-to r-r-r—" I can't bring myself to say the word, and West takes pity on me.

"But you got away?"

I nod, my cheek dragging along the damp fabric. "Your shirt."

"Don't worry about my shirt. You got away. You're safe. I'm here. He's not going to do anything else to you."

"You told me to think," I tell him.

"What?"

"That night. I heard your voice in my head. Telling me to think."

"Michaela." My name is a pained whisper on his lips, and he crushes me to him, imbuing me with a security I haven't felt all day. "I promise you. He's never going to touch you again. I swear to God."

"But...but I lied," I say, hating to admit to something that he despises so much.

"You haven't lied about anything else, right?"

"No, nothing," I tell him quickly.

"Will you make me a promise?"

I lift my head and meet his eyes.

"What?"

"No more lies. Tell me. Anything you tell me will always be better than not being honest."

"I promise."

"Nothing you can tell me will drive me away. I'm here."

I let out a breath, the tension loosening but not disappearing completely. For the first time since I signed the record contract, since that first picture in Chicago with Jax, I can breathe.

I'm not alone.

CHAPTER 15

WEST

Need you to call me.

SAWYER

Give me 5.

My phone rings in three.

"You don't usually text me shit like that." Sawyer doesn't even bother to say hello when I answer.

"It's about Michaela."

"Mikey? Is she okay?" Worry colors his tone. He's the traditional big brother. Happy to pick on her himself, but willing to kill anyone else who dares to mess with her.

"So, two things." I blow out a breath, my stomach tightening with this first part. But I need to tell him about us first in order to explain the second part.

I need the skills he's honed by opening his own company.

"West, fucking Christ, man, I'm thinking all kinds of shit over here, so do you mind getting to the point already?"

"Your sister and I—" I don't think he needs the reminder of

the familial relationship. "Michaela and I are kind of seeing each other."

"What do you mean 'kind of'?"

I sigh.

"We're seeing each other. No kind of about it. I'm dating your sister," I say in a rush, tensing for the reaction to come through the phone.

He grunts. "And that warranted your text?"

"You're not mad?" How is he not mad?

"Why would I be? Dude, I've known you almost all my life. You're a good guy. Better than the jokers she's dated in the past."

My teeth grind together at the mention of other men. They may have happened before she and I started up, but the knowledge doesn't make me any happier about it.

"Mom and Dad know?" Sawyer interrupts my thoughts.

"Yeah." I don't tell him about how much they almost knew. What they know, what Kelly is aware of, is more than enough for me.

"They cool with it?" He crunches something into the phone, and I wince at the loud static sound.

"They seem to be," I admit.

Although Dan still eyed me warily all through dinner last night.

"Mikey happy?"

Up until today? I would have said yes. But now I'm not so sure. Is she only here because she has nowhere else to go?

"Uhh..." I reach up, squeezing at the tension in the back of my neck.

"That was a yes or no question, man."

"It's complicated."

"Why the fuck is it complicated?" The tone of his voice is what I expected all along. "Did you screw something up?"

"What? No—"

"Because if so, I'll rip your balls off and shove 'em down your throat before I beat you to death."

Well, that's...graphic.

"I haven't done anything. Not that I know of, anyway. I'm worried she's only home because she has nowhere else to go."

"What do you mean?"

I tell him the entire story I coaxed from her. My anger spikes again with every detail, a red haze encroaching on my vision when I relay the texts Michaela let me read.

"Motherfucker."

"I need your help," I tell him.

"I'm already on it." There's a staccato tapping of keys and a deep breath. "I have a contact from one of my old COs. Another special ops guy who ran security for Reverb. Fuck, I knew I should have done more research into that fucking label rep when they assigned him to her. I did a full background check on the first guy, and he checked out fine. Figured that was the end of it."

"Do you know why the other guy left? Why she got assigned to this douchebag?" I ask.

"Has she talked to you about everything that's happened over the last year and a half?" His question is hesitant.

"Of course."

I still feel like an ass for assuming the worst about her and Tucker.

"I assume Reverb was tired of taking a hit to their reputation. They were in a big enough shit storm when Jax Bryant left their label to start his own."

"How the hell do you know all this?" I ask.

"You live in LA, you hear things. Especially if you keep your ears open."

"Something you're good at."

"You don't do what I did in the military without being good at it."

He's never told me exactly what that entailed, so other than knowing he went to basic training and deployed a half dozen times, I have no idea. I don't even know where he deployed to, only that when he came back, he was hyperaware of his surroundings and had a knack for knowing if something was going on, even when no one else did.

With his unexplainable ability, Sawyer's security firm—although brand new—has been extremely successful from day one.

"You need to use those skills and find out what the fuck has been going on." I've never seen Michaela more distraught than she was this afternoon.

"Bro, trust me. I'm going to get answers, and then I'm going to go pay a little visit to Brad." His knuckles crack, and I shake my head.

"Don't get yourself arrested. I'm not there to bail you out."

"I got this," he assures me. "When does Mikey need to be in California?"

"According to the texts? Now. But we're going to ignore them. I'm not letting her get within a hundred feet of that asshole. It's only a matter of time, though, before he ups his game."

"Yep. I'm almost done with this current job and should be in LA next week. I've already sent a couple of emails and will gather whatever data I can before I get back."

I breathe a sigh of relief.

"Thanks, man. I appreciate it."

"No thanks needed. Mikey is my baby sister."

"Are we cool?" I ask, worry eating at me since he is now aware I'm sleeping with his sister.

"Like I said, West. I'm good if Mikey is good. But if you hurt her, you won't be able to run anywhere I can't find you."

My swallow sticks part way down my throat, and I cough several times.

"I'm not going to hurt her. I care a lot about her." I'm halfway to falling in love with her, but I'm not going to tell him that, especially not before I've told her.

"Good. Then we understand each other. I'll call you when I get some info."

"Stay safe, okay?"

I have no idea what he's doing now, but I've ended every conversation this way since he left for basic training.

"Safety is my middle name." His standard reply brings a smile to my lips.

I hang up and step back across the hall to Michaela's bedroom. She was sleeping when I left to change clothes and call Sawyer, but when I step through the door, her wide blue eyes meet mine.

"You're awake." I ease onto the edge of her bed.

I'm not sure how to act, other than to be there for her, however she needs me.

"Sorry I fell asleep."

"Don't apologize. You needed it." I lift my hand to lay it on her leg, but hesitate, my arm hovering above her awkwardly.

"What's wrong?" she asks, motioning to my arm.

"I..." I don't want to startle her by touching her.

You've touched her plenty since the night that asshole attacked her.

Visions of the tie, of the spanking, of all our other encounters come to mind. They harden my dick but turn my stomach.

"You don't want to touch me." Her eyes close, and she turns her head toward the wall.

"No, Michaela, you're wrong." I scoot closer, gently applying pressure to her chin with my thumb and forefinger until she's turned in my direction again. "Open your eyes, baby."

She does what I ask, and the resignation and shame clear in those blue depths have me ready to kick my own ass. Sawyer won't be necessary.

"You are the most beautiful woman I've ever known. Inside

and out. I just wish you would have told me about what happened. I'd have been gentler with you, less…demanding."

"I like how you've been with me." She sits up, her hair tickling my arm when it slides down her neck.

"I—you were attacked."

"You didn't attack me, West. I loved everything we've done. Everything. I've known all along you're not like Brad. If I didn't, I would have stopped anything I didn't like."

I study her for a long moment, reading the truth in her gaze, relieved that we're past the lying.

"You're sure?" I ask, still hesitant. Still afraid to touch her and bring up those memories again.

"Positive. I lo—have feelings for you. More than the crush I had as a teenager—"

"You had a crush on me when you were a teenager?" I smile, lifting my hand to cup her cheek.

She covers my hand with hers. "I totally did. Sawyer didn't say anything?"

"No. Are you sure he knew?"

"Ugh, yes. He teased me about it constantly."

"He never said anything to me," I tell her. "He kept your secret."

I rack my brain for memories, for anything that would have tipped me off to the torch she supposedly carried as a teen, but nothing comes to mind.

"You can trust me with your secrets too." My hand lowers only enough to allow me to draw an index finger along her jaw, down her neck and shoulder to rest against her hand.

"I know."

"Anything. Nothing you tell me will change anything between us."

Her eyes are luminous in the light from her bedside table, and I want to kiss her so badly it physically aches as I hold myself back.

"I want to kiss you," I admit, tangling my fingers with hers.

"Do it."

She doesn't need to tell me twice. I close the distance, my hands cupping her jaw as I sip at her lips, nibbling cautiously until her mouth parts on a sigh. I slip my tongue in to taste her, to revel in the flavors that are uniquely Michaela. The prick of her fingernails against my biceps barely registers against all the emotions trying to escape from my chest.

"Kayla, West, dinner!" Kelly calls up the stairs, and we break apart, smiling at each other while we both breathe deeply.

"My mom has an uncanny ability to interrupt us," she teases with a smile, and I can't help the laugh that escapes.

"She's really good at it," I agree. "But as she said, dinner's ready, and I'm pretty sure you didn't eat anything today."

Her sheepish expression confirms my assumption, and I pull her out from under the covers, grateful she tossed on a t-shirt and yoga pants earlier. I don't think I could deny a naked Michaela anything she asked of me.

"You need to take care of yourself," I lecture, and she rolls her eyes, yelping when my hand finds her backside.

"Hey!"

"I care about you too. Take care of yourself, if not for you, then for me. I don't want anything to happen to you."

She nods, stepping close enough to wrap her arms around my waist, her head finding its place above my heart. I engulf her in a hug, dropping my nose to her hair as I breathe in her coconut shampoo and thank the universe for giving me a chance with her.

CHAPTER 16

MICHAELA

"Hey, sleepyhead, still want to go out today?" West's voice drags me from a blissfully deep sleep.

"Mmm." I try to burrow against him, but his chest vibrating with laughter makes it hard.

"C'mon, rock star. Time to move it." His weight shifts from the bed, and he drags the covers with him.

We plan to do our make-up cheesesteak taste test today, but first he asked if he could take me on a walking history tour around Independence Square. Last night I had been excited, but this morning, I just want to sleep.

"Already?" I whine, trying to force my eyes open. He chuckles at my grumbling before brushing his lips against my temple. "We just fell asleep."

"Nine hours ago."

"I'm tired."

"Please?" He nibbles at my ear before sucking at the sensitive spot behind the lobe.

My eyes shoot open, and I glare at the mischievous grin on his face.

"You're evil."

"You agreed to this date anyway," he reminds me with a wink.

Dressed in a pair of shorts, a faded Eagles t-shirt, and a knit beanie a shade lighter than his eyes, he doesn't look like he's a thirty-year-old high-school teacher. He looks like the teenage West I remember.

"Like what you see?" he asks, flexing a bicep.

"Yep." I shift and drop my feet to the floor. Stretching my arms above my head, I try to wake up, even though it wouldn't take much convincing to lie down and go back to sleep.

But I've been looking forward to this date since he and I first talked about the taste test showdown, and I want to see West in his history element again.

Which is why thirty minutes later, I'm showered and dressed in a pair of shorts and a t-shirt and letting him pull me to his car. He tucks me into the passenger seat before he rounds the hood and slides behind the wheel.

"Excited?" I tease.

The vibrant energy that surrounds him reminds me of a kid on Christmas Eve.

He nods. "I've wanted to do this tour for a while, but they're usually sold out."

"Sold out? You make it sound like a concert," I tease, poking my index finger against his side.

He shrugs, backing out of the driveway. "Usually, tourists book it months in advance, but I checked the other day and there were two tickets left."

"So it's going to be a big group?" I'm not famous, so I doubt it'll be a problem.

Infamous, maybe.

I hate being recognized from the sex tape fiasco, but it still happens every few weeks. Like the students West had overheard.

"I think they try to keep the tour to about thirty."

"And we're only walking around?"

He laughs, his hand coming to rest on my knee, and my whole

body tunes to the connection. That small touch makes me feel cherished. Treasured. And not because of the physical link between us or the attraction. He's excited to share pieces of himself with me and, in turn, so am I.

"We're just walking around," he confirms. "But in all these famous places where Benjamin Franklin and his peers lived and worked."

"You haven't done this already?" I ask as he drives us downtown.

"No. I took a few others, but this one has never worked out, especially when I lived in Pittsburgh."

I cover his hand with mine, interlacing our fingers. "I'm excited to do this with you."

He stares at me, eyes sparkling. "Me too."

The tour is mostly families, and West and I appear to be the youngest adults in the group. He knows the tour guide from a seminar they both went to, and he spends most of the walks between the stops discussing some of the new tours being planned and even gets invited to join a historical society group on Facebook.

He glows with joy when he talks about the history of each building, of the places we pass by. He laughs when one of the little boys asks him if he's a tour guide too, the rich sound unfurling warmth in my belly that spreads to my heart.

As a child, I loved West, the older brother figure who was always nicer to me than my actual older brothers. But this is different. After spending time with him like this over the last few weeks, I can't help but fall in love with West, the man. I suck in a breath as the word takes shape in the swirling emotions. Love.

The man in question meets my eyes, studying me like he knows what I'm feeling, what I'm thinking. Like my innermost thoughts are written all over my face. When my phone pings with a text, I step away from the rest of the group to read the message from Mia.

MIA

You have an appointment next week with Michael Pryce of Allied Entertainment Law.

Wednesday at 11:00 AM.

What?!

I asked Garrett to look into entertainment lawyers in LA since I'm not there. We need to get you away from Reverb.

The sting of tears burns my nose. Mia doesn't even know the full story, and she's fighting for me. Sniffling, I key in a response.

Mi! You didn't have to do that.

I know I didn't have to. But you're my friend. And that place is making my friend miserable.

Thank you.

Is there a number I need to call Wednesday or are they calling me or...?

It's a lunch meeting at California Burger Bar.

I'm already working on my response when she texts me the address.

I don't have a way of getting to LA. And my credit card will have a stroke if I try to charge a ticket this close.

Already took care of that too. Check your email for your ticket information.

MIA!!! I'm paying you back as soon as I can. You shouldn't have done that!

Evie found the deal on the ticket, so thank her. And as for the money, no, you're not.

Yes, I am.

We can argue about it in person later.

eye roll emoji Don't think I won't.

In person?

Are you back in LA?

No. *sad emoji* And Garrett is out of town next week too.

I didn't want you to be all alone at the house, so I booked you a hotel room.

Mia. I can find my own place to stay.

Somehow. Maybe I can get a hold of Sawyer and stay with him if he's home.

But now you don't have to. Love you!

Love you too!

"Everything okay?" West steps behind me, his hand finding the small of my back, and I lean against him.

"I-I'm not sure," I admit and hand him my phone so he can scroll through my texts with Mia.

"She wants you to meet with an entertainment attorney?" he asks. "The one here was zero help."

"They didn't specialize in entertainment law. Just said they were familiar with it. One of the few here who were."

"So you're going to LA?" His arm tightens around my waist protectively.

Spinning, I loop my arms around his neck, pressing my lips to his.

"Just for a few days," I promise. "I'm coming back."

"Sawyer's already working on it."

Embarrassment still pricks that my big brother is aware of what happened, but I know West did the right thing when he called him.

"It can't hurt to hear what this attorney has to say."

He pulls me against him, his arms tightening. "I worry about you. I don't want you to go alone."

"If Mia and Garrett set up this appointment, it means they trust this guy. And I trust them."

"I wish I could go with you."

"I know." I press a kiss against his jaw. "And I love that."

The words are on my lips. To add another love in there, but the tour guide interrupts us, calling everyone back. We keep walking, West's hand linked with mine as he whispers bits and pieces of history to me along the rest of the walk. They aren't sweet nothings, but I'll take them any day.

"Just a few days, right?" he asks as we head back to the starting point of the tour.

"Two or three tops," I tell him. "Why? Going to miss me?"

I'm teasing, but his expression is serious when he pulls me back into his arms.

"Yes."

"I'll miss you too." I grab his hands and pull him down until our lips meet, my tongue tangling with his. His heartbeat races under my palm.

If leaving him for a few days means I'll miss him this much, what's going to happen when I leave for longer?

𝄞 𝄞 𝄞

"You ready?" he asks, spreading the paper open between us on the outdoor table at a park near both restaurants.

"How are we going to do this?" I motion to the two sandwiches between us.

He hands me the one we picked up at Pat's. My mouth waters at the smell of meat and peppers.

"You try that one first, and I'll try this one at the same time." He lifts the sandwich from Geno's. "Then we switch."

West counts down from three, and I angle my head to try to take a bite without making a huge mess, watching him do the same.

The familiar flavors mix in my mouth. This is home. A warm summer day, a cheese steak, a cute guy…this is what I was missing all those months on the tour, all those months before.

Contentment.

I grab my lemonade and motion for the sandwich he's taken several bites of.

"Hey! I want some of that one. It's my favorite."

He hands it over, still chewing, and I try the new sandwich.

He polishes off the sandwich from Pat's and asks, "So, what did you think?" His voice slightly muffled from the napkin he holds in front of his mouth.

"It was okay," I concede. "But I'm still partial to Geno's. And I think you are too, since you ate most of that one as well."

"Are you still hungry? I can grab another one."

"Are you?" I ask with a laugh.

He grins. "I'm good, but if you want another one, we can head back."

His fingers play with mine on top of the table, tracing along the knuckles of my index finger.

"I'm good right here." I say, returning his smile.

"Did you have fun today?"

I nod. "Yeah."

"You sound surprised."

"I've never had so much fun with…history." A sharp pain shoots through my stomach, stealing my breath and sending a sour tang to my mouth.

West's expression goes from relaxed to concerned in an instant.

"Michaela?"

The sour sensation continues to build, and I try a sip of the lemonade, hoping to get rid of the bitter flavor.

"Umm, I'm not sure." Closing my eyes, I take several deep breaths to clear the overwhelming nausea building in my throat.

"Baby?" His warmth slides next to me on my bench, his fingers brushing against my forehead.

"I'm—I'm fine," I try again, taking a deep breath as my stomach lurches. "Is—is there a bathroom somewhere close?"

He points to the other side of the park as my stomach gurgles again. I'm not going to make it. Instead, I stand and bolt for a copse of trees, where I drop to my knees and lose the sandwiches I ate.

"Michaela?" West comes up behind me, rubbing my back and holding my ponytail away from my neck.

I wave him away, but he stays where he is. Finally, the sharp pains fade and I stand, leaning against the tree.

"I'm sorry," I say.

"Nothing to be sorry for. Are you feeling better?" he asks and hands me a napkin.

Now if only I had some water.

"Yeah. Are you okay?"

Other than the concern on his face, he appears to be fine. But considering how quickly I got sick, it must be food poisoning.

"Me? I'm perfectly fine."

"I think one of the sandwiches was bad." I lean against him as we walk back to the car.

"They didn't taste bad to me. Maybe too much time in the sun?"

"I'm not sure."

The smell of food grows stronger the closer we get to the two restaurants, and I hesitate as the sourness rushes back.

"Here. I'll run in and grab a bottle of water. How about you sit here until I'm done?"

I nod and practically collapse on the bench he pointed out. Leaning my head back, I close my eyes and concentrate on my breathing to keep the nasty sensation away.

"Babe?" West joins me, and I open my eyes to see the bottle of water in his hand.

I accept it gratefully, taking two small sips.

"Let's go home, okay?"

I nod. "Yes, please."

We walk slowly back to the car. Once inside, I relax against the back of the seat, frustrated that our date is ending with me getting sick right in front of him.

Is this going to be the theme of our relationship?

CHAPTER 17

MICHAELA

The rest of the weekend is a blur of normalcy. By the time we got back to the house, my stomach was fine.

Sawyer called mom to tell her he's coming for a visit later this week. She knows something is up, but she doesn't say anything at dinner that night or the next day. I think she trusts us enough not to ask questions until we're all together.

As my trip to LA on Tuesday looms, my anxiety spikes, and each time I check my email, the dread in the pit of my stomach tightens.

By Monday I've almost talked myself out of going. I'm looking for something to eat for lunch when the doorbell rings, and I find the mailman holding a certified letter addressed to me, the Reverb logo grinning like the devil from the top left-hand corner.

Mom and Dad are both back at work, and West is gone too, so I'm alone when I close the door and lean against it.

"Come on Kayla, open the letter," I say to the empty living room. "Bad news doesn't get better with time."

Boy, am I the walking, talking example of that saying.

I convince myself to move to the couch and fall numbly against the cushions.

I should have ignored the doorbell.

Blowing out a breath, I slide my fingernail along the fold, opening the envelope and letting the folded piece of paper flutter out. Only flutter is the wrong word for the thick, expensive paper tucked inside.

Ms. King,

We have been notified by your label representative, Bradley Russell, about attempts on three separate occasions to contact you regarding your work with Reverb. After these attempts went unreturned, Bradley notified us that you were in breach of contract. Pursuant to the last clause of your contract...

The rest is a bunch of legalese, hard to wrap my brain around, considering it took me ten minutes to work out the first paragraph. The only words that jumped off the page were *breach of contract.*

A small part of me wonders if Brad is under contract, and if assaulting me would be considered a breach of his contract.

Does it matter?

He did exactly what he said he was going to do. He turned me over to the lawyers and gave them his half of the story.

"Shit. What am I going to do now?"

I ask West the same question when he gets home that night.

"You'll want to show this to the attorney, along with your contract. Do you have a copy?"

Standing from my bed, I open my top dresser drawer and pull out the contract I had "filed" there after signing it almost two years ago.

"We should send this to Sawyer, too." He lays the letter flat on the bed, snaps a picture, and texts it to my brother.

So far, we've sent Sawyer copies of the texts and the emails, but he said he already had a copy of my contract. I don't even want to know how.

"What if"—I swallow around the lump of uncertainty growing

in my throat—"what if they can't do anything? What if my only choices are to get sued or go back? What if—"

He pulls me onto the bed with him, silencing my uncertainty with a kiss that leaves me clinging to him breathlessly by the time he lifts his head.

"We won't know unless we try, right? Whatever happens, I'm here." His hands come up, chafing warmth up and down into my arms before his fingers interlace with mine. "We'll tackle this as a team."

𝄞𝄞𝄞

The alarm cuts through an amazing dream I'm having.

I'm on stage, singing to a huge crowd full of lights and cheers while West smiles at me from the wings. They love my music. They want more, and I open my mouth, but words don't come out. Instead, it's the screech of the alarm.

The lights and crowd fade, and so does the smiling West on the side of the stage. Thankfully, I can burrow against the real version whose chest and shoulder I'm currently draped over.

"West." I press against his chest, shaking him gently as the alarm continues to blare. "West. The alarm."

"What?" His fingers come up and tangle with mine.

"Time to get up."

He groans, reaching over and silencing the annoying sound.

"We need to get up," I murmur, glad I packed last night.

"Just a few more minutes," he says, arms tightening around me. "I hit snooze."

"I can't be late for my flight." I press my lips against his warm chest. I don't want to leave him, but the meeting with this attorney is important.

"I wish you didn't have to go." The words echo my own emotions.

"I'm going to miss you," I tell him.

Propping myself up on an elbow, I fuse our mouths, tangling my tongue with his until the alarm sounds again.

The silence is tense. Like my nerves about what comes next are a tangible weight in the room with us while we get ready. We don't say much in the car either, but the warmth of his hand around mine is a balm I wish I could take with me to LA.

We pull into the departure lane at the terminal, and he parks the car, turning to me.

"I—" His eyes search mine, and he clears his throat before bringing his hands up to cup my face. "I'm going to miss you."

"I'll miss you too." The pressure of tears builds behind my eyes, and I close them, leaning my cheek into his palm. Why is saying goodbye this hard? It's for a few days. And I'll talk to him on the phone. "I wish you could come with me."

"You got this, baby. I'd go if I could, but I have no doubt you'll text me with good news after you meet with the attorney."

"I hope so." Opening my eyes, I meet his gaze, clinging to the certainty I see there.

"I know so."

Slowly, he closes the distance between us, teasing my lips from corner to corner before claiming them fully. His thumbs brush my cheeks, and he tilts my head to deepen the kiss. With a moan, I wrap my fingers around his wrists.

A horn honks behind us, and we jump apart at the reminder of where we are and the minutes slipping quickly by.

Meeting me at the back of the car, he pulls my suitcase out before wrapping me in another hug.

"Call me when you land." His lips brush my hair, and I shiver at the contact.

"You'll still be in school," I remind him.

"Text me then. I need to know you're safe."

"I will."

I'm still not ready to let him go. It takes several more breaths before I can release my death grip on his shirt, and a dozen more kisses before I step onto the curb and watch him walk around the car.

"Don't miss your flight," he reminds me.

"I won't." Even though I'm in danger of doing just that.

Blowing him a kiss, I grab the handle of my suitcase and head for the check-in kiosk inside. At the doors, I glance over my shoulder to see him still there. He watches me and winks when my eyes meet his.

With a wave, I turn toward my destination, fighting the urge to run back to him.

It's just a few days.

𝄞 𝄞 𝄞

I'm here. *palm tree emoji*

West responded an hour later to say he got the text and wanted to call me later.

I'm lying on the bed in my hotel room when his name finally pops up on my screen.

"Hey," I say with a smile as I answer the phone.

"Hi, baby. How was your flight?" I can almost imagine the vibration of his voice under my cheek instead of the soft pillow I'm resting on.

"Uneventful. But I don't think Mia was completely honest about the 'good deal' on the flight Evie found. It was first class."

I've never flown first class, even when Reverb first flew me to LA, so the high-end treatment was a surprise.

He whistles into the phone. "Living that rock star life, huh?"

"Oh yeah." I snort a laugh. "Total rock star. Currently watching a daytime talk show in my hotel room."

"Resting up for a wild night on the town?" His tone is mostly teasing, but I also catch hints of uncertainty underneath.

"If a wild night is room service and a bubble bath, you know it."

"You're not meeting up with friends?"

"Mia's still on location, and since she's my only friend, that would be a big fat no."

"I'm your friend," he reminds me.

"You're more than my friend," I tell him.

"Oh yeah? What am I?"

"My best friend." My confession is a whisper into the phone.

"Your best friend?" he asks. "I like the term boyfriend better."

"Are you my boyfriend?"

"Damn straight," he growls, and desire throbs to life in my core.

"It seems weird to call you my boyfriend." I wrinkle my nose at the term. West is so much more than that.

"What would you call me then?" he asks, and I squeeze my thighs together at the tone in his voice.

"I-I don't know." I search for a word that might better fit, but none comes to mind. "Boyfriend is probably the closest. Lover, maybe?"

He blows out a breath, and I lift a hand to my breast, the nipple hard against my palm even through the material of my shirt and bra.

"And now I'm sitting in the school parking lot with a major hard-on," he groans.

"Poor baby."

"Tease all you want, Michaela. But you'll pay for all of it when you get back here on Thursday," he warns.

"Is that a threat?" I ask, breathless as my panties go from damp to soaked.

"It's a promise, you vixen."

"Thursday can't come soon enough."

"And neither can I." His joke surprises a laugh from me. "But I'd rather not do that in a high school parking lot."

"Call me later?"

"You couldn't stop me if you tried," he answers. "And, Michaela?"

"Yes?"

"No touching yourself until I call you." His tone is firm, and I drop my hand from where I was sliding it down my stomach.

"How did you—"

"I didn't for sure. You just told me. Hands off until tonight."

I huff. "Fine. Tonight."

"I'll talk to you later, baby."

"Drive safe, West."

"Bye."

Setting my phone down, I consider continuing the exploration I was getting ready to take but ultimately shake my head with a sigh.

I can wait for him.

I'm still thinking about phone sex with West when I leave the hotel the next day and walk the few blocks to California Burger Bar, where my meeting with Michael Pryce is scheduled. My dark glasses and fedora blend with the styles around me, and I breathe a sigh of relief when I don't draw attention to myself.

Reaching the door to the restaurant, I take several deep breaths, checking my phone when it chimes.

WEST

You got this, rock star. *wink emoji*

I'll text you after.

Squaring my shoulders, I open the door and walk in with as much faux confidence as I can manage. I give Michael's name to the hostess, and she leads me to a table where three men are already seated.

Despite the baseball cap pulled low over what I know are

green eyes, I recognize one of the men and hesitate one table away.

"Ms. King?" The middle-aged man stands to greet me, but my eyes flick to his two companions before coming back to him.

"Yes. Mr. Pryce?"

He nods, gesturing to the table. "Please, call me Michael."

"Jax," I say, taking the open seat next to Michael. "This is a surprise."

"You'll have to excuse my son and son-in-law," Michael says, and my mouth drops open in shock.

"Son?" I squeak out.

"Almost. I've known him since he was born." He points to Jax before motioning to the other occupant. "And since Nick married my daughter, I now have two men to shout at football games with."

"Oh." I'm trying to process all this information as quickly as I can.

"I apologize for the surprise," Michael says. "But these knuckleheads were over for dinner when Meredith asked me about my experience with record contracts. It seems her boss, Garrett, was searching for some expertise for you."

Suddenly everything makes sense. For being such a big city, the connections between people in LA are eerily close. Especially in the entertainment world.

"Sorry for just showing up," Jax says, smiling lightly. "We both asked to come along."

"Charlie's okay with you being here?"

She had not been okay with him being around me before.

"Actually, she encouraged me to come," he admits.

"Oh."

"And since I used to work at Reverb, I have a unique perspective that might be helpful," Nick says.

I met Jax the first weekend after signing with Reverb. They flew me to Chicago to meet him and a few other artists who were all in the city at the same time. A few months later, there was an uproar at Reverb when Jax left the label that discovered him.

"You started your own label," I say.

"I did. Well, we did." Nick motions between himself and Jax. "Arrhythmic Records."

"You just signed Dylan Graves."

Nick nods. "A few months ago—"

"Like seven months ago," Jax interrupts.

"Boys," Michael jumps back in. "We're not here to talk about Dylan. We're here to talk about Michaela and Reverb."

"Reverb is saying you're in breach, right?" Nick asks.

I nod, pulling out the letter I received yesterday. I let the three of them read through it while I look over the menu, even though stress has doused any hunger pangs. It will look odd if I don't order something.

"Assholes," Nick mutters, handing back the paper. "It's standard practice for them to try this. They want to scare you."

"They succeeded," I confess. "I don't want to—I can't—Brad is—"

Nick holds up a hand. "You don't have to explain. I know that asshat's reputation. I just can't prove it."

The server comes over and takes our orders before disappearing again, and Nick continues.

"But I don't have to prove it. Reverb is a little too cocky. They haven't updated their contract language in years. Which means at least one loophole, if not more."

"If Jax's contract is any indication, more than a few," Michael says.

"Really?" Hope builds, replacing the near-constant anxiety I've dealt with since Brad's first text message.

"Do you have a copy of your contract?" he asks.

I pull the manila folder from my bag and hand it to him. "Here."

He skims the pages immediately, ignoring the server when she brings our orders as he highlights and notates the contract.

"If Mike can get you out of your contract, do you have any interest in coming to Arrhythmic?" Nick asks, taking a bite of his sandwich and studying me.

Jax watches me too as they wait for my answer.

I think back to the dream I had yesterday morning—singing on a stage, West smiling at me.

I shrug. "I thought about trying the YouTube route. It worked for Ed Sheeran."

"You could do that. Or you could come to Arrhythmic. We're not Reverb," Jax says.

"I'm just a little sour on labels after the last few years. I want to be happy and sing. If I can have that with Arrhythmic, great. But I won't settle for less again. I'll do it on my own."

Jax nods. "I understand. Hell, I was there before Nick talked about starting the label. What we do isn't a job, it's part of us. And you want that part to be happy."

"Exactly."

Nick's phone beeps, and he picks it up, his jaw clenching.

"Shit. Someone must have recognized you," he tells Jax.

He hunches in on himself. "Paps?"

"Yep. Mike, can I talk to you for a minute?" Nick motions to the back hall and leaves the table, with Michael following behind.

"Are you okay?" Jax asks, studying me intently.

I shrug. "I guess. Why?"

"Charlotte would kill me for saying this, but you look tired."

I smile at the love present in his voice when he talks about his wife.

"These last two years have been filled with one hellish descent after another," I admit, huffing a humorless laugh.

His concern is clear in his expression, and he reaches out, touching my arm in a comforting gesture.

"I know part of that is my fault," he says.

I'd only met Jax a handful of times. The first time in Chicago, recording the duet, the awards show where I met his girlfriend—well, wife, now. And the after-party of the concert he had in Philadelphia. Where I got drunk. And kissed him. He may have kissed me first, but I kissed him back. And the photo of our kiss cemented my status as a "home-wrecker."

I still don't understand why. Charlie had broken up with Jax right in front of me. We had both participated in what turned out to be a lackluster kiss. But I didn't see anyone calling him names.

"There's always been a double standard for behavior in our industry, Jax." It was a lesson I learned the hard way.

"It doesn't make it right."

"It may not be right, but neither you nor I is going to change it."

"I feel like shit. And sorry doesn't seem like enough."

"It's not your fault society is what it is. Unless you have a second career as a tabloid reporter I don't know about."

"Fuck that shit."

I laugh at the disgust on his face.

"Then don't beat yourself up about it."

Jax opens his mouth to say something else, but closes it when Michael and Nick come back.

"Car's meeting us out back in ten minutes," Nick tells Jax.

Jax nods, adjusting the baseball cap on his head.

"Hang in there, okay? Let's hope Mike can work some magic."

"I hope so," I whisper.

"And think about Arrhythmic. I really think you'd like it." Jax meets my gaze, and I get that impression too.

Maybe Arrhythmic *is* different.

I don't get to respond before Nick is pulling Jax down the back hallway, leaving me alone with the attorney that I hope can make my ability to choose a reality.

"Let me show you what I've found so far." Michael drops back into his chair, and we spend the rest of lunch going through the contract.

"Thank you for doing this," I tell him as he packs up the documents I've given him and tucks everything into his bag.

"No thanks needed, Ms. King."

"Michaela," I correct him. "You can call me Michaela."

"Only if you call me Mike." He smiles and extends his hand. "Lunch is on me today. I'm going to finish reviewing this contract, and I'll get back to you when I do. Do I have your contact information?"

I shake his hand and nod at the bag. "My boyfriend suggested I put a contact page in the folder."

"Smart man."

"Very smart," I agree with a smile.

"Take care of yourself. And avoid any further contact with Reverb. They're only in it for the scare tactics at this point." Michael says goodbye and heads to the door.

I follow behind him, ready to walk back to the hotel, when my stomach heaves.

Gagging, I barely make it to the restroom before everything I ate at lunch makes a reappearance.

My forehead and cheeks are clammy, but not feverishly warm. First the cheesesteak, and now my burger—two of my favorite foods. Finally standing up from my crouched position on the floor next to the toilet, I think about Googling food allergies, but my eye catches on the silver machine advertising pads and tampons.

How long have I been home? Quickly calculating, I come up with a month. And I've been consistent with my birth control because I like knowing when my periods are coming. So why hasn't one come yet?

My period was supposed to happen three weeks ago. Right after I got sick—

Oh.

I've been consistent with my prescription, except for the weekend I got sick. I doubled up the dosage like my doctor told me to and figured, with the stressful month I'd had, my period would show up when my next pack was done—next week.

My eyes drop to my flat stomach, covered by a dressy summer tank.

There's no way.

Right?

CHAPTER 18

WEST

I'm still waiting on Michaela's text when I drive home from school several hours later. Worry curdles in my gut.

Maybe there really is nothing they can do, and she doesn't want to call me with bad news.

Kelly and Dan are both at work, so I bound up to my bedroom, dialing her number as soon as I close the door.

"Hello?" It sounds like I woke her up.

"Baby, are you okay?" I ask, guilt eating at my stomach when she sniffles. "What's the matter?"

"I—uh—nothing's wrong." Her rushed statement triggers alarms in my head.

What the fuck is going on almost three thousand miles away?

"You were supposed to let me know how lunch went. I haven't heard from you all day."

"Sorry. I wasn't feeling well and came back to take a nap."

Immediately I feel like an asshole. She's still fucking sick, and I'm over here thinking she's up to something else. She's given me no reason not to trust her. I need to stop acting like she's up to something nefarious.

"Oh, baby, I'm sorry. Why don't you go back to sleep? We can talk later."

"No, I feel better. Just tired."

Tired from what?

I try to shut out that voice, the one that whispers negative shit. Shit that reminds me of Ashley.

"The meeting went well. The attorney, Mike, thinks there are a couple of clauses he can use to get me out of the contract."

"He does?"

"Yeah. He wanted to research it some more and let me know once he had time to do that."

"That's good. How does he know Mia?"

She laughs, and some of the tension ebbs from my shoulders —but not all of it.

"This town is crazy small sometimes. You know how Mia is married to Garrett, right?"

"Yeah." She's mentioned both Mia and Garrett a few times now.

"Well, Garrett works with Meredith Pryce. Well, Meredith Rhodes now, I guess. Unless she hyphenates. Meredith Pryce-Rhodes?"

"Baby," I interrupt, trying to get to the rest of the story.

"Sorry. Meredith works with Garrett. And she's Mike's daughter."

"And you're sure he's on the up-and-up? Not trying to take advantage of you?"

"He's not. Mia wouldn't have set up a meeting if she thought that."

"But Mia doesn't really know him," I point out.

"Garrett—"

"Doesn't really know him either."

"What do you want me to do, West?" Defensiveness creeps into her tone. "Wait for Sawyer to try to get me out of something when he has no idea what to do?"

"You haven't really given Sawyer a chance."

"I understand he's working on it. But this is on me to fix. I'm the one who has to go back to Reverb if I can't find a way out of this."

"Over my goddamn dead body," I growl out.

"If I don't go back, and I can't find a way out of my contract, I get sued. Do you have money to pay for that?"

Her mention of money burns more than it should. She knows I make less money than I can live on.

"Thanks for pointing out that I can't take care of you."

"That's not what I'm saying at all, West! God, you're twisting things."

"I'm not twisting anything."

"Yes, you are. You act like you don't trust me."

"I don't trust them. I trust Sawyer."

"Do you trust me?"

"I..." Do I trust Michaela? *Yes, you idiot*! "Of course I trust you."

"Then trust that I'm making the right decisions."

"I do."

"Actions speak louder than words, West. I-I think I'm going to go. I'll talk to you later."

"Mich—"

I don't get her name out before the phone beeps in my ear.

Shit.

How the hell did I go from worry to distrust to concern to uncertainty in the less than ten minutes?

"Thank you again for turning in your resume for the department head job," Phil says as we finish up lunch in the teacher's lounge.

It's late for lunch—my last planning period for the day—but

I'd been busy helping a student during my actual lunch. Phil had come in for a cup of coffee and ended up staying as we talked about how classes were going so far this year.

"Absolutely. I know it might be premature since I haven't been here long."

"Not necessarily a problem, given your experience prior to coming here. It looks like you were well on track to make department head there as soon as the previous one retired. What brought you back to Philadelphia?"

Fidgeting in my seat, I debate about how much to tell my boss. "Philly is home for me. I had relocated to Pittsburgh with my fiancée, but when we parted ways, I decided I wanted to come home."

"I imagine that must have been difficult."

I shrug. "Sometimes the right thing isn't the easiest thing."

He nods in agreement. "Very true."

"When will interviews be scheduled?"

"The position closed last week, so the plan is to interview the qualified candidates soon, and my replacement will shadow me next semester."

"Sounds good." I ball up the wrapper from my sandwich—the safest choice from the cafeteria since I forgot my lunch again after tossing and turning all night, thinking about my argument with Michaela.

I still feel like an ass and will apologize to her repeatedly for my churlish behavior when I see her tonight. It's been a long three days, and I can't wait to hold her in my arms again.

"Who in the world watches this trash?" Phil points to the TV mounted to the wall of the lounge as we make our way to the door. The Celebrity Gossip News logo bounces around the screen as their "news" show starts.

I roll my eyes, following Phil out, but a name catches my attention.

"Uh-oh. Looks cozy, right? Why is it every time Michaela

King is captured on film, it's for less-than-stellar reasons?" one reporter asks.

Freezing mid-stride, I turn my attention to the screen where a picture of Michaela and another man is prominent on the display with a caption in big, bold print.

Jax and Michaela...another shot in the City of Angels?

In the image, Jax has his hand on Michaela's arm. Her chin is propped on her hand as she gazes at him in adoration.

What. The. Fuck?

Another picture pops up next to it, the image older and grainier, like it was taken from a security camera. Michaela is in a short denim skirt and tight top, her head tilted while she's kissing the man in front of her. The one who looks an awful lot like the guy touching her in the recent picture.

Michaela told me the attorney's name was Michael—Mike, she called him. So why the fuck is she in a picture with Jax Bryant?

I clench my jaw so hard my head begins to throb. She told me she was meeting an attorney.

Remember, things aren't always what they seem.

Her voice echoes in my head, but it doesn't stop a playback of the awful shit I discovered a few weeks ago. Even if they turned out to be wrong.

Ask her.

Letting out a breath through my nostrils, I unclench my jaw, but the tension still locks my shoulders in place.

"West, everything all right?" Phil stands by the door, holding it open and staring at me curiously.

"Sorry," I say and join him by the door.

"You a fan?" He gestures to the TV before he steps into the hall.

"Oh, um, not really."

"No?"

Obviously, Phil doesn't recognize Michaela from the time she dropped off my lunch, and I don't want to explain who she is or what she means to me. Or why the image of another man touching her has me seeing green, the jealousy spiking hot and hard in my blood.

"No. The board presentation is coming up next week, right?" I ask, changing the subject.

"Yes. Hopefully it goes as smoothly as the first. I think everyone is aware that there isn't much more we can do," he says.

"Let me know if there's any way I can help," I offer.

He nods, waving when a student stops him to ask a question.

Getting back to my classroom, I pull my phone out of my pocket, debating whether there is enough time to call Michaela to find out why she was with Jax. To beg her to remind me things aren't what they appear.

The ringing bell negates the idea, and I tuck my phone away. Two more periods. Then I can go home and talk to Michaela in person—her flight was supposed to land about an hour ago.

Several times over the next ninety minutes, the clock either stops entirely or goes backward. That's the only explanation for why it feels like it takes eight hours to get to the final bell. There's a cacophony of scraping chairs and chatter among the sophomores leaving my class, taking the smell of hormones and acne products with them.

Dropping to my chair, I breathe out a sigh of relief at the quiet, my internal monologue finally alone instead of wrapped in the chaos around me. A small part of me wants to hide out here, in the quiet classroom, instead of facing the uncertainty waiting.

But the bigger part of me needs to know, requires answers for the questions that continue to plague me after seeing Michaela's picture on TV.

And between the questions is this insidious little voice, constantly whispering Ashley's name. Pointing out all the ways I should have noticed she was cheating before I was smacked in the face with it.

"No." I shake my head to dispel the toxic thoughts. "Michaela isn't Ashley."

Then why didn't she tell you about Jax?

What about him?

The image of the two of them kissing forms in my brain, next to the image of the seemingly innocent touch at lunch. I'm so tempted to Google the two names that my phone ends up in my hand before I realize it.

"Don't do it." I set the device on my desk. "This is not the answer."

I need to talk to her.

Knots form in my stomach as I leave the building, and they tighten as my car gets closer to the house. Even the safe-choice sandwich isn't sitting well, based on the tension clamping my stomach in a vise.

Neither Dan nor Kelly's car is in the driveway or garage, which I'm grateful for. I'd rather talk to Michaela without an audience.

Maybe she's not here. Maybe she's still in California.

She didn't text or call me when she landed, but after our argument last night, I'm not surprised.

Unfortunately, logic has no place in my brain right now. Instead, my mind flips through images—ones I haven't seen proven in pictures, and I force them away, unlocking the door and stepping out of the bright afternoon sunlight. Is it an omen that the damn door handle is molten lava in my hand? A warning to stay away?

I push through the uncertainty, closing the door and leaning against it, feeling like I've run a marathon in the time it took me to walk from my car to the house.

"Mich—" My voice cracks, and I clear my throat. "Michaela?"

No response. Eyeing the stairs like they lead to hell, I put one foot in front of the other as I climb, my hand gripping the banister tightly while the treads creak under my weight. The shower drones from the bathroom down the hall. Since Dan and Kelly aren't home, it must be Michaela.

What if she's not alone?

"You're an idiot, Abbott."

She's given me no reason to question her, but doubt still sits like acid in my stomach.

She and I have showered together dozens of times. Fuck, I've seen her naked at least once a day almost every day for the last month. I don't bother to knock before I twist the handle and push, bracing myself for what I might find.

"West!" she squeaks, sitting on the toilet seat, fully dressed, trying to hide the box in her hand.

But she can't hide it.

"What"—My throat is suddenly, painfully dry, despite the humidity from the steaming shower—"is that?"

I point to the box she grips. It's hot pink with purple writing. But maybe I'm hallucinating.

"It—I—What—"

She stutters through several starts before falling silent again, her eyes wide.

"Michaela, are you pregnant?" I force the words out, past and present colliding quickly enough to make me dizzy, and I lean against the doorjamb for support.

"I...don't know," she admits.

"What do you mean you don't know?" I snap. "I thought you were on birth control."

"I was. I *am*. But at lunch yesterday, I got to thinking that I should have started my period by now."

I clench my jaw as I think about how long she's been home. How long we've been doing what we've been doing. And no, she hasn't had her period in the last month.

"What at lunch reminded you of that?" I ask with a sneer. "The presence of Jax Bryant?"

Confusion draws her brows in, and her big doe eyes jump to mine in question.

"What about Jax?" she asks slowly.

"He was there. At your lunch. The one you told me was with an attorney named Michael."

I don't bother to phrase it as a question, since she and I both know the truth.

"He was." She doesn't bother to ask me how I know.

"Why?"

"He co-owns Arrhythmic."

"What does that have to do with anything? You told me you were going to LA to meet an entertainment attorney about getting out of your contract with Reverb."

"Michael—Mike—he's Nick's father-in-law and has known Jax for forever."

"It still doesn't fucking explain why he was there," I grind out.

"He and Nick were there when Meredith asked Mike to help me. And both have histories with Reverb."

She doesn't break eye contact, but I still can't help but suspect I'm not getting the full story.

And it damn sure doesn't explain the box she's holding against her chest like a life preserver.

"Did you know he was going to be there?" I ask.

"No."

"And now you think you're pregnant?"

Fire dances in her eyes, and her nostrils flare as her own anger comes to the forefront. "I threw up my lunch again. Right after eating it. That, added to the month of no period, is why I think I might be pregnant."

"Could be a stomach bug," I tell her. It sounds so stupid because if she had a stomach bug, she would have been sick more consistently over the last week.

She snorts her disbelief. "So that explains me throwing up

twice in the last five days? Or how about that I haven't had a period in over a month?"

I lift my hand, rubbing at my neck, embarrassed she's seeing reason and I'm not.

She reaches over, shutting off the shower. The sudden silence is so deafening I can hear my heartbeat.

"Are you going to take that?" I point to the box, disrupting the quiet that feels like a tomb.

Maybe it is.

"Not with you standing there," she snarks.

My lips twitch with a smile at her sass, even though everything is crumbling around me.

"Like I haven't seen you naked. Or had my dick so far inside you I forgot where I ended and you began."

Pink flushes her cheeks, but fire dances in her eyes.

"That's crass."

I shrug. "Might be. But it's also the truth."

She stares at me, hurt mixing with anger, anxiety written all over her face. I refuse to consider how she must be feeling. I'm too caught up in my own emotions to focus on hers.

"Are you really not going to take that until I leave the room?"

"No, I'm not."

"Fucking Christ," I groan, but spin around and take one step outside the bathroom. "Happy now?"

"Ecstatic," she deadpans, and the door closes with a snick behind me.

It's not a slam, but it has the finality of one. She doesn't lock it, but I don't bother to turn around and open it.

I like to think I'm respecting her need for privacy, but I'm also so overloaded with emotion I don't know which way is up. Jealousy. Anger. Hurt. Regret. Anxiety. They all jumble with painful memories.

The pregnancy test. The subsequent doctor's appointment.

And the slashing ache of betrayal. All of that freezes me in place, my body quivering between fight and flight.

The door opens again, and I turn in time to see Michaela retreat to the closed toilet seat. The little wand sits on top of the box, face down.

"Three minutes," she whispers, her fingers laced together so tightly they turn white.

This is going to be the longest one hundred and eighty seconds of my life.

You're a bastard, Abbott.

Either I'm a bastard for keeping my distance or I'm a pussy who forgets how I feel just so I can comfort her. And at the moment, I'm choosing self-preservation, gripping the doorframe as my eyes stay locked on purple words.

6 Days Sooner.

I can't make out the rest, the print too small at this distance. My attention shifts to Michaela, who nibbles on her lip, the normally pale pink now red under the continued pressure.

Fuck. I need to quit being a dick.

"Michaela—"

Her eyes meet mine, and her anxiety punches through my chest.

"I'm—"

My apology is interrupted by an alarm from her phone.

"I-I set an alarm."

"Oh." I snap my mouth shut, my emotions taking hold of my throat once more.

She takes a deep breath, her hand shaking as she reaches for the wand, flipping it over and blinking several times before holding it out to me.

I take it from her, eyeing the results at the same time the words tumble from her lips.

"It's positive."

CHAPTER 19

MICHAELA

"It's positive," I repeat when he doesn't react, even though, based on the pallor of his skin, he heard me.

I may be angry at how he burst in here questioning me—again—about cheating, but the bigger part of me is freaking the fuck out about the two pink lines in the little window. The second line is as bright as the first, no guessing needed.

"West?"

He still hasn't said anything, staring catatonically at the wand he holds.

I don't expect the elated cheer pregnancy test commercials portray. But a smile, a hug, some kind of acknowledgment would really do wonders for my mental state.

A baby.

My hand moves with a mind of its own to tremble against my flat stomach. Life grows under my fingers. My baby. West's baby.

The movement unlocks the spell he's been under for the last few minutes. The test clatters to the tile as his mouth compresses into a thin line, his eyes glittering as he stares at me.

"Whose is it?"

His words knock the breath from my lungs.

"What?"

He can't be serious.

"You heard me."

"Yeah, but I wish I hadn't. How can you even ask that?"

Pain lances, hot and sharp, where my heart beats against my chest.

"Can you blame me?" he spits out. "You have to admit your track record is a little sketchy."

"My—my—my track record?" Anger pushes out the pain.

What the fuck is wrong with him? He acts like he's a saint, like he's perfect. Well, I call bullshit.

"First Jax, then Tucker Winston, back to Jax. What's next? Or should I ask who?"

"Fuck you," I grit out.

"You already did." The hard tone of his voice slices like a weapon. And every perfect moment we've shared over the last month shatters, a pretty glass vase thrown to the floor. Beautiful, but not meant to last.

"You're right. I did. And you were right there with me. Doing things, t-teaching me th-things."

"Don't act like you were an innocent virgin when we started fucking."

Bile rises in my throat, burning out the tears stuck there.

"Who are you?" I ask, pushing past my own hurt and anger to figure out why he's saying all this. "What happened to the man who took care of me when I was sick? Who told me I wasn't alone?"

He rolls his eyes and makes a sound like he can't fathom why I'd ask these questions. But I don't understand. He's so different from how he's been—how he's almost always acted toward me. I've had a glimpse of a version of this West before—when he questioned me about Fucker. I don't want to admit that West isn't the perfect guy I put on a pedestal a long time ago. Maybe now is when I need to stop deluding myself.

"I told you I hate liars. And I overlooked when you lied about Tucker—"

"I didn't lie about Tucker!" I yell.

"No, you didn't tell me. A lie by omission is still a lie. Then there was the lie about how *famous* you were." He sneers, and I suck in a breath. Death by a thousand words hurts worse than any other pain I've ever experienced. "Time and again, I looked past your lies. This time you went to California to meet up with your ex."

"Jax isn't an ex."

"You want to know the problem with liars, Michaela? Eventually, their lies catch up with them. Did you think I'd just keep on believing you? That I'd be okay with fucking someone I didn't know? Someone who pretended to be something she wasn't?"

Fucking.

According to him, that's what we were doing.

I'm such an idiot. Here I was, falling in love, while he was getting off. Proof that I once again made a bad decision when it comes to men.

"I wish I never would have let you touch me."

"Please," he scoffs. "Like you weren't begging for it. Fuck, you initiated things between us more than I did. I wouldn't be surprised if that was your plan all along. You simply needed someone to warm your bed between Tucker and Jax. But maybe I wasn't the only one."

"What are you saying?" I'm done making assumptions. I need to hear him say it.

"I find it hard to believe that you were celibate between Tucker and me. That's an awfully long time for someone like you." He raises an eyebrow.

"Go to hell."

"I'm already there. Because history is repeating itself. The woman I'm screwing is trying to pass some other bastard's kid off as mine."

I cross my arms over my stomach in a protective gesture, even though the baby is so tiny where it grows.

"This baby is yours," I tell him. "Whether you want to believe it or not."

"Not. And I'm not interested in raising a kid with a cheater now any more than I was with Ashley."

"You're an asshole," I say, tears of anger and frustration burning my eyes. I don't recognize this person. He's not the West I spent the last month with. And he's damn sure not the one I remember from my childhood.

"Better an honest asshole than a liar."

"I'm not lying!"

Frustration bubbles out, and I step toward him, wishing he would believe me. Instead, he only raises an eyebrow, the condescending expression on his face shredding any hope that might be left after the last few minutes.

He lifts his hand, his finger tracing along my jaw. The touch is sweet, even if his words are nothing but poison.

"Here's the thing about liars, Mikey. They always tell you they're not lying. But eventually people stop believing them."

I yank my face away from his finger, stepping back against the bathroom counter.

"I'm not lying."

"I don't believe you." He shrugs like he couldn't care less about what he's saying. About something so beautiful turning into nothing but ash. All because of him. "I will say—I enjoyed your 'talents,' but I'm not attracted to liars. Which means there will be no repeat performances. I don't fuck a woman pregnant with another man's kid."

"Get out." I'm tired of listening to the shit he's spewing.

"Gladly," he says with a grin that has bile rising in my throat.

What the hell had I been thinking? I should have left early on when he told me sleeping with me was a mistake. But like a sucker, I stayed.

"Get the fuck out!" I scream after him as he walks away.

Slamming the bathroom door, I push the button for the lock before spinning back and dropping to my knees in front of the toilet. Tears drip down my cheeks and into the bowl as my stomach tries to empty itself of nothing.

Finally, I stop heaving. In the stillness, my heart pulses around its cracked edges, creating a new kind of pain. One I've never felt before.

"I'm sorry," I whisper, lifting my hand to my abdomen. "I'm sorry he doesn't believe me. But we don't need him."

I have no idea what I'm going to do, but one thing is certain —I can't stay here. I won't subject either myself or the little one I'm now responsible for to Weston Abbott or his nasty words.

My bag sits forgotten on the floor where I dropped it when I rushed to the bathroom, wholly intent on the pregnancy test. Reaching for it, I grab my phone out of the top and pull up my text thread with Mia.

Mi?

You're probably busy, but I need you.

My phone rings less than a minute later.

"Kay, what's wrong?"

The concern in her voice unleashes my sobs, and I tell her everything between the tears. From the awful tour, complete with the nightmarish last night, to the test still lying face down on the floor where West dropped it, and finish with a deep breath.

"I'm going to come there and rip his balls off and beat him with them," she growls, surprising a watery laugh from me.

"You're a nut." I lean over to pick up the discarded test and tuck it carefully into my bag.

"Well, this nut loves you. You don't need to stay there. Give me about fifteen minutes, and I'll find you a flight out of Philadelphia. You're coming to stay with me."

"You're not home!"

"I'm on my way," she counters smugly. "And I don't want you staying there. But if you really want to stay, I'm on your side. Whatever you want. Oh shit, I didn't even ask, how are you feeling about the you-know?"

I chuckle at her over-the-top personality, once more thanking the universe that her asshole-ex and a tape I'd rather forget about gave me the best friend I've ever had.

"I'm okay. Not loving that I apparently don't like meat anymore."

"Lots of fresh veggies and fruits in California," she sing-songs.

"I know."

"So, am I booking you a flight? Or hiring a hit man?"

"You don't need to pay for my flight, Mi."

"The hit man then?" She sounds a little too excited about that option.

"I can get myself to California," I explain.

"Nonsense. Pack your bags, baby. Evie will book you a ticket and send you the info."

I blow out a breath, exhaustion crashing over me as the entire day catches up.

"Are you sure?"

"Positive."

I groan, not sure how much I love that word right now, but I'll still take Mia's certainty. Her love. Her friendship.

"Thank you."

"No thanks needed. Now, go. I want you out of there before you have to see douche bag again."

"Pretty sure I'll have to before I leave." My stomach cramps at the thought.

"Let's hope not," she huffs. "Okay, okay, go pack. I'll text you soon."

Grabbing my bag, I stand with a groan, the muscles in my legs protesting after spending so much time on the floor. I unlock the door, opening it slowly as I listen for West. Nothing. The silence is unnerving, and I hold my breath, straining to hear anything. West's bedroom door is open on the left, but my room is to the right.

Your stuff is in West's bedroom.

Rolling my eyes at my own stupidity—again—I creep down the hallway and peek around the corner. Empty. Rushing inside, I grab the few things in his room and sprint to my bedroom, closing and locking that door as well.

Not like a locked door would stop him.

But that was before.

And a whole lot has changed between then and now.

Was he really pretending?

Maybe you didn't know him as well as you thought you did.

Story of my life.

But not anymore.

I toss as many clothes in a bag as I can, picking up my all-but-forgotten guitar from where I stowed it in my closet. My phone pings. The text from Mia has my flight details and tells me to order a Lyft on her account.

Her thoughtfulness overwhelms me, and I sniff back tears and sit on the bed. How am I going to do this?

"Same way you always have, Kayla. Exactly the same way. One foot in front of the other."

Following my own advice, I head down the stairs to the empty living room. I have no idea where West and my parents are, but the Lyft I ordered is now three minutes away. Glancing around the living room, I take in the family photos. Lucas and Sawyer standing next to each other as kids and holding me as I screamed at the camera, Sawyer and West in Boy Scout uniforms, Lucas when he graduated from high school and college, Sawyer in his Army uniform before he left. There are so many pictures, and too many include West.

What will happen when the baby comes? Will he still deny him or her when the resemblance is clear? What will Mom and Dad say? Or Sawyer? Lucas? Will they side with West? Tell me they expected this? My phone chimes, telling me the driver is here, so I grab my bag and my case, closing and locking the door behind me. It seems fitting. There's no one here to see me off.

Alone again. But not quite.

"You want some help?" the driver asks, and I shake my head.

"No thanks, I got it."

"Nonsense. My wife would kill me if I didn't offer to help." He steps out of the car, rushing to grab my bag and my guitar case before motioning to the car.

"Thank you."

"Airport?" he asks, closing the trunk.

I nod. "Please," I say and slide into the back, relaxing into the seat behind me.

We don't say much else, and I pull out my phone and send a text to my mom.

Hey, Mom, thanks for letting me stay, but heading back to CA for work.

It takes a few minutes, but her response finally comes.

MOM

Already?

I'll be home in a minute. We can talk about it then. Sawyer's coming tonight.

Shit. I'd forgotten. Too late now.

I'm already on my way to the airport.

Michaela Grace! A little notice would have been nice.

Sorry.

Off to conquer the world again?

Something like that.

Be safe, okay? And call me when you land?

Mom.

I'm an adult.

And I'll always be your mother.

Even when you're a hundred. LOL

Will I feel like that with my baby? Something tells me I will. Will Mom be excited about a grandchild? Neither Sawyer nor Lucas has any kids. Nibbling on my lip, I keep all my questions off the screen.

Ok.

Love you, Mom.

Love you too, baby.

She didn't ask me if West knew. She probably assumes he does. I breathe out a huge sigh. He and I were really good at complicating something that never should have happened.

"Traffic is crazy," the driver pipes up from the front seat.

"Sorry, what?"

"Traffic." He motions to the windshield reflecting a busier-than-normal rush hour.

"Don't worry about it. My flight's not for a few hours," I tell him.

The car falls silent again, and another question forces itself to my mind.

Am I making the right choice in leaving?

Maybe not.

But it's the only one that makes sense.

I may be running away from West, but I'm reclaiming my life.

For the baby. And for me.

CHAPTER 20

WEST

"Get the fuck out!"

The door rattles against the jamb as Michaela slams it behind me so hard I'm surprised none of the pictures fall off the wall.

"Trouble in paradise?" Sawyer is standing halfway up the stairs, his face an unreadable mask.

I don't say anything, my brain trying to hold on to the anger and betrayal of being put in this position again. Am I ever going to find a girl who doesn't fuck anything with a dick and try to pass off another man's spawn as mine?

Scrubbing my hand down my face, I groan.

"You could say that."

"Looks like you could use a beer," he says. "Come on."

Wait.

I stop at the top landing, my ear straining for any noise coming from the bathroom. What the fuck am I doing?

Shaking my head, I follow Sawyer down the stairs and out to the driveway.

"What are you doing here? Kelly said you weren't coming in until later tonight."

"I caught an earlier flight." Is all he says. "I'll drive."

He holds up a hand for my keys, and I toss them to him before rounding the hood to the passenger side. My knees mash against the glove compartment, and I move the seat back, breathing a sigh of relief as they uncurl. Only then do I remember why the seat is so far forward.

Michaela.

She's so fucking petite. The seat was up as far as it would go, and she still managed to look tiny in it.

"Where am I going?" Sawyer asks, pulling down the street as my body wars with itself over good memories being tarnished by everything that's happened in the last three hours.

Longer.

She fucking lied.

Repeatedly.

I shrug. "I don't care. A bar. Any bar."

The noise he makes is a grunt of affirmation, and he pulls into the parking lot of the first bar we come across—one of those chain sports bars with TVs everywhere, every type of athletic event imaginable playing on them.

The place is packed when we make our way inside, but Sawyer snags two chairs at the end of the bar and catches the bartender's attention

"Two Sam Adams," he orders, then turns to study me. "What the fuck did I walk in to?" he asks. "You two fighting?"

"You could say that." I take a pull on the bottle the bartender sets in front of me.

"I *did* say it. And I'm not used to repeating myself, but in the interest of time, what the fuck is going on?"

"Do I have a sign on my forehead that says 'patsy' or something?" I run my index finger across my forehead.

"No, but there is one that says annoying as fuck. Spit it out, Abbott." He takes a sip of his beer and stares at me in silence.

"Dude, she's your sister. You don't want to know."

"Wouldn't have asked if I didn't." His gaze doesn't waver, and I curse the military mumbo jumbo shit he learned that makes me want to spill my guts about every-fucking-thing.

"You don't," I warn him again.

"Fuck." He blows out a breath. "Fine. You don't want to talk? I will."

He pulls out his phone, messes with it for a second, and tosses it on the bar.

"What is this?" I ask, bending closer to review the image.

"That," he gestures to the phone. "Is Brad Russell's employee file from Reverb Records."

"How the hell did you get that?" I pick up the phone and enlarge the image.

"My contact."

"The guy who used to run security for them? He sent you this?"

He scoffs. "No. He sent me a list of names. And I took the list of names and started digging. All seven names are women who have been signed by Reverb in the last ten years. All had shown initial promise, but, after a year or two—although one was five years—they were reported for breach of contract and sued by the label."

"Like..." I can't bring myself to say her name. Doubt creeps in around the edges of my anger, and I don't like the rock growing in my stomach.

"Like Mikey, yes." He takes another sip of his drink and continues. "Every single one of these women was assigned the same label rep."

"Brad," I whisper.

Fuck.

"Brad Russell," he confirms. "Of those seven women, three still live in the LA area. Rachel Baker, Lauren Flynn, and Evelyn McBride—although she's changed her name since being signed by Reverb. Evelyn is the one who was there for five years before being sued for breach of contract."

"You talked to them?"

"Yep." It's more a grunt than a word, and he signals the bartender for another beer while mine sits nearly untouched in front of me. "Each one of those women finally opened up to me and told me that Brad made their lives a living hell. Costumes better fitted for strippers, sexually explicit comments, with the final straw being an attempt at sexual physical relations. In Evelyn's case—and I only assume this is why she lasted five years —a coerced sexual relationship."

Fuck. Fuck. Fuck. Fuck. I drag a hand through my hair as my mind starts to replay every word I flung at her.

I all but accused her of having sex with Jax, of cheating on me. I didn't say the words out loud, exactly, but that doesn't make me feel any better.

"Fuck."

"My sentiments exactly," he agrees. "So, I asked these women why they never reported this douche dick for what he was doing."

"What did they say?" I already know the answer though.

"They did. Reverb did nothing with the information except bury it so deeply it was almost impossible to find."

"But you found it?"

"Barely. The statute of limitations has expired in every instance. I didn't know if I had any options and called an attorney friend of mine. Showed her Michaela's emails and texts. I don't know exactly how, but she managed to subpoena the employee file. That's how I got that. Now, what were you and my sister fighting about?"

"I, uh—" I stutter over how to explain my stupidity, and, in my hesitation, Sawyer's expression turns shrewd. My heart gallops in my chest, my palms sweaty against the scarred wooden bar. "I-I fucked up."

I suddenly realize I made the biggest mistake of my life by laying Ashley's sins at Michaela's feet.

"What do you mean you 'fucked up'?" He hasn't moved, hasn't raised his voice, but the calm demeanor is coiled power.

The word "positive" circles my brain like a shark sensing blood in the water.

Fuck.

"She—I—fuck." I've made a massive mistake.

"Abbott, I've known you a long-ass time. Spit it the fuck out, or I'll help you do it," he growls.

"Pregnant."

"You knocked up my baby sister?" His fingers clench into fists so tight the knuckles lighten until, taking a deep breath, he releases it along with the fists. "She's mad at you because she's pregnant?"

"Mad?"

"I heard her tell you to get the fuck out," he reminds me, the corner of his mouth lifting in a smile.

A smile that fades when I don't join in.

"There's more," he says.

I nod.

"What else?"

When I don't answer, his hand slams down on the bar top, drawing attention from several of our neighbors.

"Fucking tell me."

"I told her..." I don't want to repeat it, the words carving up my insides as I remember the hurt and betrayal on her face when I uttered them the first time.

Whose is it?

"You told her what?"

Fuck.

"You told her what, Abbott?" Steel edges his voice. I've heard it before, but never directed at me.

"Hit me," I tell him and finally look at him. Unlike his sister's blue eyes, Sawyer's are brown, the color so dark they're almost black. And cold as they study me.

"Why?" he asks while his fingers once more clench into a fist.

"I-I told her…I denied the baby was mine."

But there's zero question about that anymore. I never should have doubted her.

Sawyer stands abruptly, and I open myself up for the expected punch, the one I deserve. It doesn't stop me from closing my eyes, but I want him to kick the shit out of me. When nothing happens, I open one eye and see him striding toward the door, a twenty-dollar bill sitting on the bar next to my car keys.

"Sawyer. Shit." I toss another twenty, well above the cost of three beers, and chase after him as he walks across the parking lot. "Sawyer!"

He turns, and I freeze at the pure hatred on his face.

"What?" he growls.

"Why didn't you hit me? You said—"

"You want me to hit you. To make you think you paid a price for what the fuck you said to my sister. To make you feel better. But I'm not going to do that." He closes the distance, stepping toe to toe with me. He may be shorter, but I have no doubt about his ability to kick my ass without breaking a sweat. "You don't deserve to feel better."

He starts to walk away again, but stops, turning back one more time.

"We're done. Through. You hear me?"

Twenty years. We've been friends for over twenty years, but I swallow and nod. I ruined our friendship, not him.

"Grab your shit and get the fuck out of my parents' house. As far as I'm concerned, as far as my family is concerned, you're dead."

I don't respond—what can I say? He nods once and leaves me behind with nothing but the acid of my memories to keep me company.

But his walking away still doesn't hurt as bad as the realization that I destroyed the relationship that means more to me than anything.

It's been one hell of a week. In the span of an afternoon, I lost my home, my girlfriend, my best friend, and my baby. So when I'm called down to the office the following Thursday, I'm terrified I'm going to lose my job.

"Weston Abbott?" A bored-looking man in a pair of slacks and a rumpled button-down stands from the bench next to the office.

"Yes?" I ask warily.

"You've been served," is all he says before handing me a large envelope.

"What?" I glance up in confusion, but he's already walking out of the school. "Hey, wait, what is this about?"

He doesn't respond, and I stare at the nondescript envelope in my hands with my name chicken scratched across the front.

The regret in my stomach hasn't left me in a week. Not when I got back to Dan and Kelly's to find them all gone—it was worse leaving them behind like a criminal. Without goodbye, without explanation. But I had no doubt Sawyer would fill them in. Which didn't explain why I kept ignoring Kelly's calls and voicemails.

The dread didn't get any better when I got the key to a room at an efficiency hotel on the edge of a run-down area of north Philadelphia. The couch looked like it had been found in a dumpster, and only one burner worked on the three-burner stove. But the bed was clean, if not lumpy, and eventually I grew used to the sounds of arguing and police sirens lasting throughout the night.

I'm surviving.

Searching for an apartment has been an exercise in futility. Nothing I can afford feels like home. The hotel is a place to sleep

—I come to school each morning and stay until after the janitors have all gone home. Every night I drag my ass to my car to grab fast food on my way back. If I thought I could get away with it, I'd stay at the school all night.

"What the hell is this?" I murmur to myself, twisting the envelope every which way as I search for a clue. Finding none, I lift the flap and pull out the sheaf of papers.

Order for Genetic (DNA) Testing

My vision tunnels, and I sit on the bench quickly to avoid falling over. Pain drags a razor's edge across my chest, and I suck in a breath, continuing to read.

Plaintiff, Michaela Grace King, filed a Motion and Affidavit for Genetic (DNA) Testing. Given that the Defendant, Weston James Abbott, did not contest the motion in person or in writing on or before the required date of October 17, this court has hereby ordered that the motion is GRANTED. The Defendant will contact one of the laboratories listed below within ten (10) days of receiving this order and will submit himself for genetic testing to establish or disestablish paternity of the unborn child.

"West?" Phil tilts his head as he walks up. "You're positively pale. Everything all right?"

I tuck the papers back into the envelope and attempt to smile, the movement foreign to my lips. "Absolutely."

"I stopped by your class, and one of your students said the office called you. Are you sure you're all right?"

"I'm fine. Should we talk while we walk back?"

He nods, and we move away from the office and down the muted hallway.

"Why did you need me?" I ask after several moments of silence broken only by our footfalls against the linoleum.

"I wanted to give you an update."

He stops, and I do as well, waiting for him to speak.

"There are no changes to the original plans we spoke about

last month. And interviews for my replacement will happen in two weeks."

I sputter, coughing as I choke on nothing but air.

"What?" I croak after several more coughs.

"Interviews. You *are* still interested, right?"

A year ago, I would have jumped at the chance. A week ago, I had happily submitted my resume. Now I'm second-guessing everything.

But since I've already lost so much, the job is the only thing left.

"I-I am, yes."

He nods as if he expected my answer.

"I thought as much. I'm sure Human Resources will be reaching out to you to formally schedule the interview."

"Great," I say, trying to infuse more enthusiasm into my voice. Based on the look Phil gives me, I'm not there yet. "That's great. Looking forward to it."

I say goodbye and step inside my classroom, sensing his eyes on me as I lean against my desk and watch several minutes of the film I set up when I got the call from the office. Eventually the prickling at the back of my neck disappears, and I blow out a breath.

I want this job.

Don't lie to yourself. You hate *liars, remember?*

If I'm being honest, there are things I want more than this job —my girlfriend, my best friend, my baby. They're my home.

CHAPTER 21

WEST

Following the court order to the minute detail, I show up to an approved lab feeling like a bigger ass than before. This is what they do with deadbeat dads. This is unnecessary. Michaela could have asked—

When? Before or after you all but called her a whore?

After my blood is drawn and stored, the woman walks with me toward the exit.

"Should take about two weeks."

"That fast? The baby isn't even born yet." The words fly out of my mouth before I can filter them.

"We run these tests all the time," she tells me. "Even without the baby."

"Is it safe?" I don't want either Michaela or our child to be in jeopardy to prove my dumb ass wrong.

Hypocrite. I wince.

"Oh yeah. It's called non-invasive prenatal paternity. We take your sample and one from the mother and compare fetal cells in the mother's bloodstream with the two samples. More than 99 percent accurate."

I don't care about whether the test is accurate. Because I *know*.

Only no one cares.

Not anymore.

"Thanks," I tell her.

"Sure," she says before calling the next name on her list.

I try to ignore how the waiting room is full of men who look like me and shrug on my jacket before stepping outside.

Fall is coming early to Philadelphia—either that or something else leaves me in a constant state of chill.

"West!" That voice is familiar, and I hunch my shoulders, unsure of how this conversation will go. "Weston James Abbott!" Kelly calls across the parking lot and hurries toward the entrance.

"H-hi, Kelly." I can barely speak over the lump in my throat, and I cough several times to clear it.

"Oh, honey, are you sick?"

Honey?

What the hell did Sawyer tell them?

"Sick?" I ask her instead.

"You haven't been returning my calls, and you're here." She motions to the medical center we're standing in front of. "The cough."

"No, I'm not sick," I tell her. Not physically, at least. Does heart sick count?

"Good. Now, come sit with me and tell me why you haven't returned my calls." She drags me to a bench and sits, pulling me next to her.

Guilt gnaws at my stomach. It doesn't help that Michaela's eyes are carbon copies of Kelly's and intensify the sensation.

"You probably have things to do—"

"Nonsense," she interrupts. "I'm here for some bloodwork for a physical but on a walk-in basis. Spill the beans."

"I..." God, this is awkward. I don't want to lie to her, but I also don't want to see the warmth on her face replaced by the cold hatred I saw on Sawyer's the last time I saw him. "Why are you being nice to me?"

"What?" Her nose crinkles in confusion. "Why wouldn't I be? I've known you since you were nine years old. You're like another son."

If those words don't twist the knife in my chest, I don't know what would. The pain feels so real, so palpable, that I lift a hand to rub at my heart.

"Didn't Sawyer tell you?"

"Tell me what?" she asks.

"About Michaela and me...about..." I can't. The words lock themselves behind my lips, and I squeeze my eyes shut.

"Are you sure you're not sick? You look a little gray around the gills."

I can't help the chuckle that breaks loose. "I think you mean green around the gills."

"You're not green, you're gray," she tells me. "Now, what's going on?"

"Now I know where Sawyer gets it," I mumble, but she still hears me.

"That's right. But you still won't distract me from my question." She levels me with a stare, and I give up.

"Michaela and I...we..."

"You broke up," she supplies after several moments of awkward silence when I can't finish my statement.

What?

I mean, we did. But I would have phrased it more like I was an asshole.

"Sawyer said it happened when she left for California. I got home, and he was there and said you two had broken up. And in the next breath, he told Dan and me he was taking us to dinner."

"Yeah, uh—"

"You know you didn't have to leave," she interrupts.

"I—"

"Or was it too painful to be in our house?"

Having to see pictures of Michaela every day? Imagine her in her room? In my room? In my bed?

Painful would be tame.

Agony. That was a better description.

But I'm in agony even after the change in location.

"You can always come back," she offers, and I smile through the gut-wrenching ache at the idea.

It's not home either.

Because I ruined it.

"I..." I can't bring myself to destroy the hopefulness on her face, so I stall. "I'll think about it."

"Would you also think about coming by for dinner one night next week?"

"I—yeah," I stutter. "How's Michaela?"

Her gaze turns soft with sympathy, and she rubs her hand up and down my arm.

"I haven't talked to her much. A text here or there. But Sawyer says she's okay. He's keeping an eye on her."

Don't they know she's pregnant?

I'm confused. Wouldn't Sawyer tell them everything? If he didn't, why not? Lifting a hand, I massage the bridge of my nose.

"You okay?"

"Yeah," I choke out. "Just a headache."

"I'll let you go back to...wherever you're at. An apartment by now, I'm sure. You'll have to tell us all about it over dinner." She stands, pulling me with her once again. "Stop ignoring my calls, okay?"

"Okay."

She wraps me in a tight hug and steps back with strict instructions to go home and take something for my headache before she leaves me staring after her on the sidewalk.

What the hell just happened?

Every day I think about calling Michaela. I imagine hearing her voice, fumbling my way through an epic apology. And at the end of every one is the rejection I know I deserve. Fear keeps me from contacting her.

While *coward* echoes through my head on repeat, I wait on the results I don't need. Two weeks. Then another. It could be another month or more based on the information the lab gave me.

I sit through my interview for the department head job, caught up in thoughts of Michaela. How she's doing. How our baby is doing. Somehow, I doubt my chances at getting the position, but I'll have to wait to find out for sure.

I avoid Kelly's dinner invitation, even though she calls me at least three times a week. I tell her I'm busy with after-school activities, historical society events, grading papers. But my excuses are running thin, and I'll have to go back to avoiding her calls again soon.

I'm so caught up in those thoughts that as I trudge up the stairs to my hotel room, I miss Sawyer until I'm nearly on top of him.

"Sawyer?" I blink my eyes like he's a mirage brought on by fatigue and guilt.

I don't see the right hook that connects with my jaw, knocking me to the ground.

"Congratulations, asshole, you *are* the father," he growls and drops an envelope on my chest before stepping over me.

Stars dance in my vision, and I sit up quickly, clasping it to my chest. He's walking down the stairs I just came up.

"Wait. Sawyer. How did you know where I was?"

Nobody does, including the school, since I opened a post

office box for district correspondence.

"You act like I don't have experience tracking down deadbeats." He doesn't turn around.

I wince at his description, but a part of me understands why he would say that.

"Have a nice life, asshole." He takes another step, but I stop him again.

"How's Michaela?"

The look he gives me makes me second-guess my choice to ask.

"None of your fucking business."

"Sawyer, come on—"

He's in my face before I can finish the sentence.

"Keep my sister's name out of your mouth." He all but breathes fire, nostrils flaring, teeth bared.

"I-I'm sorry."

"Sorry doesn't cut it. Not today. Not tomorrow."

"I made a mistake," I try again.

He snorts. "Yeah, so did I. In being friends with a dick."

"You're right," I agree, and his eyes round in surprise. "I am a dick. I was a massive asshole when I accused Mi"—the glare he shoots my way has me swallowing her name—"when I said the baby wasn't mine."

A muscle in his jaw ticks, but he remains silent.

"I don't need these." I hold up the envelope. "To tell me what I already know."

"And what's that?"

"She's carrying my baby."

He gives me a look that says *welcome to the conversation*.

"I-I want to be there for them. For the baby and for Michaela."

"You have a shittastic way of showing it."

"Please. I need your help." I'll beg if I must.

"I'm not helping you." He steps away and walks down the stairs.

"Why didn't you tell your mom and dad?" I lean over the banister, calling after him.

He waits until he's on the cracked, dirty concrete before looking up at me.

"Not my story to tell."

With that answer, he walks toward a car and drives away. There's no hesitation. I'm still staring after him a few minutes later when my neighbor's door opens, startling me from my position against the rail.

Reluctantly, I go inside and drop my bag on the chair. I pull the chain up and slide it across, the envelope clutched against my chest. My heart thumps painfully with the reminder that this doesn't need to be my life. I shouldn't be holding results like I'm on a private episode of some sleazy daytime talk show. Regret and sadness are my constant companions, but tonight they're a little heavier, and I sink onto the scratchy polyester couch that groans under my weight.

Running my finger against the flap, I pull out a stack of papers. The first is authorization for the noninvasive testing method in lieu of waiting until the baby is born. The next is a grainy copy of a report from the laboratory. At the top is a side-by-side comparison of my DNA and Michaela's, followed by a small box at the bottom.

Probability of Paternity: 99.845%

This hurts. Not only emotionally, but the physical ache in my chest—the regret is overpowering. I set the papers down next to me, covering my face with my hands and taking several deep breaths.

If I could go back in time and change how I reacted when I saw that pregnancy test, I would. I'd have pulled Michaela into my arms and kissed her for those three minutes we waited. Reminded her she wasn't alone anymore, that we were in this together.

"God," I groan, leaning my head back on the couch. "What the fuck do I do?"

The burn behind my eyes is telling. I haven't cried since I was a kid, but I want to sob now.

Blinking rapidly, I sit up and scan the rest of the papers. Testing procedures, the calibration of the process, another letter from an attorney indicating the intent to pursue a child support order in the state of California and, tucked between two pages, is a folded-up piece of paper with my name scrawled across it.

West,

I'm sure by now you read through the results. You're going to be a dad. I'm not sure if you're happy or sad about the news. I hope happy.

That she questions my reaction has the burning sensation back behind my eyes, this time stronger, and my fingers tighten on the paper, crumpling the edges.

I have to admit. I'm scared. Not about the baby, I mean for the baby. I've seen a doctor and everything is fine. I'm more worried about the kind of mom I'll be. I've made some crappy decisions, and I hope those don't come back to haunt our child.

I want to tell her that hindsight is twenty-twenty. That we all make mistakes. That she's worried about whether she'll be a good mom is exactly why she'll be the best kind.

Sawyer wants to bring you the results. He also wants to punch you, but I hope he doesn't.

I stretch my jaw, an ache blooming where his fist connected.

I hate that your friendship was ruined because of this. I told him that what happened between you and me was between us and shouldn't affect your relationship with him. I'm sure you can guess exactly how he responded to that. I can't get him to change his mind. I know he had his lawyer friend draw up other papers, stuff about child support and all that. I won't force it. I keep telling him, but he doesn't listen.

If you want to be a part of this baby's life, I'd like you to be. But if you don't, that's okay too. I can stay with Mia and Garrett as long as I want, which is a good thing since I'm pretty sure Sawyer would drive me nuts with his helicopter-mom attitude.

I hope you see this letter. I'm tucking it between pages so hopefully it will find its way to you. I wanted you to know the baby is okay. That you can choose to be a part of its life or not. Take care of yourself.

Two warm tears track down my cheeks, dripping onto the page and smudging the ink.

I swear she's in the room with me. The echoes of her voice, the subtle notes of her perfume—I lift the note to my nose and breathe deeply.

I *do* want to be part of this baby's life. I want more than that. I want to be there the whole time. Pregnancy cravings and doctor's appointments, birthday parties and...anniversaries.

I want this baby and I want Michaela.

For keeps.

CHAPTER 22

MICHAELA

"If that's coffee, you're not supposed to drink any."

Sawyer's voice makes me jump and spill coffee—he called it—all over my hand.

Lowering my cup to the counter, I turn to face him with a glare.

"*A.*" I hold up a finger. "Dr. Jeffries said I could drink one cup a day. This is that one cup. *B*, how did you get in here? I locked the door."

This is exactly why I took Mia and Garrett up on the offer of their guest house. I stayed at Sawyer's for one week when I first arrived and left before he could drive me bonkers.

I've heard of helicopter-moms, but never heard brothers described the same way. Sawyer is going to create his own word. If I don't kill him first.

He shrugs, stepping past the couch and table in the small living area and grabbing me into a hug.

"How's my nephew?" He ruffles my hair before stealing my half-full mug and holding it aloft when I try to take it back.

I roll my eyes with a huff, jumping at the cup. "Sawyer."

"It's not good for you. I was reading this article on *The Preg-*

nant Connection that, even though doctors allow one cup, it still impacts fetal heart rates."

"*The Pregnant Connection*?" I forget my mission of getting my coffee back.

"A website I found for pregnant women. Random questions and facts not included in books."

"Since when are you a pregnant woman?" I tease.

"Ha. Funny." He takes a sip of my coffee and grimaces. "God, what's in this? Creamer with a little bit of coffee?"

"Since that *was* mine"—I doubt I'll successfully retrieve the cup from Sawyer—"what do you care?"

"Coffee isn't good for you," Mia says, walking in with a bottle of something the color of blended grass. "Read it on *The Pregnancy Connection*."

Sawyer looks at me with an eyebrow raised, and I growl, stomping my foot like a three-year-old in the middle of a tantrum.

"I love you both, but you're going to drive me crazy before this baby even makes an appearance."

Sawyer is bad alone, but he and Mia together are like helicopter-moms on steroids.

"Here. Drink this." Mia hands me the bottle of green stuff.

I eye it warily. "What is it?"

"Spinach, mango, pineapple, banana, and coconut milk."

"That doesn't sound too bad." I pop open the lid and sniff. The scents of pineapple and banana tease my nostrils. I shrug and take a sip, then go back for more when it tastes better than it looks.

"I also have a recipe for a peanut butter and banana one we should try later," Mia says.

"I still want my coffee," I pout but take another drink of the smoothie.

"Did you take your prenatal this morning?" Helicopter-mom Sawyer tags in for this round.

"*Ugh.*" I lift my chin, dropping my head back in frustration. "Yes. You know, you two, I appreciate the…*attention*, but I'm fully capable of taking my vitamins and eating breakfast without the reminders."

"You were eating chicken tenders for breakfast yesterday," Mia reminds me.

"Haven't you ever heard of chicken and waffles?" I ask.

"Kayla, you were eating them with mustard. And not honey mustard either. Straight up yellow mustard." She makes a gagging sound, and Sawyer's face turns the color of my smoothie.

"So?"

"We just want what's best for you. Trust us."

"I do," I tell them, tears burning my nose. Stupid hormones. A greeting card commercial made me cry the other day. "I don't know what I would have done the last few weeks without you guys."

Mia had picked me up from the airport and scheduled a pedicure, manicure, facial, and even a massage for the following day. She'd asked friends about doctor recommendations until we found Dr. Jeffries.

Sawyer had worked with his attorney friend and gotten the paternity paperwork going. I didn't want the question hanging over us. And now it's done, and I can move forward.

Easier said than done. Just because I *can* move forward doesn't mean I *am*. I still go to sleep at night convinced I can feel the phantom pressure of West's arm around my waist. Each time I wake up and realize the sensation wasn't real is a reminder of what happened and is more depressing than the last. But I will not share that information with either of my bodyguards.

"Aww, Kayla." Mia sniffles and wraps her arms around me. "That's what we're here for."

"Come here, Mikey." Sawyer pulls me away from Mia, enveloping me in a bear hug. "Love you, squirt."

"Love you too."

"Love you three." Mia joins in. "That said, I need to go. I have an audition."

"Break a leg," I call after her as she darts out the door with an air kiss.

"Your friend is crazy." Sawyer drops onto a stool at the kitchen counter.

"She's sweet," I correct. "I thought you were in Philadelphia."

Perching on the stool next to him, I feign nonchalance. But it doesn't stop the way my palms grow clammy or how my heart races. He went home to personally deliver the paternity results to West, and my curiosity is killing me. I can't help but wonder how he is, what he's up to. He may not want me—us—but my heart hasn't gotten the message.

"It was a quick in and out trip." He fidgets a second before moving to the Keurig machine. "Where do you keep the coffee?"

"How was he?" I can't help but ask.

He ignores my question, pawing through the cabinets until he finds the coffee pods and pops one in the machine.

"Sawyer?" I ask when he still hasn't responded.

He grunts.

"That's not a response."

"Because it doesn't matter, Mikey. The loser is out of our lives."

"He's not a loser. He's your best friend."

"*Was*. Was my best friend."

"I don't want you to end a twenty-year friendship because of me."

"I didn't," he says.

"Yeah, right," I scoff, rolling my eyes.

"I ended a twenty-year friendship because I don't know that guy. He's not my best friend."

I prop my elbow on the counter and rest my chin in my hand. "This is stupid."

"Do you need a ride today?"

One thing about Sawyer. If he doesn't want to answer the question, he won't. He'll flat out refuse and then change the subject.

With a sigh, I nod. "Yes, please."

"What time are you heading to the studio?"

That's the other thing Sawyer helped me fix. Between what he discovered and the loopholes Mike found, Reverb was happy to let me out of my contract. The three of us had left a meeting with the owner of Reverb after she apologized profusely and not only shredded my original contract, but gifted me the rights to all the songs I worked on while at the label.

Hush money.

But I didn't care. She set me free.

Afterward, we'd met Nick and Jax at Jax's home studio. The way their contract was written provides me freedom to exit the agreement anytime in the next six months if I'm unhappy. Jax remembered my request—to be happy making music.

I also officially met Jax's wife, Charlie, and their daughter, McKenna—Ken for short. The last time I had seen Charlie was when she told Jax off at the one music awards ceremony I've been to. Our interactions are still awkward, but I hope that someday we'll move beyond one of my less than shining moments.

Seeing how everyone doted on the happy baby, I also decided to tell Nick and Jax about my pregnancy, stressing that my new little family came first. They had agreed, offering a slower ramp up that started with recording an EP and then seeing where things went from there.

Today we start recording the first song, "Whisper."

"What time do we need to leave?" Sawyer asks, checking his watch, and I glance at the clock on the stove.

"Fifteen minutes." I head toward the bathroom. "Let me brush my teeth and grab my phone."

He grunts and gives me a thumbs up, and I roll my eyes. My brother the chatty Cathy.

Like I do every morning, I study my reflection in the mirror, cataloging the changes my body is going through. But other than my shirt fitting a little more snugly, there's nothing. Most people probably wouldn't even think I was pregnant.

Teeth brushed, I grab my phone from the bedroom and nearly drop it when I see the missed call notification.

West.

There's no voicemail. I haven't seen his name on my phone in a month, so why now?

I don't have time to figure out that answer, so I clear the notification and tuck my phone into my pocket before heading back to the kitchen.

"Ready?" The awkward excitement in my voice is cringeworthy, and Sawyer studies me for several breaths before nodding.

"You all right, Mikey?"

"I'm fine. Just excited. Let's go."

I hurry him to the door, but he stops before I can push him down the path to the driveway.

"Lock your door."

"Sawyer. This is a guest house on a gated property."

He shakes his head. "Doesn't matter. Lock it."

I do as he demands, then tuck my keys back into my bag.

"Happy?"

"Ecstatic," he deadpans.

"You need to loosen up, Sawyer."

"I'm plenty loose," he grits out.

"Sure you are." But I might as well be talking to a wall, since his back is to me, and he only listens when he wants to.

We're nearly to his car when he stops so suddenly that I run into his back. He reaches behind himself to steady me.

"What?" Craning my neck around his massive shoulder, I see Evie hoisting a big bag out of her car. "Morning, Evie!"

Sawyer's body goes rigid at my words. What's his problem?

"Morning, Michaela." She doesn't acknowledge Sawyer's presence, but he doesn't relax and move again until after she's in the main house.

"What was all that about?" I drill a finger into his side.

"What was what about?" he asks while he flinches away.

"Evie."

"What about her?" He points to the passenger door, and I sigh but follow his directions.

"Do you not like her or something?"

He grunts again, like it's an answer.

"She's really sweet," I tell him. "And an amazing assistant for Mia."

"Do you ever stop talking?" He pulls the car around the driveway, heading toward the gate. "I swear you talk more now than you did when you were little."

"I do not!"

Another grunt.

"You know, if I talk too much, you don't talk at all. Grunting is not a foreign language."

"I talk when I have stuff to say."

"You're irritating." I cross my arms over my chest.

"Part of my job description as your big brother."

Just to be a pain in his ass, I grunt, and he barks out a laugh.

"Glad to see I'm rubbing off on you, Mikey."

𝄞 𝄞 𝄞

Thanksgiving is approaching, and California in November is a far cry from what I'm used to. I'm still adjusting to how different the weather is. In Pennsylvania, the impression of snow is already in the air, if it hasn't snowed already. Here in LA, I'm still wearing shorts, although they're getting tighter, and I usually have to put a hair band around the button and thread it through the buttonhole to make them comfortable. The baby continues to grow right on target, and I've gone from hating meat to craving it.

I've had a few other missed calls from West, but he never leaves a message. I could call him back or text him, but I have no idea what I would say.

After a month, I've recorded four songs, and after all the time I've spent with Nick and Jax in the studio, they're ready for release.

Arrhythmic is a dream come true. Nick and Jax remind me of my brothers. They joke around constantly until it's time to work. And the stuff they come up with together is amazing.

We've spent several hours recording today, and they're messing around with a guitar in the studio while I watch from the booth, awed by their magic. We're done, but Sawyer's on a job, so I need to order a car.

I'm not excited to head back to the quiet of the guest house since Mia and Garrett have been gone for the last few days. Instead, I'm sitting on a couch in the booth, enjoying the presence of other humans to avoid the loneliness at home, when Charlie walks in. She stops when she sees me.

Awkwardness still makes me fidget when I run into her, which is often since the studio is in a converted building behind her house. I still remember her face when I walked up to her and Jax at the awards ceremony, the anger snapping in her gaze as she turned from him to me and back again.

There's nothing like that anymore, only a quiet curiosity. What does she think when she sees me?

"Boys playing with their toys?" she asks, smiling and gesturing to the adult men who do indeed remind me of little boys playing with their favorite toys, passing a guitar back and forth and trying to outdo each other.

"Yep. Although I think if you promise them ice cream, you can probably pull them away," I tease, smiling more when she laughs at my joke.

Some of that awkwardness fades.

"How's it been going?" She sits in the vacant sound engineering chair.

"Good, I think." I still have a hard time believing I'm with a label that respects me and cares about my happiness.

"Better than Reverb?" she asks.

I snort laugh at that. "So much better. That place was…"

"Soul stealing?" she offers. "That's what Jackson used to say."

"It works. I was going to say toxic, but soul stealing sounds more accurate."

Jax spies Charlie through the window, and his eyes light up before he holds up the universal sign for just a minute, then blows her a kiss through the glass.

"He's such a nut," she says with a shake of her head.

"You guys are cute together." I wince when her shoulders tense, worried I brought the tension roaring back. "I…sorry." She seems confused, so I elaborate. "About before. The awards show and all the drama with it. If I could change it, I would."

She releases a deep breath, her shoulders relaxing. "Hindsight is great, isn't it?"

I think about my own situation with West, and the baby growing inside me as a result of our time together.

"It can be. But it doesn't always lead to regret," I say.

I don't regret my time with him. I wish I could. It would probably make these last few months easier. But from the first time I saw the little blip of a baby on the grainy screen, I had no regrets.

"No, that's true. You know"—she clears her throat, scooting the chair closer—"I'm glad you signed with Arrhythmic."

"You are?"

"Mm-hmm. I've heard some of your stuff. It's really good. Plus, you mesh well with the guys."

"They remind me of my brothers."

"How many do you have?"

"Two. You may have seen Sawyer wandering around here when he picks me up."

She nods. "I wondered. You don't have a car?"

"Nah. I don't go many places. Here and Mia's." Since Charlie works with Garrett, she's also familiar with Mia.

"Maybe we could do lunch one day? You, me, Meredith, Mia."

"I'd like that." Other than Mia and my brother, I don't have any friends.

"So," she says hesitantly. "I hope you don't mind, but Jackson told me...that you were...well, congratulations."

"Gorgeous, remind me never to tell you anything I want to stay a secret." Jax swoops into the room and wraps an arm around her shoulders, dropping his lips to her temple.

"You didn't say it was a secret." She pinches his side, and he flinches away with a giggle. His unrestrained laughter has both Charlie and me laughing too.

"It's okay," I interrupt. "Thank you. Yes. I am."

"I have some maternity clothes from when I was pregnant with Ken. Would you be interested in any of them?"

"I-I'd love that, thank you." Now I won't have to worry about scraping together the money to buy some. My regular clothes won't fit much longer, and I refuse to let Mia or Sawyer spend any more money on me.

"Great!" Her face brightens. "Whenever you want to see them, let me know."

"What is taking so long? Ken and I are ready for pizza." I've only seen Nick's wife Meredith once before at the awards show, but she's still as pretty as I remember with her darker skin and long corkscrew curls. Ken's chubby fingers are wrapped in them as she babbles from Meredith's arms. I study Meredith for any resemblance to Mike and find it in her astute gaze when it lands on me.

"Dude, we've got fifteen minutes max before hangry Meredith comes out to play," Jax jokes to Nick.

"On it." He cringes and pulls out a phone, opening an app and mumbling about toppings. "All set."

"Do you want to stay for pizza?" Charlie asks me.

I've been so caught up in watching their interactions, watching the love they have for each other, I hadn't thought about dinner.

"Oh, um…" My phone vibrates against my leg, and I check it.

WEST

Here in LA. Can I please see you?

I want to talk.

My heart pounds in my chest. Do I want to see him? Talk to him?

Hell yes! Why is this a question?

Nerves. Nerves make me hesitate. But only for a moment. I need to see him.

"Rain check?"

"Do you need a ride home since Sawyer's out of town?" Nick asks.

I shake my head. "Nah. I'll order an Uber."

Meredith and Charlie leave first, Ken making faces at me over Meredith's shoulder while Nick and Jax turn off the lights and lock up the studio.

"You're sure?" Nick asks.

"I'm sure." I nod, thinking about the texts burning a hole in my pocket.

Phone in hand again, I pull up the app and order my ride. Everyone keeps me company until it pulls up to the gate and Jax buzzes her in with an app on his phone.

"Fancy," I tease.

"Don't get him started," Charlie groans.

"They'll show you all their gadgets," Meredith adds. "Hours. Hours about apps and phones and—"

"You love my apps." Nick presses a hard kiss to her lips, and she melts, blinking slowly when he finally pulls away.

"Let me know about the lunch," Charlie reminds me as I step toward the car, opening the back door.

"I will."

Sliding into the back, I wait until the car is down the street before I stare at the texts again.

Okay.

His response is immediate, like he's been watching his phone, waiting for me to say something.

Where?

When?

30 min?

I text him Mia's address, pressing send before I can second-guess my decision.

I'm in the guest house behind the main house.

I'll see you soon.

Nerves might as well be riding next to me in the car when I think about how soon I'll see him again. But now is my chance. I have to see him again. I need to close the door once and for all.

CHAPTER 23

MICHAELA

Before I can put my phone in my purse, it rings. It's a Philadelphia area code, but not one of my contacts.

Who else would have my number?

"Hello?"

"Michaela?" I don't recognize the woman's voice.

"Y-yes?"

"Michaela, this is Rachel Abbott, West's mom. Oh, honey." Her voice sounds watery, and fear spikes through my blood. It's irrational since I was just texting with West, but what if something happened to him?

"Mrs. Abbott, is West okay?"

She sniffles. "He-he's fine. He told us about the baby, and we're so happy—another grandchild."

He told them about the baby?

"He did?"

"Yes. He's been staying with us for a about a week. He's been asking all kinds of questions about pregnancy. Did he tell you Whitney had a baby last year?" She takes a breath before rambling on. "And he left for LA this morning. The stinker wouldn't even give me your number until just a few minutes ago, even though I've been begging for it for days."

"Well, now that you have it, please use it. I'm happy to keep you all up to date on everything." I don't know that I'm doing the right thing, but they deserve to know their grandchild.

"I'd love that. In fact, Whit and I would love to drive down to LA soon and take you baby shopping. Maternity shopping," she says warmly.

"Both!" a voice I presume belongs to West's sister, Whitney, calls from the background.

"Both," Mrs. Abbott repeats.

"I-I'd like that, Mrs. Abbott—"

"Rachel, please."

"Rachel."

"Is this weekend too soon?"

I bite back a laugh at her exuberance. "Umm..."

"Mom!" Whitney speaks up again. "Ease up or she'll think you're nuts."

Rachel laughs. "Sorry. Can you tell I'm excited?"

I giggle. "A little. But I'll let you in on a secret. I am too."

"I don't want to come across as crazy though," she tells me. "So how about you figure out what day works for you and let me know, okay?"

"Okay, I'd like that."

"We'll talk to you soon, Michaela. Take care of yourself and that little one."

"I will," I say before ending the call.

West told his family about the baby. What does that mean? Sure, he got the results, but he could have kept the news to himself. I gave him an out. He doesn't need to be a part of this baby's life. Or mine, for that matter.

The ride home only takes ten minutes or so, but in my head, time drags until I'm an anxious mess, wiping my hands repeatedly on my shorts and taking several deep breaths.

"You gonna be sick?" the driver asks, and I shake my head.

"No." At least I don't think so.

"Here." He hands me a little bag. "Just in case."

I take the plastic from him, holding it in my hands as I try to distract myself and the somersaults turning in my stomach.

"Happen a lot?" I ask, and he eyes me in the rearview mirror. "People getting sick, I mean."

"A few. I learned early on spending a couple bucks on a box of those beats having to clean my car after a drunk pukes in it."

I wrinkle my nose as I consider the thought.

My stomach may not be calm, but I'm not going to be sick. I'm familiar with the signs since morning sickness and I palled around with each other for a few weeks.

"I think I'm okay." I pass the plastic back up when he pulls into the driveway. Remote in hand, I point it at the gate so he can drive the rest of the way through.

"Have a good night."

"You too." My smile is strained since I have no idea what my night is going to turn into. Dread wars with nerves as memories of my last conversation with West surface.

Whose is it?

I'm not attracted to liars.

My steps falter up the path, and I stop, strongly considering texting him to reschedule.

No. I'm straightening out the rest of my life. Time to untangle this mess too.

The paternity results were delivered. I haven't heard from him since then, but did I expect to?

He called. Several times.

But without any voicemails, I convinced myself they were accidental.

"Deep breaths, Kayla, you can do this," I say, stepping in to the one-bedroom cottage.

I flip on several lights, confirming everything is picked up. Up until recently—this pregnancy, really—I'd been a massive slob. But suddenly the switch flipped, and I now needed everything in a place that makes sense. Sawyer and Mia have referred to it as "nesting" thanks to all the pregnancy books they're reading. They've even swapped back and forth like a damn book club.

Ordinarily, I'd find it a little funny to see my six-foot-two, beefy, uncomfortable-with-attention brother trading pregnancy books with my petite famous-actress best friend. But when the two of them came at me with book reports of information, I drew the line. I tried a couple of the books but ended up imagining the worst-case scenarios, and decided ignorance was bliss.

The panel next to my door buzzes, alerting me that someone's here. Sawyer would probably kill me, but I hit the button to open the gate without confirming that it's West.

With a sigh, I step into the bathroom to check my reflection in the mirror.

The dark circles under my eyes are gone. My skin is healthy and—according to Mia—glowing. Since I was at the studio most of the day, my hair is in a messy bun. I consider pulling out the band and trying for something a little more put together, but the knock on the door tells me I've run out of time. I'm in a flowy t-shirt Mia loaned me and the shorts that are edging past the elastic-in-a-buttonhole level of comfort. I wish I had asked for an hour.

"Who cares what you look like? He won't," I tell myself firmly.

More confidence. I wish I had just a little more right now.

Another knock. I jolt, having spent more time in the bathroom after the first knock than I realized.

"Coming!"

I walk down the short hall, my breath catching in my lungs since he's clearly visible through the glass door.

Residual hurt and anger still flutter, but seeing him brings concern to the mix. Maybe I should think he deserves to look like he's lost weight, but I'm not that type of person. The hollows of his cheeks are pronounced under the dark circles that ring his eyes.

But he's still West. The chiseled jawline and bright green eyes drinking me in through the glass create a powerful pull I can't ignore. Familiarity. Attraction. And, if I'm honest with myself, fleeting sensations of the emotions I thought I was getting over.

Does he notice any differences in me?

With a deep breath, I close the distance to the door and pull it open. His cologne wraps around my senses and my heart in equal measure, reminding me of all the times I burrowed against him in bed, seeking and receiving the comfort of his embrace.

"Hi." The breathy sound betrays the emotions coursing through me.

"Hi." The tenor of his voice makes my stomach explode in a sea of butterflies, and I try to tamp down the mix of excitement and nerves.

"C-can I come in?" he asks as he fidgets with a moving box he's holding in front of him.

I don't think I've ever seen him this uncertain.

"Oh. Yeah. Of course. You can set that anywhere." I open the door wider, letting him step past me.

If anyone asks, I'll deny that I take a deep breath of the citrusy bergamot scent weaving around me. Same as I'll deny watching the muscles in his back ripple under his shirt as he lowers the box next to the couch.

Liar, liar, pants on fire.

And my pants are indeed on fire.

What is wrong with me?

The hormones. Mia showed me a book that talked all about the hormones of pregnancy, especially the chapter on the safest ways to have sex while pregnant since some expectant mothers experience a surge of estrogen leading to increased desire. Those symptoms had been non-existent…until now.

"Did—did you want something to drink?" I ask. "There's water and...well, water."

"I'll take a water if that's okay. Here, I'll get it." The small space is easy to navigate. Or does it only seem smaller because his presence overwhelms me? "Do you want one?"

I lick my lips, trying to infuse moisture back to the parched skin and nod. "Please."

He comes back with two bottles and catches me staring at the sealed box. It's plain—there's no writing on the side, no indication of what it contains.

"What did you bring?"

"It's for you. Well, for the baby," he clarifies.

"The baby?"

He nods and leans down to pull the tape across the seam. With slow movements, he peels open the lid and grabs a worn stuffed bear from the top.

"I-I asked my mom if she still had my baby stuff. I also gave her your phone number—"

"She called. You told your family about me?"

I hadn't even figured out how to tell my own parents.

"I did. I wanted them to know about you. About the baby. I also told them about what an ass I was, and Whit threatened to stick me on dirty diaper duty for the rest of my visit with them."

"Oh." I'm not sure what to say—let alone think—knowing that he's shared so much with his family.

"This was mine." He hands over the bear. "My first stuffed animal. I-I don't know why I had my mom hang on to it for so long, but I always thought I'd give it to my own child someday."

The fur is soft to the touch, the little bow tie still in place even after the years of love evident as I cradle it in my hands.

"You're giving this to me?"

"I want our child to have it. To take comfort in something that belonged to Daddy when he was little."

The expression on his face when he says the word *Daddy* creates a warmth in my chest that I haven't felt in months.

"Thank you," I whisper, trying not to cry. Clearing my throat, I motion to the couch. "Should we sit?"

"One more."

He hands me a small, folded onesie. Unlike the bear, I can tell this is new given the bright white of the soft cotton. My heart catches in my throat when I unfold it.

Daddy's Little Historian.

"West."

I want to say so much more, but tears fill my eyes, ready to fall if I open my mouth.

I sit, still clutching the fabric in my lap, and he sits next to me. I take several deep breaths and clear the unshed tears. His thoughtful presents speak for themselves. They tell me how he feels about this baby, but I have questions.

"Why are you in LA?" I finally ask at the same time he speaks.

"I'm glad you said yes."

We smile awkwardly at each other, and he motions for me to continue.

"Sorry, go ahead," he tells me.

"What brings you to LA? Shouldn't you be wrapping up the semester?"

"I, uh, I quit my job. Well, actually I first got offered the department head position, but I turned that down, and then I quit. I've been here for about a week, searching for a new job."

"Here?" Something else he said registers. "You quit your job? I thought you loved it."

"I do. And I love Philadelphia. But you need to be here. And I want to be where you are. I would have been here sooner, but it took my department head a while to locate a long-term substitute."

"Sooner?" I repeat, the butterflies flapping like mad in my stomach.

He puts down his bottle of water and takes mine, too. His fingers shake as he reaches forward, stretching to wrap them around mine. I suck in a breath, not sure how to process the emotions causing the butterflies to get seriously pissed off. Hurt, hope, anger. They're all crashing over me like waves, one right after another, pulling me under, and I'm not sure which one should win out.

"I'm an idiot. I'm the world's biggest asshole, and if I could spend a thousand lifetimes apologizing for the horrible way I behaved that day, it still wouldn't be enough, but I would try."

I can't control the tears that cascade down my cheeks as memories come back. I tried to push them down, to move forward, but they still have the power to slice like thousands of paper cuts.

"Baby," he whispers, wiping my cheeks with his thumbs. "God, I'm so sorry. I don't want you to cry."

"I'm pregnant," I remind him. "I cry a lot."

The smile he gives me is bittersweet. "Which is why you don't need me making you cry more."

I shrug and hiccup, swiping one hand across my cheeks.

"Well, you did," I tell him. "And I don't understand why. Why you said all that stuff to me about…about…"

The words lodge in my throat, refusing to be repeated.

"There's no excuse for what I did. None. I let my imagination run wild when I saw that picture, and seeing the test, it brought everything back. Everything I went through with Ashley and all the red flags I should have caught. I was so excited when she told me she was pregnant. I was ready to start a family she seemed less than enthusiastic about."

"I'm not Ashley," I say, pulling my other hand away. "And it wasn't fair for you to treat me like I was."

He dislodges the beanie covering his hair, scraping his fingers through the thick strands. "I know. And I've been in hell since I realized that. I hate myself—*hate*—what I said. How I acted. I've thought a million times about how that day could have been so different. How I wish it was."

"You can't change the past."

"No." He shakes his head sadly. "That's what my counselor says."

"Counselor?"

"I, uh, felt like I needed to work through the emotions I never dealt with. The way she hurt me. How painful it was when the idea of a family was ripped away. I thought talking to someone would help prevent you from having to bear the brunt of my issues. I can't stand to hurt you again. Or to hurt our baby."

"You believe the test results."

So many emotions crowd my thoughts—happiness that he believes me, anger that he didn't, and shock that he had kept all of what he felt with Ashley bottled up. I'm relieved that he's talking to someone about them.

"I didn't need those results to know for sure," he says. "I realized about an hour after I left that there was no doubt in my mind that you were pregnant with my baby."

"So why didn't I hear from you until now?"

"I didn't know what to say. How to apologize," he admits.

"'I'm sorry' would have been a good start."

"*I am.*" He falls to his knees in front of me, his forehead resting against my thigh. "God, I'm so fucking sorry."

"Thank you."

His eyes find mine when he lifts his head.

"Apology accepted."

"It's that easy?" he questions.

I nod. "Maybe it shouldn't be. But that's all I wanted from you. A sincere apology. To know you believe me."

"I do believe you." He leans closer like he wants to kiss me.

I pull back at his proximity. "What are you doing?" So much of me wants to lean in to him, to experience the sensation of his lips against mine again. But I've made bad choices in the past. And I have to think about more than just me now.

My stomach cramps at the hurt and confusion filling his eyes.

"You said—"

"I said apology accepted. I didn't say it meant anything more."

"But your letter—"

"I told you it was your choice. You can be in our baby's life if you want." I lift my hands to span my stomach. "But I choose who I let into my heart."

My muscles tighten again, locking the wall of my abdomen. No. The tightness is lower, almost at my pelvic bone, and I press against the area, trying to breathe through the tension. If I thought the butterflies were excited before, they're manic now.

"Michaela?" His attention shifts from my face to my hands and back again.

I take a deep breath in through my nose and release it through my mouth, only to gag as my stomach tightens again. Tears spring to my eyes, and I lean over, searching for a position to ease the vise squishing my internal organs.

"What's happening?" The panic is clear in his voice, in his wide eyes. They're the last thing I see before I squeeze my eyes closed, tears leaking from under my lashes.

"I—" Deep breath. "I don't know."

My last word is a groan as the muscles cramp harder. Oh my god, what's going on?

"The baby," I murmur.

"Maybe you'll feel better if you lie down." Gentle hands on my arms, he shifts me into more of a reclined position, but I cry out as soon as my knees drop, and he lifts me back up. "We need to get to the hospital."

Ordinarily, I would disagree, but the edges of my vision are fuzzy, and the pain is like nothing I've ever experienced. I nod, tears dripping onto my thighs and terror spiking through me.

"It hurts," I whimper.

Warm lips press against my temple, his hand covering mine where it curls protectively around the barely there bump.

"It's going to be okay." He stands, leaning over and lifting me as if I weigh nothing. The cramping intensifies with the movement, and I bite my lip on a moan, pressing my teeth so hard into the flesh the metallic taste of blood coats my tongue.

I keep one hand on my stomach and dig the other into the soft cotton of his shirt.

"Who the hell are you?" Mia's voice cuts across the patio, and the light smell of jasmine perfume mixes with West's cologne and the laundry soap scent of his shirt. "Kayla?"

"Ames, what the hell?" Garrett's voice is close by as well, even if I don't open my eyes to confirm.

"Something's wrong." West shifts his grip slightly, and I whimper.

"West."

"I know, baby."

"West? You're West? You have some fucking nerve—"

"Ames," Garrett interrupts her tirade.

"*What?*"

"We need to get Michaela some help," Garrett says. Thank god for his rational response since my stomach is being turned inside out through my belly button. "Is that your car in the driveway?"

"Yeah," West answers, taking a few more steps. They're cautious, but the jostling creates lightning strikes of agony across my abdomen.

"Why don't we drive? You can sit in the back with Michaela," Garrett offers.

Mia makes a noise like she might disagree, but Garrett keeps talking.

"Ames, look at her. She needs him."

I *do* need him. His warmth against me is the only thing keeping me sane right now. What would I do if he wasn't here?

I've never been so terrified. Panic, anxiety, and pain all center in my stomach, radiating outward and causing other muscles to cramp in sympathy. Easing me into the car, he brushes his lips against my forehead.

"Be right back," he says, and I don't even inhale and exhale before he's opening the other door, sliding next to me.

Two other doors slam, and we start to move. I try to hold myself upright and still since it seems to help the cramps a little—until we go over a bump. I cry out, squeezing West's fingers resting on the seat between us.

"I'm here," he murmurs, draping an arm around my shoulder and pulling me next to him.

"What if…what if…the baby."

"Shh. It's going to be okay."

"You d-d-don't know that."

He huffs a laugh. "You're right, I don't. But I'm going to do everything in my power to keep you safe. Both of you."

West races around the car to help me out when we pull up to the hospital's emergency entrance. I try to stand, but my knees buckle, and he scoops me up again.

"If you think I'm leaving you alone with her," Mia warns, her car door echoing mine. "You've got another thing coming."

"Ames," Garrett calls out.

"What?"

"Be nice. I'm going to park the car. See you inside."

She harrumphs but falls into step beside West as they walk through the emergency room doors.

"We need help." He says it loud enough to attract attention, and the squeak of rubber against linoleum grows louder before he lowers me to a wheelchair. "Something's wrong. Her stomach."

"Could she be pregnant?" The no-nonsense voice of a nurse breaks through the haze of pain.

"She is. She's, uh—"

"She's at the end of her first trimester," Mia interrupts.

"Either of you two family?"

"No," West admits slowly.

"Well, no," Mia says with another huff. "But she's my best friend—"

"Family only. There's a waiting room over there," the nurse directs, although I still can't open my eyes to see where she's telling them to go.

"Don't leave," I whimper, and West leans down next to me.

"I'm not going anywhere. I'll be right here, ready when you need me." His lips are featherlight against my cheek, but his warmth disappears as he rises and the nurse wheels me away.

Tears build and fall faster than I can wipe them away.

Tears of sadness. Tears of worry. And tears because he's saying everything I want to hear. Even if it is too late.

CHAPTER 24

WEST

My entire life is somewhere behind doors they wouldn't let me through.

And not being with her—not being with them—is slow torture.

For the next hour, I pace back and forth in the waiting room, ignoring the glares Mia shoots in my direction every few steps.

"You're a dick," she spits out, ignoring her husband when he tries to calm her down.

"I'm not arguing with you," I tell her.

"I hope you're ready to eat your own balls, because Sawyer is on his way." Her voice is a little too gleeful at the prospect, but I can appreciate it. Everything she's saying comes from her love for Michaela and her own stress.

"Amelia," Garrett whispers. "Enough."

"But—"

He raises a brow and cuts off any other protests with a kiss before pulling back.

"He's worried about Michaela. About the baby. Now isn't the time or the place. Let it go."

She turns back to me, and for the first time, something other than hatred fills her eyes—curiosity.

"Are you genuinely worried about them?"

"More than anything," I tell her, letting her see every emotion rioting through my body.

"You wouldn't know that by your radio silence the last several months," she says.

I sigh. "I didn't know what to say. I did call, but I didn't leave messages. Every time I heard her voice on her greeting, every thought in my head disappeared."

"She didn't tell me you called," Mia admits. "Why now?"

"Because the fear that I would live the rest of my life without her—without them—finally overcame the fear that an apology wouldn't be enough, the fear of rejection. I wouldn't know if repairing my relationship with her was possible unless I finally got off my ass and tried."

My biggest fear now is that I'm too late.

Please don't let anything happen to them.

I have no idea who I'm talking to, but I keep repeating the request.

The last sixty minutes have felt six hundred years long. I can't come this far to lose either one of them. But remembering how Michaela pulled away from me, I have so much more to do to convince her to give me another chance.

"You son of a bitch."

Sawyer charges forward, but Garrett steps in front of him, holding up his hands.

"Not the time or the place, Sawyer."

"Step outside then, asshole. That'll be the perfect time and place." He cracks his knuckles, his eyes snapping disgust at me. "What the fuck did you do?"

"I…I didn't do anything." Although guilt gnaws at my gut. Is this my fault? "We were talking, and then she doubled over in pain." My heart races at the memory, the way agony had dropped over her face between one breath and the next.

"I don't fucking believe you."

"I don't need you to believe me," I fire back. "I need you to find out what the fuck is going on. They won't tell Mia or me shit since we're not family."

I point to the nurse's station, holding his fiery gaze until he finally shrugs out of Garrett's light hold and stalks to the desk. The change in him is so instantaneous, I'm dizzy with it. Gone is the fire-breathing soldier, and in his place is a concerned older brother.

I sit down, arms braced on my knees, and drop my head into my hands.

"You okay?" Garrett asks, sitting next to me. The genuine concern in his eyes nearly breaks me.

"No. Fuck. If anything happens to her or to the baby..." The dark abyss of that gut-wrenching scenario is enough to scare the shit out of me.

Please let them be okay.

"Can I get you anything? Coffee? Food?" he asks.

I shake my head. "No. But thank you."

He claps a hand on my shoulder when he stands and walks back to his wife, pulling her a little farther away and having a quiet conversation with her. Her gaze continues to dart to me before she lets out a massive sigh.

"Fine." She starts to walk away, and Garrett pulls her back into his arms.

She buries her nose in his chest, her shoulders shaking as his hands move up and down in a soothing motion. My attention shifts to the door, the desire to soothe Michaela the same way choking me.

I'm powerless. Useless. And the lack of knowledge is another thorn in my side.

"Well?" Mia asks Sawyer when he returns from the nurses' station, her eyes shiny with tears.

"A doctor is with her now."

"What does that mean?" She asks the question I've been thinking.

"Hopefully we'll find out more soon."

He moves to the wall in the corner, leaning back and bending one knee to rest his foot against the wall behind him. If I didn't know him so well, I would think he's fine. But there's a tension around his eyes, in the thinness of his compressed lips. He's as worried about Michaela as the rest of us.

Another hour goes by, doctors and nurses bustling back and forth in the busy emergency room, but no one stops to update us on the woman I can't imagine my life without.

"West Abbott?" A new nurse stands at the open door where they wheeled Michaela earlier.

"Y-yes?" I stand, swallowing around the lump of fear still sitting on my windpipe, making it hard to breathe.

"Can you come with me, please?"

Part of me wants to say no, to run out of the hospital without a second look. What news am I going to face when I step through that door? But a bigger part is desperate to see Michaela, to feel the silk of her skin under my fingertips, to reassure myself that she's okay.

"Why him?" Sawyer growls, stepping forward. "He's not family."

I can't stop the wince at the pain his words create. Six months ago, he was the closest thing to a brother I had.

The nurse isn't intimidated, even though Sawyer towers over her.

"Listen here. I have two grown boys, both about as big as you are, and both are still afraid I'll blister their behinds faster than they can run away. So you can take your grumpy bear attitude and go stand back in the corner you've been holding up. He"—she points at me—"was specifically requested."

"By whom?" he asks, and she simply raises an eyebrow until he stalks back to the corner.

"You." She points at me. "Follow me."

"Yes, ma'am."

She turns, walking briskly in the direction she came from, and I increase my pace to catch up as we pass an empty u-shaped desk and several rooms and cubicles with curtains around them —some drawn and some not. The smell of antiseptic burns my nose, and I take several breaths through my mouth.

"Here we are." She stops in front of a glass door with a curtain pulled behind it.

"Ms. King? You have a visitor." She steps to the side, and I release a breath I wasn't aware I was holding when I see the woman who took my heart with her when she left Pennsylvania. Who held it captive while I waited in the waiting room, praying she would be okay. That they both would be.

Fuck. Relief mixes with fear. The hospital bed dwarfs her. She's got an IV attached to her arm, and a drab gray gown leeches most of the color from her skin. I want to rush forward and reassure myself she's here, but I'm terrified my movements will cause her pain like they had earlier.

"Hi," I whisper, my eyes drinking her in.

"Hi." Her voice is quiet, a mix of uncertainty and exhaustion.

"I'm going to check on the ultrasound order." The nurse leaves the two of us, pulling the curtain closed behind her, and I hear the slide of the door, followed by a snick of the latch.

"I—are you okay?"

"Do you want to sit?" she asks, and my heart falls to my feet. Usually, bad news is delivered sitting down.

Terror must be visible on my face because she keeps talking.

"No. Oh, god, no. Everything's fine. Just sit, please."

Everything's fine. Everything's fine.

I take several deep breaths, trying to calm my racing heart, and lower myself carefully to the side of her bed since there isn't a chair in the room.

"Everything's fine?" I ask. "You? The baby?"

"We're both okay." She cups her stomach over the blanket, wincing at the IV band pulled tight across her arm.

"Take it easy there." I untangle the line from her bedrail, my hand hovering above hers where it rests on her abdomen.

"Here." She takes my hand and gently places it on her stomach. "You can't feel anything yet. But I can't stop touching it."

I nod, understanding. The warmth radiating from her through the gown pulls me to her like a magnet, and I never want to let go.

"What happened?" I finally pull my attention from where my hand rests and meet her eyes.

"They ran a bunch of tests. Throwing out scary words like placental abruption and miscarriage." Her voice wobbles, and my free hand finds hers on the covers. "But they were relieved there wasn't any spotting, so they started an IV and an exam."

She grimaces.

"Did they stop the cramps?"

"Not until after the exam," she whispers, and I want to take away all the pain she endured.

"But they're gone now?"

She nods. "Once the IV had a chance to work, I started to feel better. The cramping finally released. Turns out I was dehydrated."

"Dehydrated?"

She nods. "I didn't think I was. But I guess so."

I release a breath, most of the tension finally ebbing from my shoulders in a painful wave of relief.

I lift my hand to her cheek, loving when she leans into my touch.

"I was so worried about you. Both of you," I admit. "The last hour felt like it took a thousand years off my life."

"We're okay," she reassures me. Flipping her hand over, she interlaces her fingers with mine. "They want to do an ultrasound to check on the baby."

"You probably want some privacy then." I shift to stand up.

"Wait." She clears her throat and lowers her voice. "Did you—um—would you like to stay?"

Her question surprises me.

"Stay?" I don't want to be anywhere else. I just didn't think it was my place to ask.

"I thought you might want to see the baby for yourself." Her entire face shows her hesitation. She probably expects the asshole who showed up the day we found out she was pregnant.

But he's never going to make an appearance again.

I smile so big it hurts and nod. "I'd love to. If you wouldn't mind."

Over the next few minutes, she fills me in on her pregnancy while we wait. She found an OB she loves. This is the second time she's had an ultrasound, and she admits to a love of yellow mustard on almost every food. I vow to buy every bottle I can.

"Knock, knock." The nurse from earlier opens the curtain, and another person in scrubs wheels in a small cart.

"Did you know your nurse is a badass?" I ask Michaela.

"She is?" Her attention shifts from me to the nurse, who shrugs. "Cathy, why are you a badass?"

"She made Sawyer go stand in a corner," I tell Michaela.

The sound of her laughter releases more tension through my neck and down my back. I love that sound.

"You did?" Michaela giggles again. "I can just imagine. My hulk of a brother facing off against a woman half his size."

"Like I told him. I have two grown sons as big as he is. They don't scare me. Why should he? Besides, you know what I found out about those big boys?"

"What?" Michaela asks, her gaze full of amusement when it meets mine.

"They may be all crust on the outside, but the inside is nothing but marshmallow."

Michaela laughs until she clutches her stomach, scaring the hell out of me and having Cathy pause.

"Pain scale of one to ten," she asks in a no-nonsense tone.

"It was just the laughter," Michaela explains. "Not even a one right now."

I think I lost a year off my life, but Cathy nods.

"Well, I'll leave you in Jeanne's capable hands, but will check to see if there are any other tests the doctor wants to run before we release you."

"I get to go home?" she asks, her eyes lighting up.

"We'll see."

The smile on Michaela's face fades slightly before she shifts her attention to Jeanne.

"Have you had an ultrasound before?"

Michaela nods. "At my first pre-natal appointment. The doctor wanted to confirm gestational age."

"That first ultrasound was probably different, but you're further along now so we can do a normal ultrasound. Ready?"

Michaela nods, and I mirror the action, even though I have no idea what to expect. Jeanne pulls her gown up, using the covers as a sort of curtain to expose only her softly rounded belly.

Possessiveness zips through me.

Mine.

Jeanne squeezes some gel along Michaela's stomach and grabs the wand, pressing it against Michaela's skin to spread the goo around as she presses several buttons on the keyboard. After several beats, a loud whooshing fills the room.

I meet Michaela's gaze. "Is that..." Words fail me as wonder fizzes through my body.

She smiles and nods. "That's our baby."

Our baby.

Fucking hell. It hits me in the solar plexus. My nose burns, and pressure builds behind my eyes, but I don't care.

"Our baby." I shift, pressing my lips to Michaela's temple, relieved when she doesn't pull away.

Several measurements are captured—including the gestational age putting the baby between twelve and fourteen weeks—before Jeanne prints out several pictures on her portable printer.

"Baby's first photos?" she asks, handing me several.

I check with Michaela for confirmation, and she nods. "I didn't get one at my first ultrasound. Not a ton to see."

"These are incredible," I tell her, my lips drawn to her forehead in a way I can't resist.

"I need to buy a frame for these," I tell her after Jeanne leaves.

She smiles. "I bet your mom or Whitney will know where to find one."

"They're really excited to take you shopping. And I think my mom is over the moon that her second grandchild is in California too."

"Your parents live close to your sister, right?" she asks.

"Yeah. It's only about a five-hour drive from here."

"What about you?" she asks.

"Every job I've applied for is in the LA area. I'm not living five hours away from you."

I love the faint pink that fills her cheeks at my words. It gives me hope.

"I was going to give you something earlier, but didn't get the chance."

She tilts her head with a curious look. "What?"

I reach into my pocket, pulling out a small box I haven't been able to let go of since I bought it. My good-luck charm.

"This is for you."

Her breath catches in surprise as she eyes it suspiciously. In her defense, it looks like a ring box.

"Open it," I tell her, watching as she pulls in a deep breath. It isn't a ring.

Not yet anyway.

"What is it?" she asks, lifting the lid and pulling out the smaller box inside.

"Guess you better open it and see."

She rolls her eyes but lifts the lid slowly, her free hand lifting to her mouth at what she sees nestled against the velvet.

"Oh."

"Do you like it?" I ask.

Right before I left for California, I was wandering near Independence Square and found the pendant in a shop window. It's white gold, the image of a mother in profile, her forehead touching a child's. Some might call the image Madonna. But I just refer to it as my heart.

"I-I love it. Thank you." Her eyes sparkle as unshed tears line her lashes.

"Good tears or bad tears?"

"Good," she says, sniffling. "So good. Would you put it on me?"

I nod and take the box, carefully lifting the necklace out and shifting until I'm behind her. She pulls her hair up and out of my way, exposing her long, slender neck, to give me access. Closing the clasp on the necklace, I run my hands along the chain and resist the urge to press my lips against the back of her neck.

"Thank you." Her eyes meet mine over her shoulder, and time stops, a heartbeat stretching to two, then four, and my attention zeroing in on her lips. Her tongue peeks out to moisten them, and I want to groan.

"You said that already," I tell her.

"Well, I meant it."

"You're welcome."

My breathing slows as I lean closer, watching her eyelashes flutter shut.

"Ms. King?" Cathy, the nurse, scrapes back the curtain. "The doctor is reviewing your ultrasound now. So long as nothing shows up there, he'll be by to discharge you in the next hour or so."

"Great, thank you, Cathy," Michaela says with a smile.

The curtain shuts again, and I want to pick up where we left off, close the distance, taste her again. But I hold back. We rushed into a relationship so fast before, and I lost them both. I'm not willing to risk her or our child again.

CHAPTER 25

WEST

Almost two and a half hours later, the doctor still hasn't come by. Michaela is dozing in the hospital bed, our hands joined over her abdomen. I started to pull my hand back once, afraid she was uncomfortable, but she gripped my fingers, her murmured *Stay* enough to keep me right where I was. She shifts, and the necklace catches the light, drawing my attention.

I'm going to be a father.

The thought is quickly followed by another.

I will do everything in my power to protect my family.

"Michaela," I lean close to whisper in her ear.

Her cornflower blue eyes flutter open, training hazily on me.

"I'll be right back."

Doubt furrows her eyebrows, and I shift my lips to the lines, kissing them gently.

"I promise." My throat tightens under a fist of regret.

I hate how she still doubts me. But it's my own fault.

And I'm going to make sure I never give her reason to doubt me again.

It's almost midnight. The sounds from the ER are muted, quiet. Cathy glances up from her spot at the nurse's station, and I point toward the exit. She nods, and I turn my attention back to what I need to do next.

A handful of people still sit in the waiting room, including Mia and Garrett, while Sawyer leans against the wall. Has he moved at all from his sentry? Three sets of eyes lock on me, concern for Michaela and the baby coloring their features.

I asked Cathy to come out and update them all earlier, reluctant to leave Michaela's side, and she'd agreed once Michaela had given her permission.

"They're fine," I say first, watching tension drain from all three of them.

Even though they know she was dehydrated, I don't tell them about the other words Michaela mentioned.

I plan to Google placental abruption later, but I completely understand miscarriage, and my stomach still clutches thinking about what could have happened.

"The nurse mentioned she might go home tonight?" Sawyer asks.

I nod. "We're waiting for the doctor to review everything and start her discharge."

"They're not keeping her overnight? Just to make sure?"

"I don't think so. But that's up to the doctor."

He nods but doesn't say anything else.

"Can I talk to you for a minute?" I ask him, and his eyebrows lift in surprise. "Outside."

Garrett's gaze bounces between Sawyer and me, his concern clear. I'd like to tell him he has nothing to worry about, but I can't speak for Sawyer. My jaw twinges at the memory of the right hook he delivered alongside the paternity results.

Sawyer jerks his head once, walking away without saying another word, and I follow him, preparing myself for what his reaction to me might be as soon as we step outside the automatic doors.

"What the fuck do you want?" He rounds on me the second

the balmy air hits us, and I gesture for him to step off to the side of the entrance. I'm not interested in putting on a show.

He stomps over, his eyes never leaving me.

"Well?" he asks.

"I'm sorry you hate me," I tell him calmly, not letting his temper ignite my own. "That I fucked up a twenty-year friendship by being an idiot. But I'm not going anywhere."

"What the hell is that supposed to mean?" His nostrils flare, his fists clenching, but I refuse to flinch.

Michaela and the baby are too important to me. I'm less afraid of Sawyer than I am of losing my family again.

"Whether you like it or not, I am the father of Michaela's baby."

"Could have fooled me. More like sperm donor," he snorts, and I wince internally at the dig.

"I made mistakes. Mistakes I'm not denying. Ones I will work every day for the rest of my life to make up for. And I will. Whatever it takes, whatever she needs from me—I will do it."

"Some mistakes can't be taken back."

Which is my biggest fear, but I won't tell him that.

"I know. But I can try."

"I'm not going to let you hurt her again. I trusted you. You were more than my best friend. You were my brother. And you destroyed my sister."

"I'm sorry. It's all I can say since I can't go back in time and kick my own ass before I hurt her." I let him see the regret, the pain I caused not only her, but myself. "And regardless of how you feel about me, I'm not giving up. I'm not walking away."

He steps toward me, coming toe to toe, and I stand straighter, meeting his gaze with mine.

"Why?"

"Because my life is meaningless without her," I say. "Because I love her. More than I thought was possible, more than I could imagine. I wasn't looking for her, but I was powerless to fight the fall. It started before I knew it, and I didn't realize it until too late. Until I pushed her away so hard, the chances of her returning my love are minimal. But I'm not giving up."

"Even if I kick your ass?"

I open my arms. "Take your best shot. But I'm still not going anywhere. As much as I want your blessing, I don't need it."

He studies me for several moments before finally lifting a hand, extending it, palm open.

"Finally," he says with a smirk.

"What?" Tentatively, I slide my hand into his.

"I was wondering when you were going to show up," he tells me. "You may not need my blessing, and I may still want to punch you, but the decision is up to Mikey. And if she loves you too, then I'll be on board."

I hadn't expected his reaction. Anger and disappointment, sure, but not acceptance.

"But if she gives you another shot, and you hurt her again..." He leaves the threat lingering.

I swallow and nod. "I won't."

"Then you have nothing to worry about. Except convincing my baby sister to give you another chance."

"So, we're cool?" I ask.

"Getting there."

"I'll take it." It's better than I could have hoped for. "Here."

Reaching into my pocket, I pull out one of the ultrasound images.

"What's this?" He studies the picture, his eyes softening when he realizes what he's holding. "The baby is really okay?"

"Everything looks good. But we're still waiting on the doctor to confirm."

Please be okay.

"How's Mikey?"

"Tired," I say with a sigh. "She's resting as best as she can in a hospital bed."

He nods. "Been a long night."

"That's an understatement."

"Well, get back inside. Find out what's going on."

I start to head back inside, but stop, turning to find Sawyer watching me.

"Thank you."

"For what?"

"For taking care of them for me."

"Figured you'd pull your head out of your ass eventually," is all he says, surprising a crack of laughter from me.

"Sorry it took me so long."

He waves me away, and I head back inside.

Two conversations down.

Now to win back my girl.

"I can walk, you know," Michaela protests as I carry her from Garrett and Mia's car toward her house. Sawyer said his good-byes at the hospital, heading back to his mysterious "job" and promising to call Michaela the next day.

It was nearly two in the morning before the doctor finally cleared her and sent her home with a list of instructions that include drinking more water and resting.

"You're supposed to be taking it easy," I remind her. "At least for the next few days."

Instead of clinging to me as she did when we trekked this path earlier, she harrumphs, folding her arms across her chest. My attention flicks down, more aware of her breasts the way they press against her shirt.

Not the time, I counsel my dick, who hardens against the fly of my shorts.

"We'll let you guys sleep," Garrett says, pulling Mia back

toward him and their house when she moves to follow us. "Say good night, Ames."

"But—" She sighs. "Fine. Goodnight, Michaela. I'll check on you in the morning, but text me if you need anything."

I don't miss the warning glare she fires in my direction, and I tighten my hold around Michaela's knees.

"I will," Michaela calls over my shoulder. "Night, Mi."

"Thank you both," I say, turning around and meeting first Garrett's gaze and then Mia's. "I don't know what we would have done if you weren't here."

Mia huffs, but Garrett nods, an unspoken agreement connecting us.

Garrett interlaces his fingers with his wife's, pulling her toward the house, and I spin, continuing down the path to Michaela's. The first time I walked up to this door, my shoulders had been tense with uncertainty. Now there's a sense of rightness, the way Michaela's warm weight settles against my chest.

"I didn't lock it," I say. My only thought had been to get her the help she needed.

She shrugs. "It should be okay. The gate closed when we left, right?"

Garrett and Mia weren't overly concerned, so I assume so. I was a bit preoccupied at the time.

"It was closed when we got back."

"It's fine." She turns the knob, and I maneuver us both through the door, reaching back with my foot to close it quietly.

The little guest house looks exactly like it did when I first walked in. Warm, inviting, comfortable. I'm glad Michaela has had a place like this to stay for the last few months. Compared to my hotel room, this is a palace.

"Here or your room?" I ask quietly, my voice husky at the lower volume.

Her yawn is a sufficient answer. Since the house is small,

there's only a tiny hallway with a bathroom on the right and the bedroom straight ahead.

But when we make it to her room, I find I can't let her go. Physically, it should be as easy as setting her down, but emotionally, my body craves the contact with hers. So instead of fighting that need, I sit on the edge of the mattress with her still in my arms.

Her blond hair is still up, but large strands have fallen to brush my bicep and incite goosebumps to shiver down my spine.

"How are you feeling?" I search her face for any signs of pain.

"I'm fine. Tired, but the cramps are gone," she assures me, and I release the breath I've been holding.

"God, I was so worried about you. Both of you." I place my hand gently along her abdomen, closing my eyes at the soft swell of warmth pressing against my palm.

"I was scared, too," she admits. "Especially when I overheard the doctor say something about miscarriage."

Her lip quivers, her eyes filling with tears from the residual fear her memory invokes. I raise my hand to cup her cheek.

"But it wasn't. And according to the doctor, the baby looked really good. Healthy. Strong," I tell her reassuringly.

Her eyes flutter shut, a tear dropping to tangle with my fingers, and I wipe away the moisture with my thumb.

"I'm glad you were here," she whispers, her hand covering mine where it caresses her cheek.

I hate that she worries about what would have happened had she been alone.

"Mia and Garrett weren't far. They would have taken you."

"No." Her eyes blaze open to lock on mine. "I'm glad *you* were here."

"I should have been all along." Regret stabs sharply, and I suck in a breath.

"I'm not going to disagree," she tells me wryly. "But you were here when you needed to be. And you're still upright and breathing after seeing Sawyer."

"We had a talk."

"You did?" she asks. "When?"

"When I stepped out for a few minutes earlier."

"Did you two kiss and make up?" God, this woman. She's teasing me even after this nightmare of a night. It makes me love her even more.

I lift the corner of my lips in a half smile. "I think we're on the way."

"Good. I never meant for you guys to fight about me. I'd like to say that if I had known, I never would have gotten involved with you. But I don't regret it. I can't regret this."

Her fingers spread over her abdomen. And the poignancy of this moment isn't lost on me.

"My only regret is the way I acted," I tell her. "I deserved Sawyer's hatred. And yours."

"I don't hate you, West."

"You should. I was a jackass."

"That word was used to describe you several times," she teases again, and my lips ache with the need to taste her smile.

"Justifiably."

"What did you and Sawyer talk about?" she asks, fidgeting slightly in my lap, the friction having a predictable effect.

"How sorry I am. How much I wish I hadn't hurt you, and how I would do anything to make up for it."

"So what we talked about."

"About how I'm not walking away again. I won't give you up without a fight. Even if it means only being the father of your child."

Her gaze flies to mine. "What did Sawyer say?"

"He asked me why." A half smile pushes at the corners of my mouth.

She snorts. "Sounds like Sawyer."

"Do you want to know what I told him?"

Her expression turns curious, and her tongue slicks across her lips before she nods.

"Y-yes."

"I told him whether he hated me or not, I couldn't give you up. That my life is meaningless without you," I begin, and she takes an audible breath. "I told him how much I hated that I'd hurt you. That I wished I could travel back in time so I could kick my own ass before I did. That even if I never get another shot with you, I love you. More than I could ever imagine loving another person. You came into my life when I wasn't looking for my soulmate, and I was powerless to stop our connection."

Tears stream down her cheeks, and I shift both of my hands to capture the moisture.

"Don't cry. I love you so goddamned much. I was the idiot who didn't see how you were the center of my universe until I pushed you away and was left with only darkness. You're it for me. Even if you never return those feelings. I'm not going anywhere. I'll be here where I can be a part of our child's life, a part of your life in whatever capacity you'll allow me. I love you. And until the breath leaves my body, I will never stop."

Her eyes sparkle, luminous with tears, both falling and filling her eyes.

"I hate to see you cry," I murmur. "Hate that you're crying because of me. Again."

She doesn't say anything, just watches me with those bright eyes, and I resign myself to letting her go. It's time to go back to the hotel and dream of her like I have every night since she left. Every night since I destroyed us.

I resign myself to the half-life of remembering what it's like to hold her in my arms while knowing I can't keep her.

CHAPTER 26

MICHAELA

"I should probably go. Let you get some sleep." He shifts, and I all but lunge for him, wrapping my arms around his neck and keeping him in place.

"No!"

He opens his mouth to say something, and I press my fingers against his lips, halting whatever he was going to say.

"You got to say your piece. Now it's my turn."

He nods, and I move my hand back to clasp with the other one behind his neck. The emotion in his eyes connects with my heart, with everything I feel for him. And I have no idea how to express the sentiments pressing against my lips, but I take a deep breath and let memories swim to the surface.

"When we were little, you were like the best older brother. You didn't tease me like Sawyer or Lucas, and you watched out for me. And I loved you for it. At some point, that love turned into a crush. I couldn't look at you without my tongue feeling thick, my words trapped behind all these emotions. But you still showed interest in me. You asked me about school and my friends. About singing. When you left for college, I felt like my world was ending. The drama of a pre-teen girl." I roll my eyes and smile while amusement lights in West's gaze. "I crushed on you forever," I admit. "And I hated Ashley when you brought her to our house that Fourth of July."

I spent that entire holiday locked in my room, hating the girl who was able to touch the man I always imagined would someday confess his undying love for me.

"I was so jealous I couldn't see straight. But I had to resign myself to the fact that she was with you, and my crush was only a crush. That I 'loved' you like I loved Channing Tatum or the Hemsworth brothers." I want to laugh at the mutinous glare he sends my way. "Don't be jealous. I have more to say."

"I admit, the crush faded as I got older, relegated to my imagination. I squeaked through school and then thought all my dreams were coming true when I signed with Reverb. Dreams. Ha. More like nightmares." I shudder, and his arms tighten around my waist.

"But everything—Reverb, tabloids, Tucker, Brad—all of that led me home. I let myself in the house that night and figured Mom and Dad would expect me to explain why I was home. Why my dream was dying. Until you stumbled into the kitchen. And every memory of you looking out for me, of keeping me safe, filled me with a warmth I hadn't felt in years."

"With that warmth, my crush came back too. In case you're unaware, you're really sexy."

He smirks but remains silent, and I squirm as new memories zing through my blood. "I could tell you were fighting your attraction to me, but I was old enough to know what I wanted. What I wanted was you, and you were no match for my stubbornness."

Laughter vibrates his chest.

"I didn't plan on getting pregnant. And I definitely hadn't planned on falling in love with you—the real, adult kind of love versus the teenage crush—as quickly and completely as I did. But I didn't anticipate you. This time it was me who didn't stand a chance. Which was why what you said that day hurt so much—"

"I'm sorry—" he interrupts, and I cover his mouth with my hand.

"Still talking." My words end on a gasp as he licks my palm. "What I didn't realize is that all of that led me to this moment right here. And you know what's important about this moment?"

He shakes his head, and nerves scatter the butterflies to swirl in my tummy.

"This is the moment I finally tell you that I love you. From pseudo big brother to crush to lover, how I feel has only grown stronger over time. And that love isn't going anywhere anytime soon."

I lift my hand, replacing it with my lips, nibbling at his until they part to let my tongue slide along his. Warm hands grip my hips and shift me to straddle him as he deepens the kiss, rubbing me against his growing erection and pulling a moan from deep within me. The friction is pure bliss.

My eyes flutter open to find concern lining his face.

"What?" I ask, confused by the worried expression.

"Are you okay?"

"Huh?"

"You made a noise. Did I hurt you?"

I smile, leaning forward to nip at his earlobe, loving the groan that resonates from his chest to mine.

"I've moaned before," I remind him, rotating my hips against his lap. "Never been a cause for concern."

"But earlier—"

"I'm fine," I promise him. "More than fine. And I missed you."

He holds my hips hostage, stopping my movement.

"I missed you too," he whispers, eyes shiny with tears. "I love you so much."

"Prove it," I challenge, lifting an eyebrow, my panties growing damper at the desire on his face.

"That mouth," he tells me. "What am I going to do with it?"

"Guess you better find some other way to occupy it."

He sighs and tries to lift me off his lap. "The doctor told you to take it easy."

"I am," I tell him, refusing to budge.

"It means no sex. As much as I want to." He groans when my tongue dips to his ear.

I lift my head enough to tell him a secret.

"I talked to Cathy about sex."

"Fuck. You did?" His fingers grip my hips hard enough to make me squirm, and I nip his earlobe in return.

"She said it was fine, so long as we weren't into acrobatics."

He chuckles. "Why can I see her using that exact word?"

"She did." I giggle. "So, what are you waiting for?"

"When did you ask Cathy about sex? I was with you the whole time."

He's putting up a valiant effort, but he won't win this battle.

"When you stepped out to talk to Sawyer."

He pulls back to meet my eyes, and I watch as they grow darker when the realization hits him.

This time, he closes the distance, plunging his tongue past my lips as he shifts us on the bed. He lies next to me, his hands reacquainting themselves with my body. I sit up, shedding my shirt, and straddle him once more. His knees come up behind me while his hands reach up to cup my breasts, flicking my nipples through the fabric of my bra.

"Yes," I encourage him to do it again.

"You're too far away," he complains and tugs me back down, my breasts crushed against his chest as he drags open-mouthed kisses along my jaw. He squeezes my ass and moves me up and down against his erection, driving my need for him higher.

"We're wearing too many clothes," I say with a pout.

"Easily remedied." He shifts me off him and stands, quickly

shedding his shorts and tee, but leaving his boxers to hug every mouth-watering inch of him.

My fingers fly to the button on my shorts, and for a moment, I'm embarrassed because I forgot they're being held together by an elastic.

"What's that look?" he asks as he kneels on the bed.

"I forgot." I point to the buttonhole, a flush warming my cheeks.

His hand brushes against mine. "Let me."

With a flick of his fingers, the two sides separate, and he lowers me back down to the bed, tugging my shorts down my hips until I lie in only my bra and panties.

"You are absolutely gorgeous." He meets my eyes before leaning over, his lips pressing against the slight bulge where our baby grows.

My fingers tangle in his hair, holding him to me even as tears prick my eyes at the image. I will never forget this moment.

"Touch me," I beg, lifting my hips.

"I am." He caresses my thighs, the touch featherlight, to prove his point, and I moan when he slides under the elastic of my panties.

"*West.*"

He smirks, the heat of his gaze positively volcanic. "Patience."

Painstakingly slow, he shifts my panties down my legs, following them along my thighs and calves before grabbing them from my feet. I expect him to speed up then, but he seems content to slowly move back up my body, finding spots to stop and press his lips. My knees. My hips. My belly again. His fingers trace down my shoulders to my hands, lacing them together and lifting until I'm leaning up enough for him to undo the clasp of my bra.

In the same unhurried fashion, his fingers move back up, rolling the straps down until he can pull the bra off and toss it over his shoulder. Breaths saw in and out of my lungs, and every nerve ending begs for his attention.

"Fuck," he groans, teeth sinking into his lip as he palms himself through the thin fabric of his boxers.

"I need you." I lift my arms and open my thighs in invitation.

"Michaela."

"Please?"

That one word breaks the spell, and he yanks off his boxers, then lies on his back and pulls me on top of him. His dick presses against my opening, sending fireworks to spark in my toes and fingers. Slowly, heartbeat by heartbeat, he lowers me down until he's fully seated inside me. The intensity is almost too much.

I lean my head back, pressing my breasts into his hands when they lift to cup them. Euphoria overwhelms me at the sense of rightness of being with him. It drives out all the doubts, all the loneliness I was determined to endure without him.

"I can't—" He grits his teeth, the muscle in his jaw working furiously. "I'm not going to last."

His hands shift to my hips, the grip almost painful. But exactly what I need.

I bend down, my breasts rubbing against the light dusting of hair. "Me neither."

He squeezes my ass, and he moves a hand lower, brushing his fingers where he and I meet, finding my clit and teasing it until I'm writhing against him, begging him to let me up, to let me move. Something, anything to find release. I sit up, grinding into his pelvis as he thrusts to meet me.

The tendons in his neck stretch as he lifts his head up, and I lean down, nipping at one of them.

He jolts, his eyes opening.

"What? I couldn't resist," I tell him.

"You'll pay for that. Later," he promises. "But now, I really need you to fucking come."

He shifts us until I'm leaning back slightly against his knees, his hips still driving up as his thumb rotates against my clit.

I lose my rhythm, my orgasm taking control of my body in pulsating white-hot heat. I fall forward, and his arms lock around me as he increases his speed, pistoning his hips against mine until he freezes, moaning into my neck with his orgasm.

"I love you," he whispers, brushing his lips against my temple.

"Mmm. Love you," I tell him and sprawl on top of him. "I don't want to move."

His hands make large sweeps of my back as his heart thuds to normal under my cheek.

"Who says you need to?" he rumbles.

I smile, tightening my arms around him. "No one."

"So stay."

I don't move, except to press a kiss to his heart, settling against him and letting the steady beat relax me further.

"Sweet dreams, baby," he whispers as I drift to sleep.

𝄞 𝄞 𝄞

I wake to the murmur of voices, blinking my eyes open as the sun filters through the blinds on the bedroom window.

What time is it?

Stretching, I sit up, ready to find out what's going on, when West steps through the door wearing his shorts and t-shirt. His hair is sexily disheveled from my fingers.

He's mine. And that knowledge has my blood heating.

"Where do you think you're going?" he asks with a lift of his eyebrow.

"I heard voices." The breathy quality of my voice tells both of us how turned on I am by his presence alone.

Maybe pregnancy hormones aren't so bad after all.

"Mia," he sheds his shirt and stalks toward the bed. "Checking on you."

"Is she still here?" I bite back my smile as he kicks off his shorts and climbs under the blankets with me.

"I told her you were still sleeping." He pulls me flush against him, my back to his front, his hand splaying across my abdomen.

"How long was she here?"

"Not long. Just a few minutes."

"What were you guys talking about?" I smile at him over my shoulder when he drops a kiss to my nose and wraps me even closer.

"You. She's worried."

"But I'm fine, and I'll drink more water."

"Not that." He grimaces. "Me. She doesn't want me to break your heart again."

"Oh."

"Yeah. She was pretty graphic in her description of how she would hurt me if I ever screwed up again."

I giggle as I imagine Mia's over-the-top personality and what her brain came up with.

"I'll protect you," I promise and turn to face him.

"Do I need protection?" he asks, eyes wide, but a smile twitches his lips.

"Did she tell you she's a black belt in karate?" I try to keep a straight face, but fail as soon as my eyes meet his.

"You're evil." His fingers find all my ticklish spots, not relenting until I'm breathless.

"You still love me," I tell him when I can breathe again, sticking out my tongue.

"Always." His eyes are so earnest, so open, he takes my breath away.

And I don't expect him to reach up and lick my tongue with his.

I can't help but laugh, the happiness bubbling out of me as I shift, leaning down to put his tongue to better use. Breaking the connection of our mouths, I trail kisses down his jaw, nibbling at the same tendon I did last night.

His eyes pop open, glittering as they take me in.

"I remember now," he growls. "I promised you'd pay for that last night."

"You did," I say, trying to hide my smile.

"And I always keep my promises."

And he keeps them really, *really* well.

EPILOGUE

WEST

2 months later
New Year's Eve

"Are you sure you're okay with this?" Michaela motions around us at the guest cottage, *our* home for the last two months.

I've been working as a long-term substitute at a private school in Malibu, but we aren't ready to move out yet. Hopefully soon. It helps that I'll start full time after Christmas break.

"What?" I ask, capturing her hand to play with her fingers.

Any time she's within touching distance, she draws me to her like a magnet, and somehow I doubt the pull she exerts over me will fade with time.

"This. Movies. Pizza and popcorn on the couch." She gestures to the TV—paused on *Clueless*. I tried to talk her out of this one, but since she let me watch both *National Treasure* and *National Treasure 2,* I figured she was entitled to the movie of her choice.

Although my attention has mostly been focused on her and

the clock as it ticks closer to midnight. A new year. A new beginning.

Her, me, and our baby.

"What else would we do?"

"I don't know." She shrugs. "A club? Dinner out? A party?"

"Do any of those sound appealing to you? More than this?" I ask.

We're cuddled on the couch, her between my legs and my hands resting on her ever-growing stomach. Ever since Michaela first felt the baby move, she's told me to stay close. She wants me to experience it too. At her last ultrasound, the doctor asked if we wanted to know the sex of the baby, but we want to be surprised. And no one understands how we don't feel the need to find out.

But, like we've explained to everyone who's asked, we've had good luck with surprises—falling in love with each other had been a surprise.

The best surprise of my life so far.

She cranes her neck to look at me before settling back against my chest.

"This is perfect."

"I agree." I brush my lips against the crown of her head. "Do you need more water?"

Since that terrifying night, I've made sure she always has a full bottle of water nearby. As the baby has grown bigger and spends more time bouncing on her bladder, she likes to complain, but I refuse to risk another night like that.

"Nope. All good," she says, lifting the bottle tucked next to her on the couch.

I glance at the clock.

11:50.

My palms are beginning to sweat, and the need to fidget is overwhelming, but I keep my legs where they are. I have a plan, but my well thought out design is starting to blur around the edges.

She yawns, and I nuzzle her ear with my nose.

"Tired?" I whisper.

"A little," she admits. "I used to be able to stay up all night."

My cock perks up at her observation, and I roll my eyes.

Calm down.

"You're growing another person inside you." One I want to feel move, but so far, no luck. "That's exhausting work."

"All I do is sit around. Either here or at the studio. I'm not doing that much."

"You're doing plenty."

She's still working on her first album with Arrhythmic, but spending a lot of planning time with Jax, Nick, and even another artist with the label, Dylan. I haven't heard everything they've recorded yet, but what I have has nearly brought me to my knees. The emotions her voice can inspire are breathtaking.

A pressure slides along my palm, and I still, hardly daring to breathe.

"Do you feel that?" she whispers, lifting her hands to cover mine.

Another pressure shift, but this time under the opposite palm.

"Holy shit," I say, awed by the sensation, the realization hitting me now more than ever—this baby is real. And we'll be meeting him or her sooner rather than later.

"Crazy, right?" She turns and lifts her face to glance at me again, and I capture her lips with mine.

"There are no words," I tell her. "I love you."

"I love you too." Her soft smile morphs to a light grimace, and she starts to wiggle out of the cradle of my hips. "But I need to pee again."

I bark out a laugh, standing as well to get the blood flowing back to my legs.

"Hurry. You don't want to miss the ball drop," I call after her.

11:54.

Tucking my hand in my pocket, I confirm the box is still

there, palming it and hiding it behind the pillow I was just leaning against.

"You okay if I turn it over to the drop?" I ask loudly.

"Okay," she calls back, and I hear the water turn on in the bathroom.

The recording from New York City is full of people singing and dancing and waiting for the magical moment when the new year begins. And my heart feels like I've sprinted the thirty-yard dash.

"I didn't miss it, did I?" she asks, rushing back to the living room.

"No. But we're getting close. Cider?" I ask, pouring two glasses of the sparkling cider we picked up for tonight.

She giggles, but nods. "I feel like a kid again."

"No champagne for you." I waggle my finger at her.

"Doesn't mean you couldn't have any."

"I'm drunk on you," I tell her. "I don't need champagne."

She groans at the line but wraps her arms around me anyway.

"That was bad," she says.

"You love it."

"Have you been hanging out with Dylan?" she teases.

I've heard stories. The man's lines are nothing short of cheesy.

"Nope. All me, baby," I say, winking at her.

The TV draws our attention, the announcers' voices getting louder as they count down, and I hand Michaela her cider as we both turn to watch the TV. As soon as she's focused there, I set my cider down, wiping my clammy hands on my pajama pants.

"Seven…six…five…four…three…two…one. Happy New Year!"

I sink to the floor, and she spins around, her eyes widening when she takes in my crouch.

"What are you doing?"

Without looking, I reach behind the pillow and pull out the box, opening it while my other hand finds hers.

"I love you," I tell her. "You were the best surprise I ever received. Every day I wake up convinced I couldn't love you more, and every night I go to bed more in love with you than before. I didn't think it was possible to love someone so much. But I do. I love you. I love our baby. I can't picture a future without you in it. Tonight's a new year, a new beginning, and I want to begin it with you by my side. Planning our future together. Michaela Grace King, will you marry me?"

Tears shimmer in her eyes, and she stares at me long enough that I worry I rushed this.

"Yes," she whispers against her hands.

"Yes?" I ask, the smile stretching across my face.

Flinging her arms around my neck, she squeezes me tight, her lips finding mine.

"Yes," she says against my lips. "I love you so much."

I kiss her again quickly before pulling back to bring the ring box between us. I slide the simple solitaire band down her finger, kissing her knuckle where it rests.

"It's beautiful," she says.

"I wish I could afford something more—" I start, but she stops my words with a kiss that leaves us both breathless.

"No. This is perfect," she says. "Absolutely perfect."

"Happy New Year, baby," I whisper and pull her closer to me.

"Happy New Year." Her smile is bright, her eyes full of love.

I love the way she looks right now, and I'm never going to forget this moment.

My lips are almost to hers when her phone rings, vibrating against the table.

"Nick," she tells me with a shrug.

"Answer it."

She puts the phone on speaker.

"Hello?"

"Don't you ever check your texts?" he asks.

"Not when I'm busy getting engaged," she retorts, grinning at me.

"Engaged?" he asks, and a squeal comes from the background. "Congratulations. From both of us."

Meredith echoes the congratulations.

"Thank you," we say in unison.

"What did you text me?" Michaela asks.

"A link. Billboard Top 100."

"Okay?"

"'Whisper' is number seventy-two."

"Seriously?" she asks.

"You heard me," he says.

She glances up then, her eyes finding mine, the unspoken question clear. My cheeks stretch in a smile, and I nod.

"Oh my god," she says, and I watch as the news starts to sink in.

"I wanted to be the first to tell you. Congratulations. Welcome to your dream, Michaela." Nick says his goodbyes, already planning how to keep the momentum going for "Whisper."

She studies me for several moments before lifting her hand—the one with the ring that tells everyone she's mine—to lay it on my heart.

"My dream," she murmurs.

Looking at her, I can't help but agree.

An amazing, unexpected dream I never saw coming, but one I can't imagine not living.

The End

~

Thank you so much for reading!

Before you go! You are cordially invited to attend the wedding of Weston James Abbott and Michaela Grace King. Turn the page and watch the two of them get married surrounded by family and friends.

BONUS EPILOGUE

9 MONTHS LATER

MICHAELA

Butterflies and me? We've become close, personal friends, so I'm not surprised when they flutter madly in my stomach as I apply the finishing touches to my make-up.

"You look beautiful," Mia says. Her dark eyes shine as she meets my gaze in the mirror.

"Don't start that. You start, I start, and then the last twenty minutes were wasted," I tell her sternly, handing her a tissue and dabbing at my eyes with another.

"Sorry, sorry," she says. "I can't help it. That dress was gorgeous on you before, but even better now. West is going to eat his tie."

My body heats at her word choice, and I remember a little over a year ago when I learned *exactly* what West could do with a tie.

I could show you what I can do with that tie. If you want.

The memory of his husky offer is so strong that I swear he's in the room with us and survey the space to make sure he didn't break protocol.

You didn't mind breaking protocol this morning.

The sun was barely cresting when he'd started to get out of our bed. He'd promised me we wouldn't see each other until it was time, but neither of us slept well without the other, and I wasn't ready to let him go last night. And when the sun started to rise, I still didn't want to. I finally let him leave after several orgasms and the promise of more later.

"You okay?" Mia asks, glancing around as well.

"Yeah, sorry, thought I heard something." I step back to check my reflection in the full-length mirror.

This moment is surreal. I'm standing in the bridal room at Holly Hedge Estate while two hundred people settle into their seats outside on a gorgeous fall day. Somewhere close by, the love of my life is getting himself and our nearly five-month-old son ready for our wedding.

"Benji is fine. Better than fine. He's such a happy baby," Mia says with a sigh. Baby fever has gotten her good, and I wouldn't be surprised to see another baby join our mix soon.

Benjamin Sawyer Abbott made his way into this world after fifteen hours of labor on a warm April day a week after we got notice that my first album with Arrhythmic had gone platinum. And Mia was right. Since the moment Benji was born, he's spent most of his time studying the world while chewing on his fingers or babbling.

"Are you sure you're okay with Garrett and me taking him for the week?" she asks, and my heart squeezes in my chest as mom guilt rears its ugly head.

After the wedding, West and I are heading on a weeklong honeymoon at a cabin Sawyer owns on the coast in Alaska. It's his wedding gift to us. How Sawyer has managed to own something like that without anybody finding out is a question he has yet to answer.

Mia and Garrett volunteered to keep Benji while we're gone since all his stuff is in their guest house. But not for much longer. Once West and I get back, we're moving to a house a few minutes away, despite Mia's protests that we can live with her forever. Since most of the furniture belongs to Mia, we don't have much, so even though we'll be doing the work after school only, it should only take us a few days.

West took paternity leave when Benji was born near the end of the school year and considered staying home permanently once the summer was over. But he's passionate about teaching, and Benji can come to the studio with me, so it feels like we have a solid routine.

Once our honeymoon is over, I'll be hard at work with Jax and Nick, working on my next album. It's slated for a January release. There's still a lot to be done, including the tour planning for next year. No way am I leaving West or Benji behind, so the tour schedule will be unique for sure. But I wouldn't change my life for anything.

I wake up each morning running and don't stop until my head hits the pillow at night—but I'm so happy I wouldn't be surprised if I exploded into rainbow confetti.

"Yes," I say hesitantly. "And before you ask, my hesitation has nothing to do with leaving him with you. It's the mom guilt eating at me. I haven't left him overnight since the day he was born."

My nose burns, and I blink rapidly to keep those tears at bay. There's no time to fix my make-up before we need to head downstairs. I spin, craning my neck to check out the back of my dress and the veil. Mia and I found the bohemian style wedding dress at a boutique in LA and immediately knew it was meant for me.

Wide shoulder straps of lace appliqué fall down to a sweetheart neckline with a deep V—thank god for fashion tape keeping the dress in place. The bodice is an illusion peek-a-boo lace over beige lining, and the skirt is layers and layers of tulle.

My hair is pulled back in an intricate twist at the top and flows down my shoulders, covered with a veil trailing out beyond the dress. As soon as I tried it on, I knew I wanted West to see me in this dress.

"Kayla?" Mom knocks before sticking her head in the door. "Oh, honey."

Her eyes fill with tears, and I hold up a finger.

"Don't," I croak out.

"If you start, I'll start, then she'll start," Mia explains, and I laugh.

"You look beautiful, sweetheart," Mom says. "Are you ready? The boys are lining up now."

I press a hand to my fluttering stomach and take a deep breath before releasing it.

"I'm ready."

"Here." Mia hands me my bouquet, bronze ribbons trailing from the pale pink and mauve colored roses that have pops of white scattered among the green.

"Hold there, please."

I'd forgotten the photographer was in the room with us, but do as instructed for several shots before she lowers her camera with a smile. She's been with Mia and me all day while her husband follows the boys.

I leave the room and nearly run over Dad.

"Sorry." I laugh, brushing imaginary wrinkles from the arm of his suit jacket.

"My baby," he says. "So beautiful."

He steps back to get the full effect.

"Thanks, Dad." I kiss his cheek and loop my arm with his. "Ready to give me away?"

"Only to West, Kayla. Only to West."

The photographer snaps several more photos on our way

outside before Mia steps in place in front of me where the path veers around to the house.

The music starts, and I watch her walk down the curved aisle until I can no longer see her from my spot on the side of the house. The song changes again, and this is it. Our cue.

"Ready, Dad?"

We turn the corner, and the world disappears. The only thing I can see are my two favorite men. West stands straight at the altar, the black of his jacket setting off the bronze vest. His hair is combed, but he hasn't shaved—at my request. His green eyes light up when he sees me, his smile stretching across his face.

Sitting quietly in his father's arms, Benji is a mini version of West in his black suit and cute little bronze vest. I have no idea how Mom found a suit to fit my chubby cheeked five-month-old. He is adorable, his hand shoved into his mouth as a gummy smile overtakes his face when he spots me.

Sawyer leans in to whisper something to West, and he nods, not breaking eye contact with me.

My vision blurs, and I blink back the threatening tears, keeping my eyes fastened on West's until I meet him at the altar.

"Who gives this woman to this man?" the officiant asks, and Dad clears his throat.

"Her mother and I do." He squeezes my hand once before extending his hand to West. Benji thinks the gesture is meant for him, and Grandpa takes him happily to sit with his grandma.

"Wow," he mouths, and I can't stop the giggle that escapes.

"Wow, yourself," I whisper back, and the officiant clears his throat to begin this next chapter in our lives.

WEST

Ethereal.

The only word that comes to mind as I get my first glimpse of Michaela in her wedding dress. In this moment, I swear I die and go to heaven based on the vision she makes as she walks toward me.

Benji squirms, the warm weight of him in my arms grounding me.

This is real.

The baby in my arms is real.

The woman walking toward me is real.

And she is breathtakingly beautiful.

I can hardly focus on the officiant as he goes through the ceremony we planned, the vows we asked for. But I hear him clearly when he says, "You may now kiss your bride."

I don't hesitate, cupping her jaw and capturing her sigh with my mouth as she grips the lapels of my jacket. I bend her back slightly, dipping her, taking the kiss deeper.

My wife.

"Ladies and gentlemen, may I introduce you to Mr. and Mrs. Weston and Michaela Abbott," the officiant says, and I pull away reluctantly, tugging her down the aisle with Sawyer and Mia hot on our heels. But I couldn't care less about any of them.

Michaela's breathless laughter reaches my ears as I pull her up the stairs and back to the bridal room. I've watched this door most of the day—I could find it blindfolded.

"West," she laughs my name, the sound making me light-headed. "Where are we going?"

I pull her into the room, closing the door and pinning her against it with my hips pressed against hers.

"You take my breath away, Mrs. Abbott." I drop my lips to her jaw and trace the line to her ear.

"Say it again," she murmurs as her hands fist in my jacket.

"Stunning," I whisper against her skin.

"No, not that."

"What? Mrs. Abbott?"

Her hips lift to mine, and I curse the layers of fabric preventing me from touching her more easily.

"You like that?" I ask and tangle my fingers with hers.

"Mm-hmm," she whimpers as I cuff both her wrists in one hand above her head.

At this angle, her breasts thrust forward, barely concealed by the lace that dips almost to her navel. With my free hand, I trace the deep neckline until it ends, following the V back up. I trace it again, loving the way her chest heaves at my touch.

"You were concerned your dress wouldn't fit," I remind her.

"I still haven't lost all the weight since Benji was born."

If she hasn't, I don't see anything wrong. Her hips and breasts are fuller from carrying and nurturing our son. And nothing could be sexier.

"You are fucking gorgeous. And all mine," I growl, ready to claim her mouth again.

"I've always been yours." She tugs slightly against the grip I have on her wrists.

She wants to touch me, but I haven't unwrapped my present yet.

I start to trace the line between her breasts a third time when a knock vibrates against the wood behind her.

"Quit making out with my sister and open the fucking door."

"Sawyer," she says with a groan.

The man has an uncanny knack for cock-blocking.

"If you'd leave us alone for a few more minutes, I would do more than make out with her," I respond and watch a flush pinken Michaela's cheeks.

"Dude." Even through the thick door, I can hear the warning.

With a sigh, I step back, bringing Michaela with me. If I don't let him in, I have no doubt his next move will be to take the door off the hinges.

"It's open," I tell him and mouth *later* to the woman by my side.

Sawyer walks in, but he's not alone. He's holding Benji while Mia, Garrett, and Evie trail him.

"The photographers are looking for you," Mia says. She and Evie take hold of Michaela and touch up the lipstick I very much enjoyed kissing off.

"Come to Daddy, big man," I say and reach for Benji at the same time he reaches for me.

If I've learned one thing about love with Michaela, it's how overwhelming it is. Holding my son for the first time in the delivery room? It was everything.

His little hands cup my cheeks, and I pretend to snap at them, my heart lifting at the sound of his light giggle. His white-blond hair reminds me of his mother's when she was young, but his eyes are the ones I see in the mirror every day. Benji is a solid mix of both of us, although I hope he inherited more of his mother's personality traits than mine.

"Benji." Michaela's voice comes from behind my shoulder, and he stops, searching for Michaela, confused when he doesn't see her. "Benji."

The expression on his face is pure joy when he spies her. He makes a happy sound and reaches a hand out for her to nibble on.

"We make cute kids," I murmur low enough for only her to hear.

"We do," she agrees. "Maybe we should do it again."

I nearly bobble the baby, my eyes finding hers as everyone else in the room fades away.

"Seriously?"

She shrugs, her finger gripped in Benji's chubby fist.

"I'm not saying tomorrow, but I don't want to wait too long."

"Maybe we should practice," I offer with a smirk.

"Great minds think alike, Mr. Abbott."

"How soon do you think we can ditch the reception?" I ask.

The clearing of a throat sounds from behind me, and I turn to find Sawyer glaring.

"She may be your wife, but she was my sister first. You've

played kissy face enough, and like I said, the photographers are looking for you."

"Kissy face?" Michaela asks with a laugh. "Did you seriously use that phrase?"

"So what if I did?" His attention strays to Evie, who is deep in conversation with Mia.

He catches me studying him, and I raise my eyebrows, nodding toward Evie.

He shakes his head, the muscle in his jaw working.

I consider asking him about it, but Kelly shows up at the door.

"Found them," she says, and is soon joined by my parents, Whitney, her husband, Dan, and the two photographers.

"We'll talk about siblings for Benji later," I promise Michaela.

She nods, her eyes lit with amusement as a smile tugs at her lips.

"You always keep your promises."

"Always," I say, switching Benji to one arm and interlacing my fingers with hers. "Forever."

I watch pink color her cheeks, and she stops, reaching up to press a kiss against my lips.

"I'm counting on it."

PLAYLIST

Michaela and West's playlist is the first of the playlists that repeat a song from two different artists. "Broken" by Noelle Johnson and the same song from Jonah Kagen reflect Michaela and West's battles with their past. "You" by Lucy Daydream and "Sanctuary" by Welshly Arms hit you in the feels interspersed with haunting melodies like Tommee Profitt's "Hold On For Your Life" and Taylor Swift's "All Too Well."

Want to listen to the music that inspired *Embracing the Beat*? Check out the playlist on Spotify by searching for the "Embracing the Beat" playlist or scan the QR code below.

You can find all the Heart Beats playlists on my website:

https://www.breannalynnauthor.com

ACKNOWLEDGMENTS

To you. Yes, you. The one who just read Michaela and West's story! Thank you for taking the chance on the two of them. I hope you enjoyed reading *Embracing* as much I enjoyed writing it!

For my family—thank you for supporting me in this dream. For asking for a signed paperback, for sharing my work with others, for your love. I couldn't have done this without you! I love you!

Claire and Alina—Thank you for your ideas (Claire, you know what I'm talking about!) and messaging me after getting chapters calling me all sorts of names since I wouldn't share more (Alina Lane, I'm looking at you!). You both are two of the best things I've gained from this writing thing!

Editor Jess—Thank you for the reminder that the foundation is the foundation for a reason and the advice that every author gets to that point that they need that reminder.

Beth—For sanity checking me and continued words of encouragement! For LOL moments and every moment in between! I'm so grateful for our friendship!!

Kate Farlow—Thank you for another beautiful cover! For talking me off the creative ledges I put myself on (and try to drag you along with me)!

Chris, Eric, & Skyler—The cover photo is absolutely magical! Imagine my surprise when I was scrolling randomly on Facebook and it's like my characters jumped into my social media feed!

Stevie—who would have thought that a random message would have led to not only our friendship but your AMAZING PA skills! You keep me straight when I need it, inspire laughs, and keep me keeping on! I couldn't have done this without you.

To my Alpha Readers, my Betas, and my ARC team—your excitement as you read through Michaela and West's story kept me going and helped mold this HEA into what it turned out to be!

I can't imagine this journey without any of you! XOXO

ALSO BY BREANNA LYNN

HEART BEATS SERIES

Written in the Beat

In The Beat of the Moment

Keeping the Beat

Betting on the Beat

Embracing the Beat

Falling for the Beat

STAND ALONE NOVELLAS

Rockin' Around the Christmas Tree

Jessie Bryant may be the baby sister to rock star, Jax Bryant, but it doesn't means she dates them. Not anymore. So what if she's attracted to Just One Yesterday's bassist, Topher Rivers? She can ignore that attraction since she won't be seeing him. Until she learns that Topher Rivers is really Chris Rivera and he needs a nanny for his four-year-old son. Jessie can't help but fall for Chris's son. And it isn't long before Chris shows Jessie he's more than the rock star stereotype. Can Jessie give her heart to another rock star? And if she does, what will he do with it?

TURN THE PAGE for a sneak peek of *Falling for the Beat.*

FALLING FOR THE BEAT

CHRIS

"God dammit."

The phone ringing for the second time in as many minutes distracts me from the chord progression I'm working through. I need to finish this song since it's been partially done for months. But finishing will have to wait—again. With a sigh, I drop the pick and snag my phone from the table.

"Hello?"

"Chris?" Frank Nguyen has been my attorney since I was old enough to need one. And since he was my parents' attorney first, he's been a fixture in my life for a lot longer than that.

"Frank. How's it going?" I set the guitar aside and lean back against the couch.

"I want to say fine, but I just got the strangest phone call. From an attorney named Nathaniel Ramirez."

Fuck.

I should have known. I massage the bridge of my nose where a headache is now taking root.

"Which band member is being sued for paternity now?"

On the surface, it sounds like a strange question. But with the number of times Milo, Finn, or Noah have been accused of fathering a child, it's one I ask far more than I ever thought I would.

For over twenty years, we had more than our fair share of women claiming that one of us had fathered her child. Miraculously, none of the accusations had ever been legitimate. But our luck wouldn't hold out forever. And as the leader of our band, it's my job to handle this. *They* are my responsibility.

Thank fuck Evan is too quiet to cause this kind of shit. I'd bet money Frank is calling me about Milo, since our drummer has chased more pussy than the rest of us combined.

"Er, it's not that. Not really."

"Not really?" Surging off the couch, I walk the length of my music room without finding the comfort it usually brings me.

"Does the name Melanie Sanders mean anything to you?"

I freeze mid-stride and take a breath. Melanie and I met almost seven years ago at a party here in LA. Her friend had somehow scored invitations. The friend had been swooped up by Finn, and I swooped in on Mel, who leaned against a wall seeming more than a little out of place. She had looked at me with those big hazel eyes like I was some kind of savior.

More like Lucifer.

I wasn't her Mr. Right. But our on-again, off-again fling had lasted two years before she broke it off completely when she wanted the monogamy I couldn't give her. But I wasn't overly heartbroken. With the constant tours, I was rarely in LA, and even when I was, we were in the studio recording the next album. I never expected her to wait around for me.

No way was Frank calling me about a paternity issue there. Melanie had my number. And the last time I slept with her had been almost six years ago.

"Melanie? What about her?"

"She's dead."

What the fuck?

I pull the phone away from my ear, staring at it like it will somehow tell me the truth.

"She was thirty-two." As if her age is some sort of protection.

"Car accident." He clears his throat in the awkward silence. "Nathaniel Ramirez is the probate attorney in charge of Melanie's estate."

I'm still struggling to process that Mel is dead. Probate? Estate?

"What? Why did he reach out to you?"

"Chris, Melanie named you in her will as the father of her four-year-old son, Gage Christopher Rivera. She identified you as his guardian in the event that something should happen to her."

I'm overwhelmed by dizziness and reach blindly for a wall, leaning against it as I take several breaths. That first night, Melanie knew me as Topher Rivers, my stage name. But it didn't take long before I tired of her calling out another man's name in bed. So I confided in her and gave her my real name—Christopher Antonio Rivera.

"Son?" I gasp.

I have a son. A four-year-old. Gage. One corner of my mouth quirks at the unique name that reminds me of Mel. She may have seemed like a conservative, librarian type, but she had a wild streak she showed to very few people.

"I already requested that Nathaniel initiate a paternity test—"

"He's mine." I don't need a fucking test.

Mel wouldn't name me as the father otherwise.

"Chris." The lecture is obvious in Frank's tone.

"Frank. I don't doubt he's mine."

"I know you want to believe that. But it would be better to confirm it."

"I don't need a fucking test." My molars click together. Why isn't he listening to me?

"Think about it from the child's—"

"Gage."

Frank sighs. "Gage's perspective. He's already lost his mother. We need to be sure before we upend his life again."

Fuck. I didn't think about that.

"Where is he now?"

I don't care what Frank thinks. If Gage is in foster care, I won't hesitate to go pick him up. No child deserves to lose his mother and his home all in one day.

"Melanie's parents have temporary custody."

I never met her parents. But the stories she told me assure me that my son is okay with them for the time being.

"Find somewhere quick, Frank. I want this test over and done with and the results confirmed."

As soon as we hang up, I send a text to the guys.

CHRIS: Congratulations, you're all uncles.

Four weeks. A month since Frank called to tell me I have a son. But finally, the results are in, and Gage's grandparents can't postpone anymore. They have—twice. But today is the day.

It's been a long four weeks. Once I told Mamá and Papá that they were grandparents—again—I had to beg them to not immediately rush to the Sanderses and meet their new grandson. Fuck, I still hadn't met him.

"This is bullshit," I mutter quietly, but loud enough for Evan to hear me.

"Don't worry. I'll make everyone clear out once they get here."

He and the rest of the guys showed up this morning, despite knowing that the Sanderses are dropping Gage off any minute now.

"What?"

"The guys. I'll get everyone to clear out when they get here." Evan glances up at me from the pool lounger he's kicked back on while Milo and Finn take turns cannonballing into my pool. Noah is on another chair, dark glasses concealing most of his face and a silver flask glinting in the sun where it presses against his lips.

"I know. I figured that. I just can't believe it's taken a fucking month."

I gesture to Noah, and Evan fixes his attention on our keyboardist. His shoulders tighten despite the heavy sigh he exhales.

"Shit. I'll take him home with me. Make sure he stays out of trouble."

"We need to record the new album. Cornerstone is already breathing fire since it's taken this long. We can't afford for him to go to rehab."

Again.

I don't say it, but I don't need to.

In the last three years, Noah's had three separate stints in rehab. It's been hell on our schedule, and we've barely kept our touring commitments, forget recording anything new.

My phone chimes with a notification from the guard at the gate.

"They're on their way." My heart gallops in my chest and my palms grow clammy. I'm amazed the phone doesn't slide out of my grip.

"All right, boys, that's the signal. Time to go. Milo, Finn, dry off. No way am I letting you in my car soaking wet."

They grumble but grab towels from the outdoor chest before following a surly Noah and a silent Evan to the front door. I bring up the rear, rolling my eyes at the trail of water they leave behind. The guys are barely in Evan's car when another one pulls up behind them.

I was expecting two adults. Instead, three meet me at the front door while Gage hides behind the woman.

"Mr. Rivera?" The man dressed in a suit steps forward with his hand extended. "I'm the Sanderses' attorney, Stephen Chen."

"Attorney?" I shake his hand distractedly. "Do I need to call Frank?"

"Mr. Nguyen? That won't be necessary. I'm here at the request of my clients to ensure the transfer goes smoothly."

I bite back the attitude I want to sling at his smarmy little speech. My son is watching.

"I don't anticipate any issues."

"It shouldn't have to happen at all." If looks could kill, the one Mrs. Sanders shoots my direction would have me six feet under.

"Excuse me?" I turn my attention from the attorney to her.

"He doesn't even know you. Who do you think you are to take our last piece of Melanie away from us?"

"Is that what you think I'm doing?" Her words are sucker punches to my gut. I didn't choose for Melanie to list me as guardian. But if she hadn't, I would have never known about Gage.

"He loves us. He's used to us." Mr. Sanders takes up where his wife left off.

"Mr. Sanders. Mrs. Sanders. I'm terribly sorry for your loss. But I can't be sorry about meeting my son. I don't want to take him from you. I *want* you to have a relationship with him."

Mr. Sanders opens his mouth to reply, but the attorney cuts him off.

"Tom, Bethany." He shakes his head, and I want to know what the fuck he's thinking.

The two other adults say nothing else. I'm missing something here. What the fuck does it take for their attorney to only say their names to shut them up?

"Gage," the lawyer addresses my son and snaps his fingers. "Come here."

My hands clench into fists at my side.

Stay the fuck away from my son.

The little boy steps forward, moving out from behind his grandmother's legs. Light brown hair falls across his forehead, and I can't help but trace the similar fall of my hair. Wide hazel eyes remind me of Mel, and his cheeks still show the baby he used to be—the apples dusted pink while small lips purse together as he studies me.

He lets go of his grandma's hand. She gasps and keeps her arm extended awkwardly in the air, like she's ready to snatch him away from me, even though she has no reason—and no right—to do so.

"Does he know who I am?" He approaches me slowly, and I hold my breath.

"We told him we were bringing him to meet his father." The attorney's voice grates against my ears. I can't wait for him to leave.

Gage now stands directly in front of me, and I lower to my haunches and smile at him.

"Hi, buddy."

"Hi."

"Do you know who I am?"

His little head bobs once. "Daddy."

Tears burn behind my eyes, and I blink several times to clear the sensation.

Fuck.

I'm a goner.

I've fallen in love with a kid I just met. No, not simply any kid. My son.

I don't regret my life as a rock star, but for the first time in thirty-six years, I can see the appeal of being a family man.

"That's right, Gage. I'm your daddy."

At that, he steps forward, and his little arms wrap around my neck. I inhale his strawberry and little boy scent. Mrs. Sanders sniffles, and the attorney clears his throat.

"Tom, Gage's bags?"

Mrs. Sanders follows her husband to the car, but she gets in while he and the attorney grab two suitcases and two boxes—one labeled "Books" and one labeled "Toys"—and set them by the porch.

"That's everything."

Mr. Sanders looks at me and then at Gage before waving half-heartedly and joining his wife in the car. The attorney is the last to get in, and I don't relax until his door closes behind him.

"Daddy?"

My attention shifts from the departing car to the little boy standing next to me.

"Yeah, bud?"

"I have to go potty."

"Okay. Let's go potty."

I got this.

I don't got this.

By the end of the first month, even with the help of Lois, my part-time housekeeper, who increased her hours to help, I'm still floundering. I'm practically catatonic from lack of sleep. Every night this week, Gage has either woken up with nightmares, had an accident, or climbed into bed with me for no reason. I had no idea such a small human could take up so much room on a king-size bed, but inevitably, his little foot digs into my kidney whenever he falls asleep.

"Why don't you find a nanny?" Evan asks. He showed up after Gage was asleep so we could work on song selections for the next album.

"I asked my mom to help me find one. Anytime I try to do it, I'm yanked back into band shit."

Band shit. Noah high as fuck last weekend. Milo and Finn whoring and partying it up all over town.

"Are you still meeting with Jax and Nick?"

The co-owners of Arrhythmic Records reached out to me about a song I wrote that Just One Yesterday wouldn't record—not our sound. But it's perfect for one of their artists, Dylan Graves, and they want me to work with him on the song.

"Yeah. I managed to eke out some time tomorrow afternoon." Trying to add that to my already chaotic schedule has proved almost impossible. It's the weekend, but neither of them balked when I suggested it.

"What about Gage?"

"Mamá." One word, but it's explanation enough.

"He hasn't said anything in days?"

Over the last month, Gage has become less and less talkative. He's gone from a vibrant little boy to a quiet shell of himself. He hasn't uttered a single word since breakfast two days ago when he asked for waffles like he used to have with Mommy. Only I had no idea what kind of waffles she made for him. Apparently, they were Eggos, like the ones in my freezer. But I didn't know.

I didn't understand.

I'm failing. Otherwise, my son would still be speaking.

"No." Sighing, I flop down on the couch next to Evan and run my hands through my hair.

"What's your mom say?"

"She said I need to take him to a therapist. That it's probably his way of grieving."

"You gonna do it?"

Having known Evan since junior high, I ignore his usual snarky tone.

"I need to find someone first."

"Sounds like a lot of work."

"Yeah." And all I want to do is fucking sleep.

But there's no rest for the weary. Or the wicked. And I definitely fall into both categories.

~

Does Chris find the help he needs for Gage? What else is in his future? Want to find out?

Grab Falling for the Beat now!

ABOUT THE AUTHOR

Breanna Lynn lives in Colorado with her two sets of twins (affectionately referred to as the Twinx), their two dogs, and two cats. A classy connoisseur of all things coffee, Breanna spends her time keeping the Twinx from taking over the world. When not coordinating chaos, Breanna can be found binge reading, listening to music, or watching rom-coms with a giant bowl of popcorn.

To stay up to date on the ramblings of her (often over-caffeinated) mind, Twinx Tasmania, or the latest news on her latest happily ever after, sign-up for her newsletter at breannalynnauthor.com/subscribe. Subscribers receive exclusive news, content, specials, and giveaways!

Want to follow Breanna? Scan the QR code for all the ways to stay caught up!

Made in the USA
Monee, IL
15 January 2024

50925563R00184